EVERY DAY A
LITTLE DEATH

EVERY DAY A LITTLE DEATH

CRIME FICTION INSPIRED BY THE SONGS OF
STEPHEN SONDHEIM

EDITED

BY

JOSH PACHTER

LEVEL BEST BOOKS

LEVEL SHORT

Praise for *Every Day a Little Death*

"Stephen Sondheim loved puzzles and mysteries, and no doubt he would be pleased how his songs provide a jumping off point for twenty short stories of murder and espionage—sometimes dramatic, sometimes humorous—and inventively take readers to places his original works never imagined."—Wm F. Hirschman, editor of *floridatheateronstage.com* and member of the Executive Committee of the American Theatre Critics Association

"This outstanding collection honors the legacy of the great Stephen Sondheim while richly exploring a new side of his themes. Sondheim fans should flock to these entertaining short stories that meld mysteries with Sondheim's music."—Oline H. Cogdill, mystery-fiction critic

"What a delightfully macabre idea to pay tribute to Stephen Sondheim with a collection of crime fiction inspired by his many works. From a corpse lying at the feet of Gypsy Rose Lee in a Chicago dive bar to the mysterious death of an actor in *Sweeney Todd* to a dark twist on *Sunday in the Park with George*, there's plenty here to fascinate readers—and unnerve them, too. Attend these tales!"—Richard Schoch, author of *How Sondheim Can Change Your Life*

Scenes and Musical Numbers

Overture

Crime Fiction Inspired by the Songs of Stephen Sondheim? Seriously? What in the *world* do Sondheim and crime fiction have in common?

Well, nothing…unless you remember that *Sweeney Todd* is the story of a murderous barber, and *Assassins* is the story of, well, multiple killers and would-be killers, and *Into the Woods* tells (among others) the story of a wolf who eats grandmothers, and *The Last of Sheila*—not a musical comedy for the stage but a devious whodunnit Sondheim co-wrote with Anthony Perkins for the screen—won the Mystery Writers of America's Edgar Allan Poe Award for the best mystery film of 1973.

About that Edgar….

In early 1974, I was teaching film history and television production at Cass Technical High School in Detroit. I'd been publishing short crime fiction in *Ellery Queen's Mystery Magazine* since 1968 and in *Alfred Hitchcock's Mystery Magazine* since 1972, and—perhaps because I had earned my bachelor's degree from the University of Michigan in film history and appreciation—I was asked to serve as one of the five members of the MWA committee charged with selecting the recipient of its coveted Edgar for the best motion picture of 1973. The four finalists, in alphabetical order by title, were *Don't Look Now, The Last of Sheila, Serpico,* and *The Sting,* and the committee members held an in-person meeting in New York to choose the winner. Because school was in session, I wasn't able to travel to the Big Apple for the confab, but I got a phone call from the committee chair, who told me that he and the others had cast two votes for *Serpico* and two for *The Last of Sheila*. The organization didn't want to give out two awards in the category, so it was up to me to cast the tie-breaking vote that would determine the

vii

winner.

Serpico, I thought, was a better movie, but this award was being given by the Mystery Writers of America, and *Serpico* wasn't a *mystery* movie. *The Last of Sheila*, on the other hand, most definitely *was* a mystery, and though perhaps not a *great* movie it was certainly a *good* one.

So I voted for *Sheila*, and it was my vote that got Sondheim and Perkins their Edgar.

That was the closest I ever came to a direct encounter with Stephen Sondheim—although I have another Sondheim-adjacent story I'll share with you at the end of this introduction.

This is my eighth "inspired by" anthology, following volumes of crime fiction inspired by the songs of Joni Mitchell, Jimmy Buffett, Billy Joel, Paul Simon, the Beatles, the Grateful Dead…and the films of the Marx Brothers. For this one, I reached out not just to established crime writers, but especially to crime writers with a personal connection to the theater, whether as playwrights or simply people with a love of the stage: Fleur Bradley, John Copenhaver, Brian Cox, John Floyd, Joe Goodrich, Cheryl Head, Julie Hennrikus, Alison Hubbard, Becca Jones, Jeff Marks, Jeff Sweet, Marcia Talley, Gabriel Valjan, Joe Walker, and Kristopher Zgorski.

I also decided to go out on a limb and solicit stories from people who *hadn't* previously tried their hand at crime—or, in a couple of cases, *any*—fiction, but who were involved in one way or another with matters theatrical, as playwrights, critics, and/or historians. That brought Cheryl Davis, Lisa Nanni-Messegee, Michael Portantiere, and David Spencer into the fold.

Some of these folks were fortunate enough to have had personal contact—even friendships—with Stephen Sondheim.

Jeff Sweet, for example—whose first professional sale was to EQMM but who later moved on from writing crime fiction to writing straight dramatic plays—shared the following with me: "*Evening Primrose* began our friendship. I was one of the five people who watched it on ABC in 1966, when it was originally broadcast. When Stephen and I were introduced in the early Seventies, I asked him about it, and he said, 'My God, you *can't* remember that.' I started to sing 'Take Me to the World' from memory—this was way before anybody had recorded any of those songs—and he was startled. He'd been getting a lot of shit that none of his tunes were memorable, and here was this kid singing from memory a chunk of a song which he'd heard something like six years before. He asked me for my address, and very shortly, I got an acetate disc of the soundtrack. Not long after that, I had a little one-act for which I wrote the words and music performed Off Off Broadway. He showed up, took notes, took me out for a bite, and gave me useful feedback, and then we just *talked* for two hours. I was a kid, and I was in heaven."

And David Spencer says: "Steve generously took me under his tutorial wing to observe the process of *Sunday in the Park with George* through workshop and preview performances, which we discussed the day after I saw them. The one lesson he taught me that made the most impact was: 'The biggest danger is getting used to things.' You can get lulled via repetition of not only a song or a scene, but a killing *detail*. I remarked to him about the phenomenon of tiny adjustments making enormous differences, and he replied, with joyous exhilaration, 'I know! Isn't it astonishing?' Thirty-five years later, I reminded him he'd taught me that principle, and he said, 'Oh, yes! I remember sitting behind Jerry Robbins during a run-through of…might have been *Gypsy*, but I think it was *West Side*—when he saw something he didn't like. He turned to his assistant and said, "Remind me tomorrow that I hate this."'"

Readers of crime fiction will find plenty to enjoy in these pages: murders, robberies, kidnappings, a cornucopia of crime in all its permutations and combinations.

But there's more here than "merely" crime. Since Sondheim was an avid fan of puzzles and word games, I've encouraged the contributors to include lots of Easter eggs—those hidden treasures that casual readers are likely to miss but that'll give the sharp-eyed Sondheimer a sense of accomplishment upon discovery. Fair warning: the authors have taken me at my word, and in the twenty stories that follow, there are literally—by which I literally mean *literally* and not figuratively—*hundreds* of buried treasures to be found.

I should probably say a few words about the shows and songs represented here.

Saturday Night, Sondheim's first musical, came close to a Broadway production in 1960 but never actually received a professional performance until 1997. I've chosen to include it here with *West Side Story* and *Gypsy* as a show of the 1950s, though, since it was *written* in 1955.

Evening Primrose was written for television, not the stage—but it's a musical, and Sondheim wrote it, so it seemed silly to exclude it…and, given his reminiscence quoted above, it should come as no surprise that it's the show Jeff Sweet selected as his inspiration.

Follies was originally performed in one act, although revivals have sometimes split it into two acts with an intermission. For the purposes of this anthology, I have listed its songs as they appeared in its original one-act version.

Road Show went through a complicated development. It first played at the New York Theatre Workshop in 1999, titled *Wise Guys*. Rewritten and retitled *Bounce*, it had a run at Chicago's Goodman Theatre and then moved to the Kennedy Center in DC in 2003. Finally, as *Road Show*, it played Off-Broadway at the Public Theater's Newman Theater in 2008.

The *Playbill* for *Here We Are,* Sondheim's final show—which premiered at the Shed in New York on September 28, 2023, and ran through January 21, 2024—didn't list any song titles. It proved well-nigh impossible to find a writer willing and able to take on the challenge of writing a story "inspired" by a song when not even the *titles* of the show's musical numbers, let alone their lyrics, were available. When the cast album came out in mid-2024, though, Alison Hubbard jumped on the chance to contribute a story, and I think she did a fine job under considerable time pressure.

And the songs? As theatergoers will be aware—but others may not—songs are cut and others added during a musical's production process, during tryouts and previews, and sometimes even after a show has opened. I have attempted here to list the songs that were performed on each show's opening night, and with one exception the contributors have selected as their inspirations songs that can be found on the various OCAs (Original Cast Albums, for the uninitiated). The exception was my friend and former officemate Lisa Nanni-Messegee, who picked "There Won't Be Trumpets," which was cut from *Anyone Can Whistle* during previews. (The song was recorded for the OCA, but wasn't actually *released* until 1989. Today, scripts and scores for *Whistle* almost always reinstate it.)

At the beginning of this introduction, I shared a personal Sondheim story from 1974 and promised you another one at introduction's end. Well, here we are, so here you are:

Also in 1974, *A Little Night Music*—which had opened on Broadway the previous year—embarked upon a year-long national tour, with Jean Simmons, George Lee Andrews, and Margaret Hamilton in the lead roles. As I mentioned earlier, I was teaching at Cass Technical High School at that time, and Frances Hamburger, my department chair, was able not only to get tickets to a weekend performance but to arrange a backstage visit with the cast.

For reasons I've long since forgotten, I wasn't able to join my colleagues that day, but I vividly remember telling Frances, "If you don't bring me back Margaret Hamilton's autograph, I'll die." (My classes were housed in the Performing Arts Department, so forgive me for being dramatic!)

First thing Monday morning, Frances came to my office and handed me a program from the show. And there on the cover, the Wicked Witch of the West had scrawled:

Dear Josh,
Don't die!
Margaret Hamilton

That was excellent advice, and today—half a century later—I continue to follow it.

That story told, the orchestra is all warmed up, and it's time to raise the curtain and begin Act I of *Every Day a Little Death: Crime Fiction Inspired by the Songs of Stephen Sondheim.*

Happy reading—and, for the Easter eggers amongst you, happy hunting!

Josh Pachter
  Midlothian, Virginia
  September 13, 2024

Act I

The 1950s

Saturday Night

originally scheduled to open on Broadway in 1955

ACT I

"Overture"
"Saturday Night"
"Class"
"Delighted I'm Sure"
"Love's a Bond"
"Isn't It?"
"In the Movies"
"Exhibit A"
"A Moment with You"
"Saturday Night" (reprise)
"Gracious Living Fantasy"
"Montana Chem"
"So Many People"
"One Wonderful Day"

ACT II

"Entr'acte"
"Saturday Night" (reprise)
"I Remember That"
"Love's a Bond Blues"
"All For You"

"That Kind of a Neighborhood"
"What More Do I Need?"
"One Wonderful Day" (reprise)

Music and lyrics by Stephen Sondheim.
Book by Julius J. Epstein and Philip G. Epstein.

Class

by Michael Portantiere

A wall of rain turned to sleet as Gene Gorman plodded down a sidewalk in Brooklyn Heights on a late Friday afternoon in December, barely protected from the elements by his threadbare coat. The wind and half-frozen water seemed to slice through him as he proceeded, so much so that he found himself wishing he might be gifted with a nice, warm Harris tweed coat for Christmas. But that was a ridiculous thought. Gene wasn't expecting anything in his stocking other than a few lumps of coal, as he had been a very bad boy this year.

The 1920s were said to be "roaring," but not so much for Gene. He told everyone he was a musician, which was technically true, but he made very little money with his clarinet, as his hot-headedness frequently got him in Dutch with other musicians, and it's damned hard for a clarinetist to find solo gigs. The "Great Experiment" of Prohibition had reduced to a trickle the amount of available club work, so he was pretty much limited to earning a few bucks here and there playing for social events with guys he hadn't yet managed to alienate.

Possessing no other skills or talents to speak of, Gene had been relying on gambling and pool to get him through. Currently flat broke, he was forced to turn to his only other viable source of funds: a pawn shop. There was a particular place where he had been going to unload stuff, but the owner had recently told Gene he was no longer *persona grata* there, due to his constant profanity-laden complaints. When Gene railed against the proprietor as a "miserable Hebe," that was the straw that broke the camel's back, so he was now about to try his luck at a shabby little shop on Nostrand Avenue.

"A buck twenty-five," the grizzled guy behind the counter said impassively, after examining the cufflinks Gene handed him.

"You gotta be kidding me!" Gene exclaimed. "Those are ivory!"

"Sorry, pal. If those are ivory, I'm Babe Ruth's ugly sister. A buck twenty-five, take it or leave it."

Gene grouchily accepted the offer, cursing under his breath. He took the money and bolted, mentally crossing another pawn shop off his list.

His next stop was a meet-up with three of his buddies at their favorite speakeasy, an under-the-radar place in the shadow of the Brooklyn Bridge, where Gene and the boys had become fixtures as permanent as the sconces on the walls.

Ted, Artie, and Ray were sitting at the bar when he blew in around six o'clock. Unlike Gene, all three were gainfully employed: Ted as a plumber, Ray as a shop assistant, Artie in construction. They each had a beer lined up behind the ones they were currently downing.

"Hey, sport," Artie shouted as Gene entered, and the other two raised their glasses to him.

"Gentlemen! Sorry I'm rather tardy, but I had to run an errand."

"Which pawn shop did you hit up this time?" asked Ray, who could be a real jerk when he wanted to.

"Nostrand Avenue," Gene grimaced, taking a seat at the bar. "You must have been there at some point, Ray—I saw your mother's earrings in the window."

"How do you know they were Ray's mother's earrings?" asked Ted.

"Never you mind," replied Gene with a leer, and Ray cheerfully gave him the bird.

"Anyway," Ted said, "we're glad you scrounged up enough coin to join us for a few."

"Always a pleasure," Gene grinned, adding a curt "Pabst" to the Irish bartender.

The boys talked and drank together for more than two hours. Their subjects of discourse ranged from women to family to sports as the other three got drunker than Gene, who was good at handling his liquor. Typically, he voiced his aspirations for a tonier lifestyle than the one he knew at present, going on and on about the places and events in Manhattan—great shows, fancy restaurants, exclusive parties—that he was determined to be a part of someday, in contrast to his current meager existence in Flatbush and environs.

It was after eight when the quartet left the bar. The wind and precipitation had ceased, and a nearly full moon shone through the clouds. Gene fell quiet as he gazed upward at the magnificent superstructure of the bridge that towered over them.

"There she is, boys," he murmured in boozy wonder. "What a beauty."

"I dunno," Artie commented. "I think it looks kinda creepy."

"Nah," Gene replied softly. "That bridge is my rainbow."

"Oh, really?" Ted snickered.

"Yes, and I know there's a pot of gold on the other side. I just have to figure out how to get my hands on it."

* * *

The rest of the winter was bleak for Gene, with only one lousy gig playing a bar mitzvah and more failure than success at gambling. But in the spring, he got lucky, with a tip from an acquaintance on a long-shot horse in a race at Belmont Park, and in mid-June, he found himself at a semi-fancy restaurant with a girl named Celeste, who he'd met at a dance a few weeks before.

Gene never had much trouble finding female companionship; he was a good-looking chap with wavy hair, steel-blue eyes, and a square jaw, so it was easy for him to attract interest from the ladies. But he had never yet had a long-term girlfriend, as anyone he dated was soon repelled by the personality he exhibited whenever things weren't going well for him.

Celeste was a nice girl, far too nice for Gene—but that hadn't become apparent to her yet. This evening, Gene was in full show-off mode, acting as if he were a sophisticated *bon vivant* at the most expensive restaurant in Paris. In reality, Gene was no Maurice Chevalier, and Schrafft's wasn't Maxim's. But that didn't stop him from putting on airs.

"Oh, Captain," he called when he was ready to order.

"Captain?" Celeste repeated the word with a quizzical smile.

"Sure, you gotta know how to behave in a place like this," Gene explained. "You gotta have class." He sipped his non-alcoholic approximation of a cocktail, the closest thing to booze that could be found in a reputable place during Prohibition. "We'll order the priciest items on the menu, I'll buy a Havana cigar for later, and I'll leave a five-buck tip when we're done. Then they'll treat us like royalty when we come back."

"It sounds like you're planning on becoming a regular."

"You know it, toots!"

The waiter trotted over to their table, and Gene ordered as if he had just broken the bank at Monte Carlo. Then he dismissed the fellow with a jovial, *"Merci, monsieur."*

"Gene," Celeste said gingerly, "this is a lovely place, and I really appreciate you bringing me here, but I want you to know I'd be just as happy if we were eating at a greasy spoon. I think it's wonderful that you came into some money from your uncle"—Gene had lied to her about that, choosing not to divulge the true source of his windfall—"but I don't want you to feel you have to spend it all quickly, and certainly not on me."

"Not to worry, my dear," Gene replied with a beneficent smile. "Tonight is only a taste of what's in store for you if you stick with me. Don't you *like* pricey restaurants, fashionable clothes, and jewelry?"

"I like all that as much as anyone," Celeste answered sincerely, taking Gene's hands in her own. "But honestly, that's not what's important to me. I've got *you*, Gene. What more do I need?"

* * *

Gene and Celeste only lasted two months together, as he soon decided he couldn't be happy with a girl who didn't lust after the finer things in life. In September, broke again, he headed to a pool hall in the Hell's Kitchen section of Manhattan, hoping to set in motion there a plan that would earn him enough money to live out his days in the style to which he desperately wanted to become accustomed.

The day before, Gene had read in a newspaper column that the world-famous musician Bix Beiderbecke would be playing a concert in Carnegie Hall with the equally renowned Paul Whiteman and would be staying at the Plaza Hotel while in New York. Beiderbecke's cornet was worth a small fortune—about a hundred times the amount Gene made in an average year—and a guy named Bobby, who Gene had met at the pool hall, was a porter at the Plaza. So….

The smoky pool hall was a stereotypically raffish place. When Gene arrived, Bobby was already there, halfway through trouncing some poor son of a bitch in a game of one-pocket. Gene waited patiently while the unfortunate was dispatched, then sidled up to his potential accomplice.

"Hey, sport," Bobby greeted him. "It's been a dog's age. What are you up to?"

"That depends on you, my friend. Can you take a break, so we can talk outside for a few?"

Bobby assented, and they exited the joint to an alley off the 46th Street side of the building, where they could converse in private while sharing a smoke. Gene provided the cigarettes, purchased with the last of his loose change.

"Okay," said Bobby, "what's on your mind?"

After double-checking that no one was in earshot, Gene unveiled his scheme: he would borrow Bobby's porter's uniform, bring it to the Plaza in a suitcase, rent a room where he could don the uniform, and steal Bix Beiderbecke's cornet, which would be worth thousands of dollars on the black market.

Bobby listened with a combination of interest and amusement, then asked: "And how exactly would you get into Bix's room?"

"I haven't figured that part out yet," Gene acknowledged. "But when I heard he'll be staying at the Plaza, I remembered that you work there, and I—"

"Hold on," Bobby interrupted him. "I got fired last month for behaving inappropriately toward one of the female guests."

"Jesus H. Christ!" Gene exploded. "You got sacked? That's the story of my miserable life. When the hell am I gonna catch a goddamn break?"

"Maybe sooner than you think," Bobby said with an evil-looking smile. "I stole my uniform when they canned me, and it's hanging in a closet at home right now. And not only that—I've got a master key to all the hotel's rooms!"

* * *

Gene strolled into the Plaza that Saturday afternoon with the key in his pocket and Bobby's uniform in a suitcase. He drank in the ornate entrance lobby and the Palm Court for a few moments before heading to the check-in desk.

"Good afternoon, sir," chirped the prissy gent behind the counter. "May I help you?"

"I have a reservation in the name of Dino Martini," Gene said, having chosen a combination of the names of two reprobates he used to know.

"Ah, yes, Mr. Martini," replied the clerk. "Is that with a twist, or with two olives?"

Gene forced a laugh in response to this lame stab at humor. The clerk, embarrassed that his joke had gone over like a lead balloon, gave a feeble smile as he handed Gene a key and said, "Room 519."

Flush with excitement and nervousness, Gene went up to his room—which, if all went well, he would vacate within a few short hours. He took Bobby's uniform from his suitcase and put it on. It was a near-perfect fit. Regarding his image in a full-length mirror, Gene was satisfied that he looked for all the world like a genuine, honest-to-God Plaza Hotel porter.

After also retrieving from the suitcase a box of premium Lilac chocolates, Gene rode the elevator to the penthouse level, where he had learned that Bix and his entourage would be staying. The car was already occupied by an elderly man and woman, who smiled sweetly at the handsome young porter.

"Ma'am, sir," Gene said politely. "I hope you enjoy your stay," he added, when the couple exited on the ninth floor.

No one was in the hall at the penthouse level, and Gene walked briskly to the door of Bix's suite and knocked. His heart was pounding, but he was counting on his natural acting skills to get him through the next few minutes.

"Yes?" said the man who opened the door. Gene recognized the owl-faced, pencil-thin-mustached fellow as Paul Whiteman, whose distinctive visage was familiar from countless photos in newspapers, magazines, and on album covers.

"Mr. Whiteman," Gene stammered, barely managing to hold himself together. "I, ah, I just wanted to welcome Mr. Beiderbecke to the Plaza on behalf of the management." He awkwardly thrust the box of chocolates forward.

"What a lovely gesture," Whiteman smiled. He turned away and called, "Bix! Someone's here with a gift for you."

Gene tried to remain calm as the famous clarinetist approached. "For you, Mr. B." He handed the box to his idol and potential mark. "Compliments of the Plaza."

"Why, thank you, son," Bix said. "I'll share these with the boys in the band. Do you think they'll enjoy that, Paul?"

"Indubitably," Whiteman replied. "I know I will!"

During this brief exchange, Gene stole a glance into the suite's bedroom and gasped as he saw on the bed what he guessed had to be the case containing Beiderbecke's cornet. Collecting himself, he said, "The manager would like to offer you some other welcoming gifts he's asked the staff to deliver this evening, if you're planning to be here."

"Ah, no, I'm afraid Mr. Whiteman and I are leaving around six for two social engagements, so we'll be out for quite a while. Please thank your manager, and I'll be sure to do so personally tomorrow."

"Of course, sir," Gene responded with a grin, thrilled to learn that the suite would be empty for several hours. "If you require anything at all, please don't hesitate to ask. We are completely at your service." He gave a little bow and left, closing the door behind him.

* * *

Back in his room on the fifth floor, Gene decided to wait until seven o'clock, just to be safe. He hoped and prayed that the cornet would be left in the penthouse while Bix and Whiteman fulfilled their social obligations.

Gene paced about the room, keyed up with thoughts of what he was about to attempt. He gazed out one of the large north-facing windows at Central Park, which unfolded before him in the late afternoon sun beneath a cloudless sky—quite a different view from the one he had from the single window in his Flatbush hovel, which basically consisted of an inch of sky above a dark alleyway. He removed his porter's jacket, lay down on the bed, took a few deep breaths, and tried to glean some enjoyment from what would be a very brief stay in a well-appointed room at the storied Plaza, a foretaste of how much better his life would be when he became a member of a much higher economic class....

* * *

Three hours later, Gene was hiding underneath the bed in Bix's suite and realizing for the first time in his life how extremely difficult it can be for a person not to make the slightest sound when it's really, *really* important to keep quiet.

He had re-donned Bobby's jacket, elevated back up to the PH level, and knocked gingerly on Bix's door to make sure that he and Whiteman had indeed gone out. In his hands was a bottle of champagne with a card reading "Welcome to the Plaza," a cover for his return to the room in case the men were still there for some reason. Relieved that his knock got no response, Gene hustled back to his own room, left the champagne on an end table, grabbed his suitcase, and high-tailed it back to the penthouse with the pass key in his pocket.

There was a moment of panic when the key wouldn't turn at first, but with a little jiggling, he got it to work and entered, closing and locking the door behind him. A second wave of alarm ensued when he entered the bedroom and saw no cornet case on the bed. He checked the closet, behind the curtains, even in the bathroom, all with no luck, and had begun to sweat bullets when it occurred to him to look beneath the unmade bed—where, in fact, he spied the case. Again holding his breath, he dragged it out from under the bed and heaved a sigh of relief to find that it did indeed contain the instrument. The cornet didn't look like it was worth big bucks, but he understood that its value was due to its ownership, indicated by the letters "BB" engraved on one side of the bell.

With trembling hands, Gene removed the cornet from its rightful place and stashed it in his suitcase. As he was doing so, he heard a key in the lock in the other room, a sound that nearly caused him to ruin his underwear. Moving faster than he ever had, he shoved both cases beneath the bed and crawled under there himself.

Based on what he could see and hear from his hiding place, he knew that a maid had come in to make the bed and change the towels. As she did her job over the next fifteen minutes, Gene remained quiet as a mouse, despite strong urges to cough, sneeze, or become flatulent. When the woman finally left the suite, he let loose all three noises almost simultaneously.

He escaped from beneath the bed, left the empty cornet case there, and hurried back to his room with the cornet in his suitcase. He stripped off the porter's uniform, got back into his street clothes, and headed down to the lobby.

"Ah, Mr. Martini," said the prissy fellow behind the check-in desk. "You're not leaving us so soon, are you?"

Gene had his lie well prepared, having read *The Great Gatsby*. "Yes, sadly. An urgent matter has arisen at one of my properties on Long Island."

"Oh," the clerk responded, impressed.

"I was hoping that my associates could handle the crisis," Gene continued, counting out a few bills to pay for his room, "but they insist my presence is required. Terribly sorry I won't be able to spend more time at the Plaza on this trip."

"So are we, sir," the clerk said, "but we surely hope to see you again soon. Would you like any help carrying your suitcase to a taxi?"

"No, thank you," Gene replied, a little too quickly. "I can handle it. *Arrivederci* and *au revoir*, my good man!"

He gave the fellow a toothy grin and was gone in a flash.

* * *

"What can I do for you, son?" asked Clarence Fletcher.

The mousy stockbroker's tiny office was located on the outskirts of the Wall Street area. Fletcher had been recommended by Gene's cousin James as someone who might help him invest the very large sum he had left after paying Bobby twenty-five hundred dollars for his help with the theft of the cornet. (He'd told Bobby he had only been able to get five grand for the instrument, when actually he'd sold it for twice that amount. In cash.)

A full year had passed since the heist at the Plaza. Gene had been on tenterhooks for weeks afterward, in fear that he might somehow be tracked down as the thief of the cornet, but he had seen absolutely nothing in any of the newspapers about the crime. The Plaza wanted to avoid bad publicity, he guessed, and they'd likely reimbursed Bix handsomely for the stolen instrument and convinced him to remain silent about the matter. The concert with Paul Whiteman had gone off as planned on October 7, with Bix using a backup cornet or one he'd borrowed from a fellow musician— though again there was no press coverage of the substitution.

It had taken Gene several weeks to fence the cornet for a price he felt was fair. For months afterward, he kept the cash he'd gotten for it under his mattress—figuring that was the only viable hiding place for it, clichéd as it might be. After handing Bobby his share of the booty, he'd walked away with seventy-five hundred bucks.

That would have been more than enough for him to live off handsomely for quite some time, but given Gene's mindset and personality, he wanted more. So once he felt confident the heat was off, he decided to invest most of what still remained in the stock market. He would have liked to deal with someone more reputable than this Fletcher guy, but given the shadiness of the provenance of his funds, he couldn't be choosy.

"I'm only interested in stocks and securities that will give me a high, quick return," Gene replied *sotto voce* to Fletcher's question.

"Aren't we all? But why are you whispering, son?"

"Oh, sorry, I didn't realize. No reason."

"Hmm," Fletcher reacted, his beady eyes becoming steady for a moment as he assessed the young man before him. "Have you broken up the total amount into four separate bank checks, as I suggested?"

"Got them right here," Gene said, patting his satchel.

"Good. We're talking about a sizable sum, and it will look better if we deposit several smaller checks to your new account, rather than one enormous one. We wouldn't want any red flags about the source of the money, would we?"

"No. We definitely wouldn't want that."

"Any specific thoughts on where and how you'd like to invest?"

"I have no idea," Gene replied in complete honesty, "so I'm going to go with your recommendations. I know a couple of guys who've made a killing in the market, but lately, I've heard some concerns."

"Well, yes, there's been volatility in recent months, but I don't think it's anything to worry about. Just a necessary correction or two, which will be followed by some huge gains. Of course, there's more risk if you want quick and large returns, but I think you'll be fine if we stick to leveraged-investment products like the Blue Ridge and Shenandoah Trusts from Goldman Sachs."

"Ripping!" Gene enthused. "Sign me up."

"Will do. We'll get you in on those two and, for safety, we'll put some of your funds in a few other solid investments, like Bank of the United States and Atwater Kent. I'll set up your account today, make some phone calls, and you'll be all invested by close of business on Wednesday. I hope you can stand to wait till Thursday to start watching your money grow."

"Yes, capital! That's grand!" Gene's language became more pretentious by the minute, though he was among the newest of the *nouveau riche*.

The sign-up process was soon completed. Gene handed the checks to the little fellow and left the office on a cloud. He hailed a cab as a sign of his new financial status and instructed the cabbie to take him on a mini tour of Manhattan before transporting him to Brooklyn, where he planned to treat Ted, Artie, and Ray to a magnificent night on the town.

Relaxing into the ride, Gene noticed that the cab's previous occupant had left a copy of the *Herald Tribune* on the back seat. He picked it up to leaf through it, but first took note of the date indicated on the front page—a date that, in Gene's opinion, ought to have been printed in big red letters, marking his entry into the world of high finance.

It was Tuesday, October 22, 1929, and Gene Gorman was on his way to Easy Street.

West Side Story

opened September 26, 1957, at the Winter Garden Theatre, New York

ACT I

"Prologue"

"Jet Song"

"Something's Coming"

"The Dance at the Gym"

"Maria"

"Tonight"

"America"

"Cool"

"One Hand, One Heart"

"Tonight (Quintet and Chorus)"

"The Rumble"

ACT II

"I Feel Pretty"

"Somewhere"

"Procession and Nightmare"

"Gee, Officer Krupke"

"A Boy Like That/I Have a Love"

"Finale"

Music by Leonard Bernstein.
Lyrics by Stephen Sondheim.
Book by Arthur Laurents.

Tonight

by John Copenhaver

If you tell me that what I feel isn't love, this conversation is over. Grant me that, and I'll explain everything. You'll see, I'm only guilty of being romantic, a Romeo calling up to his Juliet, his Riccardo.

Falling in love with Ricky was an accident. Ask anyone: the pandemic was hard on dating. I'm thirty-five and haven't ever had a long-term boyfriend. Sure, I used the apps, but that faded when I was promoted to technical director for the Richmond Rep.

The Rep had recently received a windfall, and we moved to a community center next door while construction was underway on a new wing. I was assigned to design and build a stage from scratch for *Starcrossed*, an uber-gay reimagining of *Romeo and Juliet*. Romeo, in this version, was infatuated with Julien, a flirty teenager. I support a queer twist on the classics, but this script was juvenile, like something from Season 6 of *Glee*.

My point is: I wasn't looking for love. I didn't have the time.

I kept my head down, blinders on, nose to the grindstone—but when gorgeous Riccardo Pazzano entered stage left (literally!), he shone too bright. He was beautiful: a tennis player's rangy body, curly black hair, brown eyes that swirled with color like agate, Tom Hardy lips. But Ricky was more than the sum of his parts; he had charisma and intelligence that imbued *Starcrossed*'s sophomoric dialogue with subtext.

At thirty-two, he was old for Romeo, but he sold it. I'd take breaks from building the set to watch him rehearse. Whether it was him killing Tybalt—

Ty in this version—or wooing Julien in the balcony scene, his skill was apparent. For many actors, beauty is their Achilles heel, a wall between the audience and the character; our inclination to objectify them limits our imagination. For Ricky, this wasn't true. His physical beauty dissolved into his character, and he expressed that ineffable vulnerability that's so rare.

Before long, I had fallen for him. Most of the cast was in love with him, too—except for that prick Russell Feist, playing Julien, a sneering, self-obsessed demon twink who always thought he was being upstaged when in fact he was being outperformed.

Ricky's effect on the show was to transform a blah production into something exciting and honest. The energy was humming and—Russell aside—positive.

Until, of course, I opened my mouth, took a chance, and shared my feelings.

Tell us more about that, Woodrow.

Woody, please.

Okay, Woody. What did you say to him?

It was a Sunday night, three weeks into rehearsal, and someone decided we should watch other interpretations of *Romeo and Juliet*, including the 1961 *West Side Story* and 1996 DiCaprio. Jerry Roberts, the director, wasn't jazzed about it. He didn't want those versions seeping into his actors' performances, but the cast said they'd watch the films with or without him. So he invited us to his cramped Cape Cod in Midlothian, and we opened beers, ordered pizza, and streamed the movies.

Ricky sat on the carpet with his back against the sofa, his long legs crossed at the ankles. Sore from construction work—we'd finished the tiered risers and the Capulet home's exterior flats—I snagged Jerry's weird pleather bean bag.

During the fire escape scene in *West Side Story*, when Tony and Maria profess their love in Technicolor, I glanced at Ricky. Flickering in the TV's glow, his strong profile and parted lips overwhelmed me. Or maybe it was the swelling music, Jimmy Bryant's voice dubbed over Richard Beymer's performance of "Tonight."

I warned you I was a romantic.

My attraction was carnal but not purely carnal. I was grateful for Ricky's ability to transform the play into something we could be proud of. It motivated me to level up the design and focus on the details.

He suddenly turned and met my gaze. If the room hadn't been dark, he would've seen my face bloom bright red. He could've scowled or pretended not to notice. Instead, he smiled as if this were something he was used to—all the lovestruck men and women dazzled by his sun—and a lurid satisfaction crept onto his lips.

The movie paused suddenly, slicing off the soaring song, leaving Tony and Maria frozen on the fire escape, the world blurred out around them.

"You know," Russell said, pointing the remote at the screen like an accusatory finger, *West Side Story* doesn't capture how obsessed and impulsive those two are. The romance is so sanitized."

"It's love at first sight," I grumbled. He was overanalyzing it.

"It's the Hays Code," Jerry said from the back of the room. "*Everything* was sanitized, then."

"And I'm remembering," Russell said, "Maria—unlike Juliet—doesn't die at the end."

Cutting my eyes at him, I said, "Then it's a good thing Julien dies in our version. Come on, press play."

Between the movies, Ricky went outside to vape, and I followed him. After our flirty exchange during *West Side Story*, I wanted to talk to him. We'd only had a handful of perfunctory conversations; our workplace Venn diagrams rarely overlapped. He leaned on the exterior wall, took a drag, and offered me a puff. I inhaled, and the soothing vapor rolled through me. I handed back the pen. "I'm sorry," I said, shivering in the chilly October breeze. "I didn't mean to stare during the movie."

"Don't worry about it."

"You're just...very attractive."

He chuckled. I was telling him something he already knew.

"Are you used to it?" I laughed. "I can't be the first."

"Not really." He took another drag. "It's weird."

Trying another angle, I said, "I appreciate everything you're bringing to this production. I wasn't excited about the show until you signed on. You're pushing us, even the lowly tech crew."

He smiled and offered me the pen again. "Thanks," he said. "It's hard for me to know what Jerry's thinking."

"He's diplomatic to a fault," I said, taking another drag, feeling looser, mellow.

"And Russell always makes me feel awkward, like I'm getting on his nerves."

"Russell is evil."

He laughed. "A little, maybe."

"When you look under 'evil twink' in the urban dictionary, there's a photo of him pouting, spray-tanned, with frosted tips."

Ricky laughed and bumped my arm, accidentally on purpose. I took that for a green light, so when I returned the pen, I grazed his finger, a lowkey but erotic gesture. His eyes fluttered, and he pulled away. "Look," he said, "you're a cool guy and a fab designer, but I—"

"Don't tell me you're not gay."

"I'm bi."

"I'll forgive you," I said, meaning it as a joke, but it didn't land right.

"That's not the point.," he said, worry creeping into his brow. "I'm in a long-term committed relationship." When he said this, a shadow fell over him, as if the person he was in a relationship with was perched on his shoulder, imp-like, twisting his black curls.

"I'm flattered," he whispered, "but I can't. Kaye's dealing with some pretty traumatic stuff and needs me to focus on her. I don't want to lead you on."

Poor guy. He was trapped. I know the look. I saw it on my father's face growing up, my mother's iron grip squeezing the life out of him. "Kaye," I said, not concealing my distaste. "That's a beautiful name."

21

Go on.

Over the next week, I observed Ricky from a distance. He seemed withdrawn. Something was eating him. Kaye?

Russell noticed it, too. "Ricky," he bitched, "I feel alone up here!" Or "What's wrong with you? It's like I'm acting to a wall." Or "Jesus, are you high?"

One evening, Ricky's car was in the shop, and I drove him home. We chatted about theater politics, and I mentioned that I disapproved of how Russell spoke to him. He shook his head and said, "He's right. I haven't been present for him."

"Everything okay?"

He paused. "Yeah. It will be."

I knew he wanted to share something with me. He trusted me. It was about Kaye. She's a handful, I suspected. But he didn't want to "lead me on." My heart broke for him.

"Good," I said. "But I still think Russell should be kinder. His bitchery isn't helping."

He smirked. "Honestly, sometimes I want to kick him in the balls."

Ricky lived in a two-story white-brick apartment complex circa 1965 in Northside. After he wished me goodnight, I noticed he'd left his messenger bag on the floor of my Honda. I flung the door open and dashed after him, following him into the complex's C-shaped courtyard, past an empty swimming pool, and up a flight of stairs. I called to him as he approached his apartment. He was startled at first, then melted with relief when he saw the bag. "God, I'm totally out of it," he said, taking it from me. "Thanks, you saved me a lot of grief." His eyes flashed with traces of flirtation.

After we parted, I glanced back at him. His hips shifted languidly from side to side as he walked four doors down to his apartment. His shoulders were burdened by an invisible weight—a deep loneliness that made him utterly irresistible. I suddenly knew that seeing Kaye would explain something to me. So I strolled to the outfacing side of the building and slipped into the underbrush, a mixture of partly bare trees, evergreens, and hydrangea bushes that provided the building privacy from the street.

On the balcony of the fourth unit from the end, I spotted a woman sitting with her bare feet propped on the railing, leaning back in a vintage metal porch chair and smoking a joint. She wore jeans and a knit wrap-around sweater that fell loosely from her neck, exposing a series of vinelike tattoos across her chest and neck. Ricky appeared on the balcony, greeted her with a kiss, and took a drag from her joint, the smoke curling into the air.

I immediately understood what kind of person she was: imperious, demanding, controlling. How could I tell? My years in theater have made me sensitive to body language. For instance, she didn't meet his kiss but received it passively, as if he were expected to pay homage to her. Then there was the way she handed him the joint, as if she were permitting him but a mere modicum of the pleasure she got to enjoy in full. She also never took her feet off the railing, which was so blasé, so hideously ungrateful. Didn't she appreciate the beauty of the man standing beside her, a man who had remained loyal to her and chivalrously refused my advances?

And those neck tattoos. Talk about attention-seeking and self-indulgent. *Please.*

Poor Ricky. Was he blind to her manipulations? Was he trapped? There was much to their story I didn't know.

As I peered up from my hiding place about fifty feet away, I could see the heaviness in his brow, his shadow-shaded eyes, and tightly pressed lips. I wanted to climb up and save him. "Wake up," I would say to my sleeping beauty. "She's no good. She's a dead end. Come with me."

What did you do next?

Nothing. What *could* I do?

Okay. So, was that about the same time as Russell's accident?

I figured you'd ask about that, but there's not much I can tell you. I wasn't there when it happened. What I *do* know is that he and Ricky had a big blowout. Ricky kept fumbling his lines during the balcony scene, and in full prima-donna plumage, Russell lost his patience and had a hissy fit. Ricky is a consummate professional, but with Kaye pushing his buttons at home and Russell upstaging him in and out of scene, it's understandable that he was struggling.

After Jerry called a thirty-minute break, Ricky appeared in the shop, breathless and pale. "Sorry," he said, "I need to hide out for a few minutes."

I asked him what was wrong, and he told me.

"Russell has gone too far," I said. "He's blaming his inadequacies on you."

"Maybe," he said, hanging his head, his dark curls falling forward. "But he's right. I don't know the lines."

"Oh."

"I'm distracted."

"Stuff at home?"

He smiled weakly. "Something like that."

It was Kaye, but instead of prying, I offered to run lines with him. We went outside in the sun and, despite the beeping backhoe and clatter of construction next door, practiced the scene several times.

The problem resolved itself a day later—happy coincidence—when the left side of the Capulets' home fell on Russell, crushing his leg. When I dashed in, he was making a terrible squawking noise, like a chicken caught in a blender, and I helped lift the flat off him. I take responsibility for not triple-checking that the scenery was secure. If you want to stick that on me, that's fine. But keep in mind that it cost me, too. I had to rebuild that part of the set.

When did you begin filling in for Russell? Wasn't that unusual?

Ricky told Jerry that I'd run lines with him and that he was surprised—even startled—by my acting skill. He forgot that many theater techs take acting coursework as well. We're not *just* designers and carpenters, thank you very much. Anyway, I found myself in the delightfully awkward position of filling in for Russell until Jerry could lock in a permanent replacement.

Balancing rehearsals with keeping the crew on track was tricky. For weeks, I only got three hours of sleep a night. Still, acting again was invigorating, and I drew energy from reserves in my mind and body, pockets of adrenaline I never knew existed.

I wasn't expected to learn the lines. My job was to move through the blocking and bring the appropriate emotional energy to the lovestruck and rash Julien, giving Ricky emotion to play off. Luckily, I'd watched one of the balcony scenes—the most important scene between the two of them—hundreds of times and had memorized it.

As Julien, I peered down at Romeo and asked, "How did you find me?"

He beamed, his features smoothing with joy and desire. "Love, of course. I could smell your cologne through the open window. I followed your laughter like cosmic GPS."

Doing my best impression of a blushing teenager, I swooned and, with no force in my voice, said, "You need to go. Now. You'll get us both in trouble if you're seen." Then, in a clumsy aside, "If he could see my face in the shadows, he'd know my words don't match my desire."

Of course, Romeo sensed all this, ignored my warning, and scaled the side of the house.

In the blocking, Ricky was supposed to reach through the balustrade and grasp the sides of crouching pajama-clad Russell's face. The bars symbolized how the lovers were separated by their feuding families—who were, in a bid for relevancy, political enemies.

But when the moment came, Ricky rose above the railing, pulled me to him—thumbs pressing gently on my jawline—and kissed me, lingering, our lips interlocked. In a single gesture, he smashed the wall of tension between us and tore open something beautiful inside me.

That's when I knew Ricky loved me, too.

I ached to talk to him in private, to mine the layers of his kiss's meaning and perhaps urge another unscripted kiss.

Being a professional, however, I understood that the scene must go on.

But you did talk to Ricky, right?

After work and away from everyone, I followed Ricky outside into the crisp evening air. Behind us, the new wing's skeleton of I beams, shot through with stars, held symbolic weight as if designed for this moment, our scene. Initially, we said little to each other, and then he stepped toward me and gathered his words. "I want you to understand something," he said, smiling a tad shamefully, his true emotions hard to bear. "You're a very attractive man, Woody. I'd be lying if I told you I didn't enjoy kissing you. For that moment, the world and all its shit went away."

I touched his arm, the warmth of his skin soothing, and said, "I'm falling for you."

That was a lie. I'd already fallen for him, and it was a wild and bright feeling, like a downed electric power line whipping and sparking in the night. But I didn't want to overwhelm him.

All the same, he pulled away, his shoulders drooped, and darkness fell across him. "I can't," he said.

"Is it Kaye?"

He gave me a pained—no, *stricken*—look and muttered, "I just can't."

His loyalty to her was frustratingly admirable. She must be adept at psychological manipulation—an expert gaslighter. What sad story had she spun to fence him in and keep him from expressing his needs? The struggle between his loyalty and his desire was palpable. He was her cult of one.

I stepped toward him, but he snapped, "Don't! You'll hurt us both." He trembled. "What a terrible mess I've made of everything. I'm so sorry."

"You've done nothing wrong," I urged. "Please believe me."

"No, no." He stepped back. "Leave me alone."

"I can't."

"Please."

"I love you."

He jerked away as if I'd slapped him, speechless, his feelings too much to process.

"Ricky," I pleaded, my heart shattered.

But he turned from me and fled into the dark.

That's not everything, Woody. You promised the whole story.

I'm telling you everything—in detail.

Hmm. Tell us about your confrontation with Kaye Wilder, then.

After Ricky bolted, I was worried. Had I thrown him for a loop? Was he overcome with confused feelings? So I drove to his place. His car was still in the shop, and I assumed he'd take a bus or Uber home.

Frankly, I didn't know what I was doing. I parked on the street, crept along the fenced property line, and peered up into his apartment, hoping to glean information through the glass doors. Kaye was leaning against the railing, puffing on a joint, staring into the night sky. She seemed to live out there. Her blond hair was up in a messy bun, and she was once again wrapped in a bulky sweater. I realized that she was older than Ricky, perhaps in her late thirties or early forties. She was objectively attractive, but I couldn't see what Ricky saw in her. Of course, if she had him wrapped around her finger, beauty had nothing to do with it.

Despondent, I turned to leave, and in my exhaustion, I lost my balance. I fell and gripped a tree to brace myself, making noise. Kaye leaned over. "Hey! You, there, Creeper. What are you doing?" she said, or something equally inane. I stood completely still, but she had eyes like a hawk. "Were you watching me?"

Instead of stepping forward and declaring myself, I backed away, attempting a stealthy escape. I moved quickly through the underbrush to the edge of the property and traced the fence until I arrived at the entrance.

But I wasn't fast enough. Flying across the pavement like a banshee, smoke trailing from her joint, Kaye barreled toward me. "You perv!" she accused, her voice like the crunching of gravel. "Why are you lurking in our bushes?"

I had no choice but to stop. I didn't say anything, pretending to be baffled. After all, *she* was the one gesticulating and caterwauling.

As she moved closer, it dawned on her who I was, her deductive powers not curbed by the haze of cannabis. "Jesus," she snarled, "you're that guy

27

from the theater. Woody something. The one that's gaga for Ricky." She chuckled. "He told me about you. He said whenever he looks at you, he can see the drool on your chin."

"I don't know what you mean."

"Oh, come on." She smiled. "He was worried you had a crush on him. He told me you wouldn't let up, mooning over him." She was twisting his words. "Listen, I get it. He's a gorgeous guy, but no means no, man. Hashtag MeToo. He's got enough to contend with." She indicated herself and laughed gloomily.

I stepped toward her and said, "So he tells me."

This rankled her, and a chill fell over her. "Get out of here."

"I kissed him today," I said. "He wants *me*, not you. You're just a problem to solve. An impediment. Baggage."

Heat rose through her. "Get the fuck out of here." I'd gotten to her. "Or I'll call the police."

I obliged and took off. I was eager to find Ricky. Doing so would scrape her version of him—the sneering, eye-rolling, haughty Ricky—from my brain. What she'd said was vicious, and her tone echoed through my skull like my mother's high-strangling harpy's cry. I needed to cleanse myself of that nasty exchange and ground myself in the reality of us, our true love, however nascent, however impossible.

Woody, Kaye did *call us.*

Of course she did. I imagine she wanted to get me in trouble at work.

It was more than that.

Do you want me to finish?

Yes.

I scoured the theater and all the usual haunts for actors and crew members, but no Ricky. Had he vanished? (Why? Where?) Was he hiding? (Not from me, certainly.) Or was I just missing him?

For the life of me, I didn't know where he'd gone, and I began retracing my steps out of desperation. I returned to his apartment complex and again found myself gazing up at his little rectangle of outdoor space. This time, no one was out—no wisps of smoke, no Kaye—perhaps because it had grown cold and late. After a while, my resolve slipped, and a deep—no, *profound*—exhaustion settled in, my shoulders slowly crushing me to my feet.

As I was about to turn away, a light came on inside, like a TV switched on mid-show. Kaye, in jeans and a baggy concert T-shirt, crossed to stage right, her arms moving this way and that, her face a scrawl of anger, her sloppy bun slipping. To my surprise, Ricky followed her in measured, thoughtful steps, seeming to float, his dreamy good looks tarnished with grave concern. Was he a miracle or a mirage? He was the rock in their troubled relationship, a locus of sanity. I knew that much. Kaye's verbal attacks were muffled but unmistakable in their rage. As Ricky approached her—palms out, a supplicant—she howled, a banshee's scream if I ever heard one, picked up something long and thin, like a poker, and swung at him.

Horrified, I made a move. I had to. Reeling from exhaustion—the gravity under me doubling, tripling—I forced my body through the underbrush.

I must save him, I thought. *I'm his salvation!*

The fingers of the branches tore at my hair, shirt sleeves, and pants legs, as if they wanted to drag me back into the darkness. Still, I pressed on, burst into the thin strip of grass between the building and the trees, and staggered toward the courtyard, my head spinning, shooting stars, and then, as I reached the steps…well, I don't know what happened. All went black. I must've passed out.

That doesn't make much sense, Woody. How did you get back to the theater?

I understand it's hard to believe from your perspective. But it was like I hit a ripple in time and, leaping forward, woke up in the back seat of my car the next day, peeling my face off old *Playbills* and other detritus. The morning sun shot spikes into my eyes, and I had a monstrous headache. Maybe I'd driven myself? But my exhaustion was too extreme. Someone else must have brought me to the theater. Kaye? Had she killed Ricky? Was I a witness to murder? Had she hit me over the head?

And what about Russell?

Well, yes. Russell. He was the one who roused me from my slumber, tapping the end of his crutch against the car door. He was still in a cast but upright now. His hair was long, and his frosted tips had grown out; he looked like a sad porcupine. His arrogance, however, remained intact, curling the corners of his mouth. He claimed he'd been trying to contact Ricky by phone, but he hadn't responded, which was unusual, so he took an Uber to the theater to try to catch him. I didn't know what to tell him. It was too overwhelming to spill my guts.

But why did you tell him you'd just seen Ricky enter the theater?

How did you know that?

   Well, he started in on me: "Why were you sleeping in your car? You look like shit. Is everything okay?"

   I didn't have the energy to invent a story, so the best way to get rid of him was to tell him I'd seen Ricky go in.

Why did you follow him?

I'm getting tired of these questions.

Why did you follow him, Woody?

I don't know. I was confused, my brain was mush. What does it matter?

So you followed him, and then what?

And then what? And then...Ricky was there. Can you believe it? My fear and anxiety were whisked away in a flash. We went into the rec center, and he was on the stage, awash in a pool of light, graceful, electric, kneeling where comatose Julien would lie during the final scene of *Starcrossed*. His hair was rimmed, halo-like, and his dark eyes were Romeo's dark eyes, filled with impatient grief. Soon, believing his lover dead, he'd take his own life. Behind him loomed the Brutalist Capulet tomb I'd designed. It was meant to contrast the vitality of the young lovers: the chill of death present, even for the young. But Ricky's beauty and perfection banished the claustrophobic set pieces, halting the play's unfurling tragedy.

What about Russell?

I was relieved to see Ricky, sure. But it was more than that. I wanted to freeze the scene, pause the world, and live forever, peering up at him. That's love, I guess.

It's not what Russell claims happened.

Russell *claims?*

Yes, Woody, he survived, even though you struck him sixteen times with a counterweight like the ones that held your precious set pieces in place.

That's impossible.

He's awake, and he's talking.

That's not true. You're lying. He's...lying.

Look at these photos.

What? These are fake, digitally manipulated.

They're not fake. They're evidence. The construction workers found Kaye Wilder's body covered with a thin layer of dirt where they planned to pour the foundation for the new wing of the Rep.

She must've fallen there.

She fell and somehow strangled herself? That's a funny trick.

She must've driven me to the theater and then—

Shut up, Woody. It's time for you to listen. Look at yourself. You're covered in dirt. When you woke up in the car, didn't you wonder why you were caked in mud? If that's even the truth.

You're setting me up. The gay guy is always an easy target. So cliché.

You nearly beat a gay man to death, so don't—

What about Ricky? He can vouch for me. He knows none of what you're saying is true.

The workers were startled to find Kaye's body in a shallow grave, and you can imagine their shock when they discovered another *body under hers. Riccardo Pazzone's.*

No, no, no!

There's your starcrossed lovers.

Damn you!

32

His body had been down there for a little longer and was better concealed. He'd been struck in the back of the head with a long, thin, heavy object. Perhaps a piece of rebar? It'll all come out in the autopsy.

Stop.

The cameras on the construction site tell a story, too.

Stop it!

We think Mr. Pazzone wasn't as into your advances as you would have us believe. He was too preoccupied with Kaye's cancer diagnosis to fool with you, Woody. After the stage kiss, he rejected you, didn't he? So, jilted and obsessed—

It was love, not obsession.

Your "love" brought the rebar down on the back of his head, cracking his skull open to the brain. And your love dragged his body into a cold ditch and shoveled dirt over him with less reverence than most folks would give a dead pet.

Don't say that; that's horrible.

Then you went to his apartment, broke in, and strangled Kaye. You put her in the trunk of your Honda, drove her to the site, and dumped her on top of Ricky—but in your exhaustion and mania, you barely covered her with dirt.

Stop it. Just stop it.

Why kill her? Did you need to invent a story for yourself? Was it too much for you to believe you killed the man you were in "love" with? Is that it?

You don't understand a thing. A fucking thing. That's not the truth.

Then tell us, what is the truth? How did it happen?

The truth is—the truth is....

You know the truth: Riccardo, gorgeous Ricky, is alive and well. After our kiss on stage and our scene under the star-streaked sky, my heart was broken, sure. But I'd never hurt him. He has too much talent; he's too beautiful to ruin. I told you: I saw him with Kaye. She's the reason for this. She's the villain in this piece. She's the one who picked up the rebar, and...I can't even say it.

But it doesn't matter because, as I explained, I saw him today, kneeling in the tomb, encircled by light, running his lines, inhabiting the role he was made for, that he perfected. That's the truth, and you know it. There he was, on stage, becoming Romeo, being Romeo, forever my Romeo, banishing all the darkness from my world. And he's still there.

It's funny, Woody. I thought Romeo and Juliet *was about young love—at least, that's what I learned in high school—but you've taught me something.*

What's that?

It's a story about violence: obsession and violence.

You're wrong, detective. It's about putting love first. Like I did last night and will do again tonight and every night. I told you I'm a romantic.

You're a murderer.

That's not—

You aren't capable of love.

I told you, don't tell me what I feel isn't love.

34

Right, right. Or you'll stop talking.

Yes.

Well, then, I'll consider this conversation over.

Gypsy: A Musical Fable

opened May 21, 1959, at the Broadway Theatre, New York

ACT I
"Overture"
"May We Entertain You?"
"Some People"
"Some People" (reprise)
"Small World"
"Baby June and Her Newsboys"
"Mr. Goldstone, I Love You"
"Little Lamb"
"You'll Never Get Away From Me"
"Dainty June and Her Farmboys"
"Broadway"
"If Momma Was Married"
"All I Need Is the Girl"
"Everything's Coming Up Roses"

ACT II
"Entr'acte"
"Madame Rose's Toreadorables"
"Together, Wherever We Go"
"You Gotta Get a Gimmick"
"Small World" (reprise)

"Small World" (reprise)
"Let Me Entertain You"
"Rose's Turn"
"Finale"

Music by Jule Styne.
Lyrics by Stephen Sondheim.
Book by Arthur Laurents.

Together, Wherever We Go

by Jeffrey Marks

Gypsy Rose Lee had arranged to meet her mother in one of the Windy City's many dives, and she was sitting at the wooden bar of the Dante, waiting for Mama Rose. The Dante's floor looked like it hadn't been cleaned in months. Little white lights twinkled behind the row of bottles across from her. Cheap brands, she noticed, suspecting that the mob had had a hand in their selection.

She ordered a beer, which couldn't be watered down like liquor, tugged her mink coat closer around her, and hoped that no one here would recognize her. She had developed an elite persona that had taken years to perfect, and she didn't want it stained and scarred like the bar on which she rested her elbows. While the cast of her burlesque show at the Empire would never believe Gypsy might patronize a dump like this, the entire purpose of meeting her mother at the Dante was to *not* be noticed.

Gypsy wasn't the most attractive woman in the show. She'd never be a film star—or so Mama Rose kept telling her—but she had a nice body, with long legs that attracted the men.

She'd brought a hardbound copy of her new mystery novel, *The G-String Murders*, released a few weeks ago. The book had been selling like hotcakes, but she doubted that Mama had bought a copy. The cover was pink and gold—a perfect combination, now that women in the 1940s were making their own money.

Gypsy's visits with her mother always followed a routine, just like their old vaudeville shows. Mama Rose would recount their days on the Orpheum Circuit, and, oh, what fun the three of them—Mama, Rose Louise, and Baby June—used to have! Mama could certainly tell a good story, but her tales were usually exaggerated, generally featuring herself as the star of the act.

Gypsy had hurried to the Dante after her last turn at the Empire, where she deserved her billing as the most famous stripper in town. She preferred to be called an "ecdysiast." That word sounded classy, covering up the shadier side of burlesque. Mike Todd, the impresario, was in Chicago now, and he had promised her a role on Broadway. Gypsy wanted to move up to his lifestyle, not fall back into the low-rent career her mother represented.

The bartender set down her beer with a thud. "What's the damage?" she said, pulling out her clutch.

"A buck for you," the bartender said, eyeing her from head to toe.

So *he* had recognized her and had set his price accordingly. "That's rather steep," she said, batting her eyes to see if that might help.

"I can serve your beer to one of those guys, if you don't want it," the bartender said, nodding at the Dante's other patrons.

Gypsy didn't bother to argue. She handed him a dollar and turned away, just in time for an older man sitting beside her to offer her a piece of paper. He might have been attractive when Coolidge was president, but too much booze and a rough life had left him wrinkled and pudgy.

"I'd be happy to buy you a beer," he said. His eyes were glassier than the mirrors backstage at the Empire. "That there's my number—just in case."

Gypsy glanced at the paper he'd pressed into her hand. It said "Manny Grimes," with a phone number scrawled below the name.

Flirting with this moke after Mike Todd, she thought, *would be like sipping this beer after a glass of champagne.*

She checked her watch—from Switzerland—and saw that Mama Rose was running late. No surprise there.

She smiled at Manny Grimes. "Thanks, but no thanks. I have someone."

Granted, Mike wasn't *hers*, not exactly, not *yet*—he had a wife at the moment, but Gypsy had been promised their marriage wouldn't last long.

She sipped from her beer and made a face.

Then she heard, "Louise? Why did you pick this hellhole when we could have gone somewhere *nice*? I wanted to go to the Theatre Café—the one on Clark."

Mama Rose knew the café belonged to Mike Todd. She also knew Gypsy had no intention of introducing them. Todd was having enough trouble with the mob, who saw the café as a place to collect protection money once, twice, sometimes three times in the same week.

Mama—a broad-faced woman with dark brown hair much like Gypsy's own—settled onto the barstool on the other side of her daughter from Manny Grimes and ordered a martini, barely glancing at the bartender. Gypsy couldn't imagine what it would cost but knew she'd wind up having to pay for it.

Mama Rose wore an older coat, one of the two Gypsy had bought her, over a plain dress that made her look of humble descent. She *had* grown up in straitened circumstances, but now—thanks to Gypsy's success—she could have the best French dresses, any clothing she wanted.

Meanwhile, Manny ordered a drink, which a waiter brought around the bar to him.

"If you want to see me," Gypsy told her mother coldly, "we'll meet here. I don't want to be swamped by people asking for autographs."

"Louise," Mama said, "aren't you getting a bit above yourself? Autographs, and drinks with producers? It's all too much."

"It's who I am, Mama, and I'll thank you to call me Gypsy."

"I don't want to annoy you, but it's hard to remember to use that name. I still think of you and your sister as Louise and Baby June."

Gypsy pointed to an empty table across the room. "Let's go over there, where we can talk. I don't like sitting at the bar with all these men."

They took their drinks to the table and sat. When their glasses were empty, Gypsy attempted to hail the waiter, but he didn't seem to notice her.

Mama launched into a reminiscence of a time when Herbie, their manager, had managed to get the three of them room and board for the length of an appearance. Gypsy didn't recall any such occurrence. What she *did* recall was Mama stealing to make ends meet, and people eventually catching on and giving her a wide berth—and, eventually, even Herbie leaving them.

The waiter breezed past them again, picking up Manny's empty glass and wiping the bar.

Gypsy let her mind wander, thinking about Mike Todd's issues with the café, her own career, and the question of what her mother *really* wanted from her. A chunk of cash, she guessed. Mama was at her most charming when she needed money.

When the story ended, Gypsy said, "The Orpheum Circuit has been gone for over a decade, Mama. Vaudeville is dead, remember?"

"But there's still burlesque, with its raunchy jokes and"—Mama's face took on a look of disdain—"strippers."

"Men will always want to look at pretty women, especially when we're taking our clothes off. That's one thing I can count on—and it means I'll always have a career."

They heard a thump and turned to see Manny sprawled face down on the bar.

"Another bum who can't hold his liquor," Gypsy said. She'd seen plenty of men like that in her audiences. And Manny Grimes had been well on his way to drunk when he'd propositioned her.

"Louise, don't be dense. That man is *dead*." Mama Rose crossed to the inert boozer and shook his shoulder—and Manny collapsed from his stool to the floor. "I told you," she said. "He's stone-cold dead."

Gypsy didn't know who it was who was screaming until Mama grabbed her by the arms and shook her. "Stop it, Louise. I swear, why do I always have to be the one with the nerve?"

* * *

Mama called the police from a payphone inside the drugstore next door to the Dante, while Gypsy rested against the wall and attempted to regain her composure. She'd been expecting a quiet evening, but now the papers were likely to run photos of the two of them, and her plan of keeping their get-together low-key had vanished. She groaned and looked in her purse for an aspirin.

"Think of the publicity, Louise. We'll be on the front page," Mama said, waiting for someone to patch her through to homicide. "Mama Rose—and Gypsy," she said, bringing her arm around in a semicircle, like the lights on the marquee.

Then an officer must have picked up, because Mama rattled off the Dante's address and said her own name twice and "Louise Hovick" once. While she might not be happy about her daughter's career choice, she did have a knack for promotion and knew full well that Gypsy Rose Lee's presence in a neighborhood dive bar would not enhance her reputation as an upper-class stripper.

"They want us to go back and wait for the detective," Mama said, cradling the phone. She looked at Gypsy's mink. "I'd be more comfortable in this Chicago weather if I had a coat like yours."

"I'll buy you one, Mama," Gypsy said, repeating a promise she'd memorized over the years. Today a mink, tomorrow it'd probably be a car.

Back at the Dante, Gypsy headed toward their table, but Mama crossed the wooden floor to the dead man, dropped to her knees, and rummaged through Manny Grimes' pockets.

"Mama, don't," Gypsy said in a stage whisper. "What will the police say?"

"I'm just looking for his name," Mama said. "The detective will want to know who he is."

"I *know* his name," said Gypsy. "He told me, just before you got here."

A newcomer strolled into the bar. He had slicked-back hair and was rail-thin, with a hungry look about him. He obviously wasn't a policeman. He was the type of smartly dressed man about town who came to a bar looking for laughs and women—both in the plural.

He leaned down beside Mama Rose and spoke to her. Gypsy couldn't hear the words, but soon her mother was giggling like a schoolgirl.

The pair of them examined Manny's clothing together, and Gypsy saw her mother palm something from the dead man's front trouser pocket. She had to admit that Mama was good at being bad.

The bartender was talking to another new patron, who stood at the far end of the bar. He had an intriguing smile and wavy brown hair that looked like it had been left too long under a White Sox cap. A curl hung nearly down to his eyes.

Twice, he pointed in Gypsy's direction, and she prepared herself for a treacly conversation and wandering hands. At last, he approached her.

"The bartender says you talked with the dead guy," he said, and whatever pick-up line she'd expected him to try, it certainly wasn't that one.

"That's Captain O'Riley," the bartender called. "In case he ain't introduced himself."

O'Riley turned his attention to Mama Rose. "That, ah, *gentleman* you're chewing the fat with, Mrs. Lee, is a notorious gangster. I wouldn't be hanging around with him, I was you."

Mama stood. "We were just looking for the dead man's name," she said. "And it's Mrs. Hovick, not Mrs. Lee. And just for the record, my new friend Mr. Wolf here didn't arrive until after the *gentleman* on the floor was dead. So there's no way he could have been involved."

Wolf was not as cordial in his reply. "I just came here to collect a thousand bucks from the guy. You might want to check these two dames out and see if they've got it."

Gypsy leaned forward. "We don't know anything about your thousand dollars, sir."

The gangster laughed. "I'd say the same thing—if I took the money." His laugh stopped abruptly, and his face grew as severe as if he'd just learned that his dog had been stolen. "It's obvious: you charmed him, took the money, and bumped him off."

Gypsy flushed. "He offered to buy me a drink and gave me his name and number, but he didn't say a word about having such a large sum of money." She looked across the bar and saw the waiter ignore two patrons but serve a third one. He'd done the same thing before, ignoring her and Mama Rose but bringing a drink to the dead man.

She suggested that O'Riley might want to check the waiter's apron.

"Hey, that's Silver Dollar Mineo," Wolf declared. "He's changed his look from when I last saw him. I heard he was hoping to make one last score before he skipped town."

O'Riley turned to ask the waiter a question, but the man dropped the tray he was holding and bolted for the door.

Mama Rose put out a foot and sent him sprawling.

In the waiter's apron pocket, O'Riley found a small vial. He uncapped it and sniffed its contents. "Hmpf," he said. "Bitter almonds."

"If he ain't got my money," Wolf snarled, "I'll say it again: one of these broads must have glommed onto it."

Gypsy knew a way to clear herself of suspicion. "I can show you *I* don't have it," she murmured seductively, letting her mink drop off her shoulders. It was clear that her tight-fitting dress couldn't conceal a thousand dollars in cash.

Her impromptu striptease riveted the attention of the men in the bar.

Mama Rose was outraged. "If you think *I'm* going to strip like some cheap burlesque performer, you've got another think coming."

"Well, then, Mama dear," her daughter said sweetly, "why don't you just show the officer what's in your purse, instead?"

Mama's cheeks reddened, and she shot her daughter a murderous glance and clutched her bag tightly to her bosom. "I—I—" she stammered.

Captain O'Riley snatched the bag from her and pulled out a roll of bills.

Wolf tried to grab the cash, but O'Riley held onto it. "Why was the dead guy bringing you a thousand dollars?"

"He liked me," the gangster said weakly. "It was a gift."

"You're coming to the station with Silver Dollar here and Mrs. Hovick," the cop announced. "We've got a lot to discuss."

Mama put on her rigid face. "You go home, Louise. Mike's probably waiting for you, and you don't need to waste your time in some filthy police station."

Gypsy thought back across all the history she and her mother had shared and sighed. "No, I'll go with you, Mama. When you're in the soup, I'm in the soup. For better or worse, Mrs. Hovick, you and I are in this together."

Act II

The 1960s

A Funny Thing Happened on the Way to the Forum
opened May 8, 1962, at the Alvin Theatre, New York

ACT I
"Comedy Tonight"
"Love, I Hear"
"Free"
"The House of Marcus Lycus"
"Lovely"
"Pretty Little Picture"
"Everybody Ought to Have a Maid"
"I'm Calm"
"Impossible"
"Bring Me My Bride"

ACT II
"That Dirty Old Man"
"That'll Show Him"
"Lovely" (reprise)
"Funeral Sequence"
"Finale"

Music and lyrics by Stephen Sondheim.
Book by Burt Shevelove and Larry Gelbart.

Everybody Ought to Have a Maid

by Marcia Talley

Eighteen months ago, after Michael Crawford hired me to work for his private security firm out of L.A., my mother thought I'd be learning how to drive fast and shoot straight, not traipsing about after a twenty-one-year-old pop star as she checked out the Forum Shops at Caesar's Palace in Las Vegas. I'd spent ten weeks on bivouac with a paramilitary group outside of Pensacola, Florida, but a lot of good that training did me on my current assignment: Abigail Owen, or "Abbie-O" to the fans who had stuck with her via YouTube and TikTok during her two lengthy rehabs at a posh hospital in the Santa Monica Mountains, not far from Malibu.

"Is she the one who shaved her head?" my mother wanted to know.

"No," I said. "You're thinking of Britney Spears."

"So she's the one who got caught trying to smuggle cannabis into Singapore?"

"Wrong again," I said. "No, Abbie just quietly drank herself out of a promising career. She's been clean and sober for over six months now. This is her big comeback. She's opening for Garth Brooks next week."

"Him, I know," Mother said. After a pause to put me on speaker because she was driving, she continued, "You babysitting this girl, Jessie?"

"Sort of," I confessed. "They've put us up in a two-bedroom suite with a hundred-and-eighty-degree view of the Strip. I'll send pictures."

"Who's *they?*"

"Her father, I suppose. Reginald Owen. He's Abbie's manager. He's the one who hired us, anyway."

"So you drive her around?" Mother asked.

"Nope. They hire a limo for that."

"You her bodyguard, then?"

"They've got that covered, too, Mom. His name's Georgi. Big. Bulky. Bulgarian. Nobody messes with Georgi."

"So what's left, then? You follow her around? Make sure she behaves herself?"

"When she's not in rehearsal, yeah. I make sure she eats properly and doesn't socialize with her old drinking buddies. And I walk her dog."

"Ha," Mother snorted. "You might as well be a maid."

"I am not a maid," I insisted, remembering the countless hours I'd spent in the Florida boondocks, crawling through the heat and the ticks and the chiggers while carrying a full backpack.

"Humph."

When my mother seizes hold of an idea, she's hard to turn, and our discussion was clearly going nowhere.

"I'm hanging up now, Mom. Bye."

* * *

I am not a maid.

I repeated those words to myself as I wandered next door to check on my client, purposely resisting the urge to pick up the trail of clothing Abbie'd stripped off on her way to the bathroom. She was still in the Jacuzzi, belting out her signature song—"How Could They Know?"—in a sweet high soprano, mercifully free of the alcohol and cigarette rasp of her drinking years. "Know, oh, oh, oh!" she crooned, while Zero—her teacup Bichon Frisé—joined in on the chorus, howling from his customary perch on a padded chair next to the tub. In my opinion, he was a welcome addition to the act.

I knew Abbie was out of the tub when Zero scampered into my room, a snow-white puffball on legs thanks to Tanya, his groomer at Buff and Fluff.

"Want something to drink?" Abbie called out. I scooped Zero up and found my client standing in front of the minibar, wrapped in a gold-trimmed Caesar's Palace signature bathrobe, sipping a Diet Coke. No danger there. Before we checked in, they'd emptied the bar of adult beverages and re-stocked it with fruit juices and diet sodas and iced tea.

"Over a hundred and sixty shops." Abbie sighed heavily. "And what are they? Victoria's Secret? Burberry? Gucci? Aren't there any *young* people in Vegas? Everything's so, I don't know, blue-haired Boomer baby."

I had to smile. "You did drop some bucks at Hermès," I reminded her.

"I must have been desperate."

Abbie, I'd learned, had a magic credit card, though its monthly three-thousand-dollar limit kept her on a comparatively short leash. She'd maxed it out at Hermès, buying a twenty-two-hundred-dollar purse-sized carrier for Zero and a two-hundred-dollar scarf. I didn't mention as the salesman wrapped the scarf that I'd once bought a similar one at Kohl's for nineteen ninety-five—and that was *before* my twenty-percent discount.

"You know that pendant?" she mused after several minutes. "At Van Cleef & Arpels?"

"Yeah," I said, remembering it well, a glossy ruby cabochon surrounded by diamonds. It cost the earth, but we'd agreed it would look perfect on stage, glittering from the cleavage of her black Spandex catsuit.

"I called Daddy. He's making arrangements to borrow it for the show. For the video, too."

"Van Cleef & Arpels," I said, checking my watch. "A Hollywood tradition. Don't you think you better get dressed? Rehearsal's in thirty minutes."

"I know, I know." Abbie drained her soda and tossed the empty can at the trash, missing the basket by a good two feet.

I am not a maid, I thought, cringing as droplets of Diet Coke decorated the baseboard. I made no move to collect the can, nor the empty Doritos packets on the coffee table, nor the breakfast dishes dropped higgledy-piggledy on the room service tray. Tidying up was housekeeping's job.

Ten minutes later, Abbie emerged from her bedroom in skin-tight cropped jeans and a sleeveless T-shirt. Her auburn hair had long ago outgrown its neon streaks. She'd twisted it into a knot at the top of her head and secured it with a red sequined claw that matched her high-heeled sandals. "How do I look, baby?" she cooed, squatting to address Zero, not me.

I answered her anyway. "Lovely. Like a pop star ready for her comeback."

She glanced up at me and grinned. "You really think so?"

"I do," I assured her, just as there was a knock on the door. "That'll be Georgi come to pick you up."

"Time for walkies," she told Zero. "Jessie will take you in your brand-new bag. Won't that be nice? The sidewalks are too hot for your itty-bitty paws."

"No worries," I said, turning Abbie over to Georgi.

* * *

Zero and I had an early lunch at Snackus Maximus, sharing a plate of chicken fingers and French fries in a lounger near the Temple Pool. The hotel's pet-relief area was not far away, a rectangle of Astroturf surrounded by a wrought-iron fence behind the Augustus Tower Building. The last time I'd brought Zero there, he'd slipped out under cover of an Irish wolfhound, and I didn't catch up with him until he'd almost reached the Mirage. I'd recommended to Abbie that she buy one of those high-tech GPS collars for him, but nobody'd done anything about it as yet. Perhaps because *they* didn't have to chase an energetic puppy up and down the Las Vegas Strip.

I reminded Zero of this shameful episode and reached into my purse to execute Plan B—transferring my Apple AirTag from my car keys to Zero's collar.

Five minutes later, with no other dogs in sight, I set Zero's carrier down on the sidewalk in front of the pet-relief park and reached to open the gate. Something struck me on the back of the head, lights flashed, and everything went dark.

* * *

"Are you okay?"

The speaker loomed over me, all six-foot-something of her, wearing a preposterous blond wig and channeling *I Dream of Jeannie* big-time in a pink silk harem outfit. As she eased me into a sitting position against the fence, the tiny bells that circled her waist and biceps tinkled cheerfully. "Do you need an ambulance?"

"No, no, I'm fine," I insisted, rubbing the bump on the back of my head and dredging up a grin. "It's only a flesh wound."

"We saw what happened," her companion told me. A full-blown Roman centurion, she was decked out in a leather bra with studs so pointed they could poke your eyes out. A coiled-up whip was lashed to the waist of her studded leather skirt. "We stepped out for some fresh air and a smoke when this Honda Fit pulled up. A punk jumped out and clobbered you over the head, snatched the dog, and skedaddled."

"Dog?" I said stupidly. I looked around in growing panic. Zero was gone. "Shit! Somebody kidnapped my dog?"

"There's a lot of that going around," the centurion muttered. She handed me a sheet of lined notebook paper, folded down the middle. "Punk dropped this on the way out."

I unfolded the paper and saw, clichéd as it may seem, this message spelled out in words and letters cut from magazines and pasted to the page: *$100,000 in small bills. Will call. No cops or the dog dies.*

I knew Abbie had paid a reputable Bichon Frisé breeder nearly six thousand dollars for Zero. That plus two thousand for the Hermès carrier brought her total investment to eight grand, so a hundred K seemed like a high markup to me. Then again, Zero *did* know the chorus to "How Could They Know?"

"Can you describe the dognappers for me?" I asked.

"The guy driving the Honda, not so much," the harem girl said. "All I saw was he was wearing a red ball cap. The other guy, the one who actually snatched your dog, might have been in his twenties. Jeans, T-shirt, and—"

"Wait a minute," the centurion cut in. "He had a tattoo, right? On his forearm? A four-leaf-clover-like thing, with lightning bolts shooting out of it."

I sighed, almost with relief. I recognized that description. Abbie's former boyfriend, Miles Gordon, individual number one on Reggie Owen's BOLO list, had a tattoo like that. "Thanks," I said, refolding the note and stuffing it into my pocket. "Is there some way I can contact you, if I need to talk to you again?"

The harem girl waved vaguely at the hotel across the street. "We're appearing at the Flamingo, in RuPaul's Drag Race. I'm Steve, and this is Kyle, but you can ask for us by our stage names. I'm Tintinabula," he said, jingling his bells.

"And I'm Gymnasia," Kyle said, extending his hand. "I do whip tricks. When Jingle Belle here doesn't impress the rubes, the whipper will."

"Sometimes it works out that way," sighed Steve. "Ah, well: I win some, I lose some."

I grinned, catching the references—but what would my boss say if he learned one of his operatives had to be rescued by a pair of drag queens? I'd made a rookie mistake; Rule Number One is *always remain aware of your surroundings.* Unless I could sort things out by myself in the three and a half hours remaining before the end of Abbie's rehearsal, there'd be a price to pay for my carelessness.

∗ ∗ ∗

At three-forty-five, Georgi deposited Abbie at the door of our suite.

I was ready for her.

She breezed in, so wreathed in smiles that it seemed like a crime to burst her bubble.

"Rehearsal went well, I take it?"

"Fab," she chirped. "I thought I'd miss the bigger band, but the new group worked out better than I expected. Patty Jessel is awesome on the electric violin." She glanced around the suite, looking puzzled. "Where's Zero?"

I delivered the news bluntly. "Somebody kidnapped him, Abbie."

Eyes wide, she gasped. "You've got to be shitting me."

Her performance wasn't convincing. "Don't pull that crap on me. You're

53

a much better singer than you are an actress. Sit." I patted the sofa cushion next to me.

She sat.

"There were witnesses," I told her. "They saw a couple of punks in a silver Honda. One guy had a distinctive tattoo. Clovers and lightning bolts? Any idea who that might have been?"

Abbie folded her hands in her lap, lowered her head, and nodded silently.

"Did you know about this?"

She looked up. "Sort of. Miles always said he wanted to hold my dad up for some serious money, but I didn't think he meant it. He talked a lot about buying a boat and sailing off into the sunset with me."

Miles was a doofus if he thought he could buy a seaworthy cruiser for as little as a hundred thou, but I didn't say so. "So, who's Miles's partner, the one driving the car?"

"Probably his brother Phil. He's not super bright." After a moment, she added, "Where have they taken Zero?"

"Oh, I know exactly where Zero is." I slid my iPhone off the glass tabletop and opened the Find My app, which pinpointed my AirTag in a position that Google Street View told me was a cut-rate motel about half a mile from the Strip, sandwiched between Pawn Palace and Bad Boy Bail Bonds. "Do you know how to get in touch with Miles?"

Her cheeks flushed. She nodded.

"Okay. Let's cut the shit, then. You're gonna call him, tell him we know exactly where he is, and if he doesn't want the cops knocking down his door with a battering ram, he's got to bring Zero back. If he gets here within the next thirty minutes, I might—just *might*—consider not filing assault charges against him."

Abbie stood up. "Okay, but I'll have to get my phone. I left it charging in the bedroom."

* * *

"It's done," she said when she rejoined me. "Miles says he'll be here in twenty minutes." She tossed her phone aside and fell back onto the cushions. "The sonofabitch can drop dead, for all I care."

That'd save everybody a lot of trouble, I thought.

I had my head stuck in the fridge, fetching us both something to drink, when Abbie called, "I swear to God, Jessie, I don't want to go on living like this!"

"Like what?" I asked, genuinely curious. I handed her a Diet Coke and sat down.

"*This!*" Her free arm swept the room. "The travel, the hotels, the room service. Georgi, for God's sake—and even you! Ever since I appeared on *The Voice*, everything's gone all haywire! I made decent grades in high school. Why can't I just go to college like a normal person?" She leaned forward and whispered, "I don't even *like* Miles very much, but I used to think he'd be my ticket out." She snorted. "Some hero he turned out to be."

"Why not quit?" I asked. "Just walk away. You're twenty-one—that's old enough to make your own decisions."

"I gotta do this gig first, Jessie, honor my contract." She frowned. "It's a lot like work, though. Buttering up the honchos when all I want to do is scream. Staying quiet as a mouse simply isn't in my genes, and it's not like I really need the money. There's sixty-five million and change sitting in the accounts my father manages."

"Fire his ass, then. Hire a new manager."

"Can't. When I was in the hospital, the court granted Dad a conservator-ship, claiming I was unfit to manage my own affairs." She smiled wistfully. "Which was true, I'm afraid. I might have blown it all on a motor yacht for Miles."

"You need a lawyer," I said. "I'm not allowed to recommend anyone specific, but if I were you, I'd Google the guy who represented Britney Spears and give him a call, find out what he has to say."

"I could make this my farewell concert," she mused, warming to the idea. "Put it up on YouTube, watch it go viral. Maybe I could even get a book deal. Britney did."

The girl was on the right track at last. I hoped nothing would derail her.

* * *

I worried about what I might do when forced to confront the odious Miles, but the situation never arose. Zero, Hermès carrier and all, was delivered directly to our door by a hotel porter. As Abbie cuddled her beloved pet, tears coursed down her cheeks. "Where are the goddamn Kleenex when you need them?" she sobbed into Zero's fur.

Although I was not a maid, I got up and fetched them for her.

Anyone Can Whistle

opened April 4, 1964, at the Majestic Theatre, New York

ACT I
"Prelude Act I"
"I'm Like the Bluebird"
"Me and My Town"
"Miracle Song"
"There Won't Be Trumpets"
"Simple"

ACT II
"Prelude Act II"
"A-1 March"
"Come Play Wiz Me"
"Anyone Can Whistle"
"A Parade in Town"
"Everybody Says Don't"
"Don't Ballet"

ACT III
"Prelude Act III"
"I've Got You to Lean On"
"See What It Gets You"
"Anyone Can Whistle" (reprise)
"Cora's Chase (The Cookie Chase)"
"I'm Like the Bluebird" (reprise 1)
"With So Little to Be Sure Of"
"I've Got You to Lean On" (reprise)
"I'm Like the Bluebird" (reprise 2)
"Finale Ultimo"

Music and lyrics by Stephen Sondheim.
Book by Arthur Laurents.

There Won't Be Trumpets

by Lisa Nanni-Messegee

Angela Fay was *the* main show at the Cookie Jar. She always danced at the coveted hour of eleven, when the Jar was full, and the drinks were flowing. When that crimson spotlight landed on her perfect form, you woulda thought Angela was the sun. In the moments I could take my eyes off her—which were rare—I could see the redneck pigs trying to sort through all the ways they could get Angela alone. But they couldn't touch her. Nobody could...till the trumpet player came along.

Now that son of a bee sting is dead, and Angela—my darling Angela—is gone, too.

* * *

Let me say this right off: I ain't pretty enough to be a dancer. I got skinny chicken legs and broad shoulders, my chest is flat as a pancake, and my brown eyes don't have that special sparkle. I think it's because I been used up. When I enter a room in my Carhartt and flannels, folks don't look up; there's no angels' choir. That's reserved for girls like Angela Fay. My darling, my beautiful Angela.

She first arrived at the Cookie Jar in Lourdes, Mississippi, two years ago, and a week later to the day, I got the bartending job. You'd think it woulda been easy getting a job behind the stick at a dump like the Cookie Jar, but it was the opposite. Henry Schub, the owner, squinted one eye at me and said if he had a dog who looked like me, he'd shave its butt and make it walk backwards. Well, the devil on my shoulder tempted me to say that his beer belly was so big he looked like a red-headed camel with the hump in front—but thankfully I kept my mouth shut and got the gig.

Henry soon learned that what I lacked in looks, I made up for in bartending skills. I got my start in my daddy's bar in the shit backwater of Yellow Holler when I was fourteen. Sheriff Magruder looked the other way, provided daddy let him have *his* way with me out in the back alley, which reeked a sour whiskey. But that there's another story for a different porch swing.

The Cookie Jar had some asinine rules. The craziest one was the dancers had to pay full price for their own drinks unless a customer bought them one. That was stupid, because I wud'n allowed to serve the girls *any* drinks till they were done with their set, even if they were bought and paid for. The thirsty ones would beg me, so I'd sometimes sneak them a Miracle, which was our house version of a watered-down Long Island iced tea.

Well, Henry started to get suspicious when the rats showed up. He spotted one licking at a cup in the dressing room during a set. I caught hell for that, and since then, I been in charge of spraying rat poison into the Cookie Jar's every corner and crevice.

One night, as I was closing, Angela stormed into the bar, tear-stained and mad as a wet hen. She was tugging at her dress and talking out loud to no one in particular, saying, "That carrot-headed, egg-suckin' dog, with his penny-pinching scheme. He thinks he can threaten *me?*"

I called out to her, "Angela? Angela, you want a Miracle? I'll make you a real good one. My treat."

She looked at me, surprised, like it was the middle of winter and I was a new shoot sprouting up in the dirt. "Well, bless your heart, Lee Ann. Yes, I could use a drink."

"It's just Lee," I said shyly.

"Right, right." She smiled an apology. "A shot'll do me. I got to get my pocketbook, and I don't want to stay here longer'n I have to. No offense." She cocked her head to one side, and I watched her false eyelashes flutter twice as she said, "You look familiar. Have we met before? Outside a this shithole, I mean."

"I guess I got one a those faces," I said, my heart pounding outa my chest. Imagine! Angela Fay thinking she recognized me! Ain't nobody ever really *saw* me before, and that moment changed my life.

I pulled two shot glasses, reached for the bottle of Jack, and filled them both perfectly, to the rims.

Angela settled in and proceeded to tell me that Henry wanted to turn a bigger profit at the expense a her and the girls. Now every dancer would have to pay the house twenty dollars a night to perform. When she confronted Henry about it, he threatened to put her on the blacklist, which is death to a dancer: it's shared with all the other clubs in a thirty-mile radius, and a blacklisted girl's name becomes mud.

After her third shot, Angela confessed she was sick of being ogled and taken advantage of. She wanted to be a *real* dancer and work in Jackson, at the Majestic. She'd been trying to save up her money, but it'd been a long road. She just needed an exit ramp, she said. She was pining for a hero to save her from her plight, and she was thinking she'd found him in a trumpet player from the city, a guy with a pock-marked face who'd been showing up every night for the last couple weeks just to watch her dance.

"His name's Gabriel," she gushed, "and I heard he's rich as Croesus. His family has a place in Wet Rock Springs. Every time he comes here, he wears silk shirts and white leather shoes and one a them Panama hats. He ain't like anybody around here. He looks like he come straight outa *Casablanca*."

I wasn't real sure what she meant by that, but Angela was convinced Gabriel was the kinda man who would propose to her. He just needed a little more encouragement, and she was desperate enough to break her golden rule and give him what he wanted.

I was horrified. "You mean private-room business? That ain't who you are, Angela! You're—you're above that!"

"If I get Gabriel to propose," she answered, "it don't hardly matter. If my moral ground is keeping me stuck at the Cookie Jar, I got to make a change."

"Henry Schub'll never let you go," I retorted bitterly.

"Will you help me convince him?"

She put the question so sweetly, I felt myself bending like a willow branch. "I'll save you," I declared, with the kind of reverence a knight would give to his queen.

Angela laughed so hard she had to steady herself on the barstool. I played it cool, but deep down, I was dead serious.

"You're funnier'n I expected," she purred.

"I used to do some theater."

Her eyes widened. "You're an actress?"

"Oh, no, well, makeup, mostly," I stammered. "I got cast in a musical once. I was in the ensemble, but then I got a small part with lines. The character had to do a live stage whistle, and nobody could do it but me, so I got the part. I even got a solo."

"Well, that's—"

"Only the director cut the song the night before we opened."

Angela's face dropped. "Oh, honey, that's a real shame."

"It was the best song in the show."

Angela tucked a delicate strand of blond hair behind her ear and stared at me for what felt like an hour. Then she stood up and put out her hand. "Come with me," she said.

An awkward smile crawled across my lips as I placed my hand in hers. Her tapered fingers wrapped around mine like a cool satin sheet.

She led me to her dressing room. She was the only dancer at the Cookie Jar to have earned her own space, and no one—not even Henry—was allowed in without her permission. The room was hardly bigger than a walk-in closet. A rack, neatly hung with colorful costumes, covered most of the left wall, along with a line of clear boxes filled with spike heels and knee-high boots. On the right was a vanity, stained honey maple, with a big mirror outlined in white bulbs. Makeup, curling irons, and brushes were neatly organized. Tucked around the mirror were pictures carefully cut out of magazines: rainbow-bright buildings along a cobblestone street, a big ol' water fountain with ladies squeezing fish, and the Eiffel Tower.

"I got a soft spot for all things French," Angela explained. "My mama was born there, and my daddy always promised he'd take me one day, but…that didn't pan out." She cleared her throat and pointed to a poster on the wall. "That there's a French movie poster. They talk in a mix a French and English. It's called *Come Play Wiz Me,* 'cuz French people can only say *wiz* and not *with.* Ain't that charming?"

"Sure is," I said, but my voice came out husky.

"Now our sizes are a little different. You're taller'n me, and your shoulders are stronger, but I think I got somethin' ya might like."

She pulled a dark suit coat off the rack and hung it on the back of the chair.

"I did some cabaret choreography at the Hapgood Gentlemen's Club, which was the last place I danced at. It went over pretty well, but the customers here don't want me to work that hard. You have a seat, Lee. I want to do one little thang with some makeup."

She worked on me in silence for a while, and I reveled in the nearness of her. Her hair still held the curl from her last performance, and she smelled like a heavenly mixture of hairspray, sweet vanilla, and musk. I didn't even mind the hint of whiskey on her breath. Her gray eyes were made up to look smoky, which added to the sadness in her face. As she leaned in close to add mascara to my lashes, my gaze had no other place to go than her cleavage. It was something I'd seen a lot of on stage, but it was much more intimate now, because this show was all for me.

Suddenly, she started to chuckle. I figured she'd caught me looking where I shouldn't. My ears burned red, and my breath quickened from shame. If she noticed, she didn't say; instead, she started to whistle. Now, Angela was good at a lot of things, but I would not put whistling on the list of her accomplishments. Hers had no melody; it just came out like a soft hiss.

"I was just thinking about those folks in that musical you were in," she said, "trying so hard to put their lips together and make a noise. And there you were, tootin' away like a bluebird." Her laughter ebbed, and her voice softened. "Lord willing and the creek don't rise, *I'll* get in a musical one day."

Angela got me standing and slipped me into the suit coat before I could take a breath. She added a top hat and pointed my shoulders toward the mirror.

"Look at you!" she said proudly, grinning from ear to ear.

She'd turned me into a man, with an angular jaw and a pencil-thin mustache. I couldn't even recognize my own self in the reflection!

"Well, I'll be," was all I could muster, which made her crack a smile and playfully slap my arm.

"I think you look good enough to sing a solo," she said.

I opened my mouth to protest, but Angela grabbed me by the hand and marched me out of her dressing room and up onto the stage, where I did something I never in a million years thought I'd do: I sang to Angela.

* * *

The gravel parking lot was empty when we finally left the Cookie Jar. My heart ripped in half when Angela drifted toward her Ford Escape without so much as a hug goodbye.

The words that were caught in my throat suddenly spilled out. "Angela, I got to ask: do you love Gabriel?"

Her brow furrowed, and she traced a gold-painted fingernail along the edge of her feather keychain. "Love don't mean squat in this insane, upside-down world we live in. That's a sad fact. I'd best be getting on, now. Thanks for the shots, and for playin' dress-up and sanging to me. You take care now, Lee Ann."

I didn't have the heart to correct her about my name. Instead, I watched her hips sway as she glided toward her SUV and unlocked the door. I thought about that jackass Gabriel and his stupid silk shirts, white leather shoes and Panama hat. I thought about him touching her like Sheriff Magruder touched me in the back alley of my daddy's bar. I may not be rich or talented or pretty, but I was serious as a heart attack when I swore that, if Angela needed me, I would be the hero that shows up in the nick of time.

* * *

Some plans come together fast, but mine hatched just like a chick. It took nearabout twenty days of careful planning before the first peep.

I bided my time by stayin' busy at the Cookie Jar. I made Miracles and sprayed for rats, while Angela danced double sets. Here and there, she'd give me a quick glance and a little smile, which made my heart soar. Deep down, I knew it was proof she felt our bond. After each set, I watched as she took the pock-faced trumpet player into a private room and closed the thick red velvet curtain, like she was a leading lady in a Broadway play. At least I kept telling myself that. How else could I allow my darling Angela to get all used up like that?

It took less than a week for the girls to start clucking like hens about the Cookie Jar's star couple and making bets on when the wedding bells would ring. Henry 'n' me were the only ones who didn't see matrimony in the cards. He saw dollar signs. And me? Well, I saw a different future, where Angela and I would be together forever. We were already the best of friends. I'd even sang for her, and for that reason alone, Angela Fay was mine to save. My darling would soon discover that real heroes don't come to the rescue blasting trumpets. They're loud in other, more clever ways.

* * *

Henry Schub was in rare form that night. He closed the Cookie Jar early and rushed the rednecks and dancers out. I stayed on, since I had to close out the cash register and clean the bar.

While I wiped down the soda gun, I took a gander at him. He looked ridiculous in his sleazy green pinstriped suit. It was a size too small, so the middle buttons were working overtime. He piddled around the empty club, nervously wiping tables and pushing in chairs. I knew he'd spent the last two weeks talking on the phone to the trumpet player, finally convincing Gabriel to meet him in his office to talk about Angela.

"Unlock the back door, git some champagne and the ice bucket, and put it in my office, Lee, then git yer flat ass back behind the bar and close up."

"Yessir," I replied.

Just to mess with him, I let him start walking before I called out innocently, "Who's it for?"

He stopped and sighed as loud as he could and slowly turned to me.

"Not that it's any of your business, but Angela's trumpet-player boyfriend is fixing to take her away from the Cookie Jar. He don't know it yet, but it's gonna cost him."

"When's he comin'?"

"In an hour, so shut your pie hole and get a wiggle on! I want that champagne bottle cold by the time he gets here."

With that, Henry hoisted up his britches and strutted toward his office.

Through the window by the door, I could see the gravel lot was empty, except for Angela. She was just standing there with her suitcase, waiting for her savior to arrive, make a deal, and take her away for good. With the music turned off, I could hear Henry in his wood-paneled office, shuffling around, farting, rearranging chairs. The bar lights were dimmed, and pretty soon, all was silent.

Only then did Gabriel appear.

He wore a deep violet satin shirt that made him look like royalty, along with his signature white leather shoes and Panama hat. The brim, tipped down low in front a his eyes, cast a shadow across his face. His shoulders were broad, and he had a confident swagger as he entered Henry's office without knocking.

Henry started in on his prepared speech about how valuable Angela was to the club, but he didn't get far.

"You ain't Gabriel," he cut himself off, his voice small and scared, like a kid looking for his mama in a shopping mall. Then a flash a anger set in.

He stomped over and ripped off my Panama hat.

"Forty hells! Lee Ann? What in tarnation are you up to, wearin' 'at outfit? Where's the trumpet player?"

I answered him with a whack to the temple, using the ice-cold Mumm's champagne bottle. I didn't say a word, just sat on his camel hump and walloped his head till my white leather shoes turned crimson, like the color of the spotlight that shone so bright on my darling Angela.

* * *

It was long past midnight by the time I pulled Gabriel's apple-red Dodge Challenger into the gravel lot. Angela was in the car putting on her lip gloss before I even popped the trunk for her suitcase.

"So I reckon it worked out, Gabriel? You pickin' me up 'n' all. What did Henry say? Am I finally free a that shithole?"

She leaned in and turned my face to hers and kissed me. Her lips were smooth and soft, like rose petals, and she tasted like a Georgia peach. Then she pulled back, like she'd been bit by a snake.

God's honest, I didn't think to rehearse how I'd *tell* her it was me underneath the costume and makeup. I figured it'd just work itself out; she'd find out it was me and see at last that I was her true hero. We'd laugh, and she'd curl her cool fingers around mine, and we'd drive into the sunset like Thelma and Louise.

Well, as they say, if wishes were horses, then beggars would ride.

Instead of a "thank you, Lee" or a "you're my savior," Angela pitched a hissy fit. She kept hollering as I put my seat belt on and shifted into drive. I tried to explain what I done in the clearest, calmest terms. I told her she wudna believed how many hills I'd had to climb for her. How I drove to the jazz club in Jackson the night before and laced the mouthpiece of Gabriel's trumpet with Henry's rat-poison spray between sets. How Gabriel hurled shrimp and grits into the audience and stumbled out the club, and I whupped him, stole his clothes and his car, and told him I was working for Henry. Then, tonight, all sweaty, with spitfire vengeance, Gabriel come in through the back door of the bar wanting a piece a me and Henry both.

Imagine his surprise, seeing me in his clothes, holding the Mumm's champagne that wud'n yet chilled. One wallop was all it took, and the hard cement floor did the rest. Funny: I killed two bodies for the price a one off that bottle. I dragged Gabriel into Henry's office, I explained, cleaned my prints off the Mumm's so it'd look like a knock-down-drag-out between the two of 'em'd turned deadly.

"You ain't right in the head, Lee Ann," was Angela's reply.

"You don't mean that. You and me, Angela, we got something special. I sang for you."

"And you did a crap job. You couldn't carry a tune in a bucket with the lid on it."

* * *

I roll those hurtful words around in my head as I watch Gabriel's car take on water and slowly sink into the Mississippi River. I think I'll get creative with Angela's suicide note. Maybe I'll tell the story of a girl who got a part in a musical—even had a solo, but it got cut the night before opening. Then she fell on hard times and wound up at the Cookie Jar, dancing for a scoundrel named Henry Schub, who pimped her out to a pock-marked trumpet player from Jackson.

As for me? Well, I was the hero who didn't show up in time. The world's still waiting for me to arrive. And when I do, y'all will know it. And there won't be no trumpets, neither. You'll know me, sure as shooting, 'cause I'll be the one whistling.

Do I Hear a Waltz?

opened March 18, 1965, at the 46th Street Theatre, New York

ACT I

"Overture"

"Someone Woke Up"

"This Week Americans"

"What Do We Do? We Fly!"

"Someone Like You"

"Bargaining"

"Here We Are Again"

"Thinking"

"No Understand"

"Take the Moment"

ACT II

"Moon in My Window"

"We're Gonna Be Alright"

"Do I Hear a Waltz?"

"Stay"

"Perfectly Lovely Couple"

"Thank You So Much"

"Finale"

Music by Richard Rodgers.

Lyrics by Stephen Sondheim.

Book by Arthur Laurents.

Bargaining

by Joseph S. Walker

NEW YORK CITY, 1965

Dexter Wakefield did not *leap* to the conclusion that Frank Serge had to die. He regarded his deliberation as evidence that the decision was entirely justified. If Dex was really the monster some said he was—the narcissist, the tyrant, the director New York actors told horror stories about—he would have started planning Serge's death the first time the movie star showed up to rehearsal late, drunk, and openly contemptuous of the production Dex had poured his life into, the production he desperately needed to work. But Dex Wakefield was a *humanitarian*, whatever the troglodytes at the *Times* thought. Dex Wakefield was an *artist*, too sensitive to all the colors of human experience, too imbued with empathy and understanding, to start thinking of murder immediately.

No, it took him almost three weeks to make up his mind.

* * *

Ten years earlier, Dex had been the toast of the Great White Way, the *wunderkind* with two hit shows under his belt. He still couldn't believe how quickly it had all fallen apart. All right, yes, there was that one dress rehearsal, when he attacked those actors with a baseball bat, but he would

70

swear to his dying day that he thought the bat was a foam prop when he grabbed it, and it's not like Carol Manning had been confined to a wheelchair *permanently*. Besides, anyone who witnessed what the actors were doing to the script would agree that his reaction was warranted.

But that didn't prevent his decade in exile. The dinner-theater staging of Shaw one-acts in French Lick, Indiana. The community-theater mauling of O'Neill in Jacksonville. The "Theater for Kids" segments on public TV, shot with secondhand equipment that turned everything into a gauzy blur. The—at his lowest points, he shuddered to recall—the *teaching*.

Oh, God, the teaching. Never again.

For the last six years, he'd poured his frustration into a script he was sure would fuel his comeback: *Merchant!*, a modern-dress musical retelling of *The Merchant of Venice*, with the action relocated to Venice, California, and the themes refocused on contemporary concerns—racial tension, political strife, abuse of municipal tax codes. After all the rough landings, all the false starts, all the misunderstandings, this one was a sure-fire winner. If those bastards Robbins and Bernstein could get away with ripping off the damn Bard of Avon, why couldn't Dexter Wakefield do the same thing?

There'd been a lot of hurdles, especially finding a composer and lyricist to fine-tune his admittedly rough song ideas. Sondheim hung up on him, then called back just for the pleasure of hanging up on him again. Lerner and Loewe laughed in his face. Dorothy Fields called him names no lady should know. Oscar Hammerstein took the easy way out—by dying. Finally, in desperation, he'd hired Eddie Damon and Jennifer Marie, a couple too fresh out of Julliard to be choosy.

Then there was the financing. Dex sank everything he had into the project, but that didn't come close to covering the cost of mounting a Broadway production, and his angels dictated such draconian terms that he wouldn't see a dime of profit unless *Merchant!* played for at least six months to SRO houses.

And then, of course, came the casting. Fritz Weaver would have been perfect for Shylock, but he was busy shy-knocking 'em dead as Sherlock in *Baker Street*. John Raitt could have made it work, if it wasn't for the damn revival of *Carousel*. Richard Kiley would have *owned* the role, except for fucking *Man of La Mancha*. At last—more desperation—Dex managed to land Frank Serge, the larger-than-life hero of dozens of Westerns. Serge's management needed a vehicle to prove he could do more than ride a horse and shoot at Indians, and Dex needed a star to get his show up and running, so they were able to cut a deal.

The ink was still wet on the contracts when Dex realized he'd made a deal with the devil.

Frank Serge was better than six feet tall and weighed close to two fifty. It shouldn't be biologically possible for a man that size to stay drunk all day, but Serge, a scientific marvel, managed it. He was routinely late for rehearsals. He rarely knew his lines and had to be reminded repeatedly that cue cards are not employed in the theater. He clomped flat-footed around the stage, ignoring Dex's meticulously arranged blocking and grabbing the breasts of any woman who wandered within reach. In his first attempt at stage combat, he put the third male lead in traction by shoving the poor moke into the orchestra pit. He was rude, vulgar, entitled, violent, temperamental, and stupid, but Dex would have happily forgiven it all…if only the son of a bitch could act or sing.

* * *

Two and a half weeks into the planned eight weeks of rehearsal, Dex sat third row center, staring up at Serge, who stood, swaying slightly, at the front of the stage. The star had just finished a rendition of Shylock's big second-act number, "Pound of Flesh (Gimme Gimme Gimme)." Dex felt like he could still hear the music, its waltz-like beat burning in his brain, though it had actually faded into silence.

Cast and crew, eyeing Dex while pretending not to, waited for his reaction. Over the last two weeks, they'd seen him cajole Serge, pamper Serge, plead with Serge, reason with Serge, go red in the face raving at Serge, none of which had any apparent effect on the cowpoke's performance, though it frequently triggered his temper.

Look on the bright side, Dex told himself. *At least he remembered the words. Although they weren't in the right order. Or tempo. Or key.*

Dex was out of things to try. He knew, with a sudden bright clarity that suffused him with hope, that Frank Serge had to die.

Accepting this reality was such a relief that Dex managed a smile. "Great work, everybody." He made a show of looking at his watch. "We'll wrap up a little early today."

"We haven't even had lunch," somebody said.

"Have a long one," Dex said. "We're back at nine tomorrow."

Then he went looking for Renny.

* * *

Renny was a thin Italian stagehand with a toothpick perpetually wedged in the corner of his mouth and a jet-black pompadour. Every show Dex ever worked on had a crew member like Renny, but they weren't there to manage props.

If you were exhausted from the stress of rehearsals, you talked to Renny, and there'd be a little bottle of pills tucked into a pocket of your costume. If you were an actress whose ex wouldn't stop hanging around the stage door, you talked to Renny, and next day he'd tell you what hospital the guy was in, in case you wanted to send flowers. If your TV was on the fritz, Renny would find you one that fell off a truck somewhere. If your roommate hadn't ponied up his share of the rent in a few months, Renny knew guys who could help him locate his wallet and show him how to open it.

Dex found him lounging at the lightboard, perusing a racing form. "Renny," he said. "Having a good day?"

Renny looked at him over the top of his paper. "Fine, boss."

Dex drummed his fingers on the console.

Renny folded his paper and set it aside. "How's *your* day?"

Dex shook his head. "Rough. You heard Frank sing?"

The toothpick moved from one side of Renny's mouth to the other. "I did."

Dex's shoulders lifted and fell. "He's not exactly taking to the boards, is he?"

"I can see he ain't a dream come true. You can always fire him."

"No, I can't. His people insisted on a no-cut clause before they'd let him sign on."

"Maybe he'll quit. He seems pretty miserable."

"Not likely. That's the clause *I* managed to get into the contract. If he walks, he has to pay a massive penalty—and on top of all his other charming qualities, Frank's a cheapskate." Dex rubbed his hands over his face. "He hates being here, and I hate having him here, but we're stuck with each other."

"Well, some guys do better in the movies than live on stage, you know?"

"*Live* on stage," Dex repeated, emphasizing the first word meaningfully. "I was thinking you might have some ideas about that."

"There's lots of things you can try," Renny said. "Some work wonders for a couple weeks. Others are more…ah, *permanent*. It depends how big the problem is."

"Frank Serge is a pretty big problem."

Renny grunted.

Dex leaned forward. "The thing is, Renny, I need this show to work."

"We all do, boss."

Dex waved this away. "No, you *want* the show to work. I *need* it to. If *Merchant!* isn't a hit, I'll be singing 'Brother, Can You Spare a Dime?' on street corners the rest of my life. If only Serge wasn't in the way, I'm sure I could get another name big enough to keep the investors on board."

"I hear you, boss." Renny picked up the racing form. "I think of anything, I'll let you know."

* * *

Two days later, Dex was back in the third row, going over plans for the stage sets and watching his young lovers work out harmonies on "I Took a Gondola to Your Heart," when Renny slipped into the seat beside him.

"Hey, boss," the stagehand said. "Listen, you know that bar around the corner, couple blocks down? Fiora's?"

"I've walked past it," Dex said.

"I'm having a drink there tonight with some friends. They maybe got an idea about that problem we talked about. Why don't you come by?"

* * *

Fiora's was a long, dimly lit room with a bar running down one wall and a series of small tables along the other. The only person in the place when Dex arrived was a middle-aged woman with a face like the blunt end of a hatchet, who stood behind the bar watching a Technicolor movie on a ceiling-mounted TV. Dex glanced up at the screen and saw Katherine Hepburn fall into a canal. When he looked back, the woman was staring at him. "Need something?" she asked.

Dex blinked, trying to get his eyes to adjust. "I'm meeting someone."

"Renny? Back room. Third door, past the johns." When Dex started walking, she held up a hand. "Not so fast, pretty boy. Two-drink minimum."

"Ah." Dex looked around. "Do you have a wine list?"

"We got beer."

"How about a whiskey and soda?"

"We got beer."

"Vodka martini?"

Her torso rose and fell in an elaborate sigh.

Dex gave up. "I guess I'll have a couple beers," he said.

"Ten bucks. Each."

He dropped two tens on the bar, holding his wallet so she couldn't see that was most of the cash he had. The woman shoved the bills in her pocket and filled two glasses from an unmarked tap. The liquid that spurted out was somewhere in the yellowish part of the spectrum. Dex took the glasses, touching them only with his fingertips.

"Thanks so much," he said.

Her eyes were on the TV, and she didn't even grunt in reply.

He found Renny alone at a table in a room barely large enough to hold it and four chairs. When he came in, Renny pointed at his beers. "I wouldn't drink those. I don't think the tap's been cleaned since the place was built." He nodded at the whiskey bottle and shot glasses in front of him. "I got us this."

Dex sat. "She said she only had beer."

"And you believed her? What did she charge you?"

"Twenty."

Renny snorted. "It's a good thing you got here before my friends. They see someone all wet behind the ears like you, they'd be licking their chops. We gotta get you ready to wheel and deal. You ever done anything like this before?"

"Of course not."

"Okay. So you tell my friends what you want, and they name a price. Then what do *you* do?"

"Pay it."

Renny made a noise like a game-show buzzer. "Wrong, boss. You accept their first number, they'll know they can walk all over you. You got to *bargain* with people like this."

"Bargain?"

"Haggle. Negotiate." Renny tipped whiskey into one of his shot glasses and pushed it across the table to Dex. "Don't look too hungry. Make 'em think you can just walk away if they get too greedy. A thing like this, whoever waits the longest usually gets the better deal." He tossed back a shot and coughed. "While it's still just the two of us, what's your ceiling? What's the absolute most you can swing?"

Dex hesitated. "We're talking about a *permanent* solution to the Frank Serge problem, right?"

"They don't get permanenter."

"How much does something like that normally cost?"

Renny shook his head. "There ain't no *normal*, boss. Every deal is different. Depends on the people and the conditions. Like, how soon you want it done? You want it gentle or painful? You want it to look accidental? Want

76

him to know it was you?"

"Jesus, no. I don't care about that."

"Don't tell *me*, boss. Tell *them*. Listen, they'll be here any minute. You still haven't said what your budget is."

The word *budget* activated the part of Dex's brain that dealt with contracts. His eyes narrowed. "What do *you* get out of this, Renny? A percentage? Some kind of finder's fee?"

Renny slapped the table. "Now you're thinking, boss. Sure, I'll get a cut, but that's not why I'm here. I'm here because I want the show to work. And killing that gin-soaked cowboy will be an act of mercy all around. Just tell me how high we can go."

Dex bit his lip, doing mental calculations. "Five thousand."

"That's it?"

"Renny, I put almost all I've got into this show. I'll have to hock everything I have left to scrape the five together."

"Maybe they'll settle for five as a down payment. I don't know. What could you give them in, say, a year, if the show's a hit?"

Dex considered the question. "Twenty?"

"Twenty-five total *might* do it. But—"

There was a rap at the door. Renny held up a silencing hand as it opened, and a man and woman somewhere in their thirties came in. The man was clean-shaven and wide-eyed, wearing casual slacks and a bowling shirt with *Ross* in script on the chest. The woman, blond and anonymously pretty, wore a yellow sundress set off by a necklace of dark red gems. They didn't look like assassins. They looked like they belonged on a ferry to the Statue of Liberty, marveling at how the buildings here were so much taller than the ones in Des Moines. All that was missing was a camera around the man's neck.

"Sorry we're late, fellas," the man said. He fell into the chair to Dex's left. "You wouldn't believe the time we had getting here."

"One thing after another," the woman said. She sat across from Dex, grabbed Renny's bottle, and poured herself a generous slug. Like the man's, her voice had the earnest tones of the Midwest.

"We were in Miami when we got Renny's call," the man explained. "Normally, we drive to our jobs. I *like* driving, you know, being in control. But the man said to hurry, so what did we do?"

"We flew, Cookie," the woman said. She downed half her whiskey in one quick swallow. "You boys been on a plane lately?"

"Madness," the man said.

"Madness," she echoed. "Delayed four hours, first of all."

"Somebody should sue," the man said. "Pour me a snort of that, Sugar. Let me tell you, we were starving by the time we finally took off. Then they brought out the food." The man gave a theatrical shudder. "Bad enough they could serve it here, huh, Renny? Go great with that piss they call beer." He noticed Dex's two glasses. "Of course, some people might like it."

The woman steamrolled over Dex's attempt to reply. "You barely get to see the food before they kill the lights and start playing a movie. What was the movie again, Cookie?"

"Couldn't tell you, Sugar. Something with Doris Day. I missed most of it, because of the kids screaming and kicking my chair."

"Kids! You ask me, they shouldn't let them on a plane until they're old enough to fly it."

"Now, last week, we were on a plane—never mind where we were going— for some reason packed full of Germans. Very dour, you know? Bitter people. Made for a depressing flight. But quiet."

"This week's plane, all noisy Americans." The woman finished her whiskey and reached for the bottle again. "Give me back the Germans, that's what I say. Or even rude Frenchmen."

The man chuckled. "Anyway, at least we didn't crash into the woods. Good to be here again and see an old pal. Everything well, Renny?"

Dex couldn't stand it any longer. "Are you two sure you're in the right place?"

The woman laughed. "We're not what he expected, Cookie."

"He was expecting somebody like Lee Marvin," the man said.

"Robert Mitchum," she said.

"Some big, tough guy. Somebody like Frank Serge."

"Instead, he gets us. Just a regular couple."

"Perfectly lovely."

"Nobody looks twice."

"Which is the point." Something hard pushed into Dex's side. He looked down, and the man had a gun held against him. Dex had no idea where it had come from. He looked at the woman, who was still smiling, though her eyes were hard.

"I'm Leona," she said. "This is Ross. Are you ready to talk business?"

Dex looked down. The gun was gone. "Sure," he said. "I'm Dex. Let's talk business."

"We hear you've got a problem," Ross said.

"Frank Serge is ruining my show," Dex said.

"Would you even *have* a show without him?" Leona was back to being bubbly. "From what Renny says, he's the reason you can make it happen at all."

"*Publicity* makes things happen. A movie star in the cast means publicity, but a dead movie star means even more publicity. Enough to get another star signed up and people in the doors, anyway."

"So they can see your work of genius," Ross said. If there was sarcasm in his voice, it was buried deeply. "How do you do it, Dex? Think up a whole show, I mean?"

"You just wake up one day with an idea," Dex said. "Should I ask how you do your line of work?"

"No," Renny put in. "You shouldn't."

"If publicity is good," Ross said, "I guess you don't want him to, like, trip down a flight of stairs or eat a bad oyster. More blood means more headlines, right? If it bleeds, it leads?"

"Of course, an obvious hit is riskier for us," Leona said. "And it's already risky, going after somebody so high profile."

"High risk, high reward," Ross said.

"Which brings us to the only question that matters," Leona said. "How much?"

Dex glanced at Renny. The stagehand was pouring another round from

79

his bottle. His face didn't twitch. "You're the ones with something to sell," Dex said. "Seems to me you should tell me what it costs."

Ross smiled broadly. "It's not like we've got a shop set up, with price tags and sales tax, Dex. We're not knocking on doors, asking housewives if there's somebody they'd like to see a lot less of. You came to us, remember?"

Dex took a slow sip of whiskey. "I understand that. But maybe I'm having second thoughts. There's a lot of risk for me here, too." He put the glass down. "I could just walk away."

"Sure," Leona said. "So could we."

"Well, now, Sugar," Ross said, "we're already into this for a couple plane tickets."

"We'll call it a vacation," Leona said. "It's been a while since we were in New York. I hear *Fiddler*'s good."

"Zero Mostel," Renny said. "I saw it. Terrific stuff."

"He'd probably make a good Shylock," Ross said. "You think, Dex?"

"Zero's a funny name," Leona said. "Makes me think of numbers. You thinking about numbers, Dex?"

"Dex wants *us* to say a number."

"We wouldn't say zero, would we, Cookie?"

"Nope."

Dex held up his hands. "How do I know I'll get what I pay for?"

"Dex wants a guarantee, Sugar," Ross said.

"Maybe a contract," Leona said. "Sign our names nice and big, so the cops can read it."

"Maybe, we don't deliver, he sues us." Ross looked Dex full in the face. Like Leona, he could make his eyes go flat and dead, while the rest of his face remained jovial. "We don't do warranties and refunds, Dex. But your friend Renny put you in this room with us, right? As a favor to him, I'll say a number. Thirty thousand."

Dex leaned back in his chair and steepled his fingers, suddenly confident. Renny said he shouldn't be the first to name a price, and he hadn't been. "I can't come up with that much right now," he said. "Not even close."

"I guess we wasted a flight," Leona said.

"I can do three thousand now."

Ross laughed. "Ninety percent is a hell of a discount, Dex."

"Let me finish. Three now, and another ten in six months. Or, if you can wait a year, fifteen."

Ross rubbed his chin. "You got that clipping, Sugar?"

"You bet." Leona reached into the top of her dress and pulled out a folded square of paper.

Ross unfolded it and put it on the table in front of Dex. It was a profile *Time* had run on him two months ago, about his attempt at a comeback. There was an old picture of him in his living room, in front of framed posters from his long-ago smashes. Ross tapped his finger on the photo. "We did some reading up on you when Renny called," he said. "You still got these red goblets?"

"I do," Dex said. Most of the furniture and books in the photo had been sold or pawned, but the matched pair of ruby red goblets were still on his mantel. They were all he had left from his high-roller days.

"Eighteenth-century Venetian," Leona said. "Right?"

Dex nodded, not trusting himself to speak.

"Here's the deal," Ross said. "Four thousand now, plus the goblets, and another twelve thousand in six months."

Dex took a long minute. "I don't know," he said at last. "Those goblets mean an awful lot to me."

"No more games, Dex," Leona said. "That's the deal. Take it or we walk."

Dex looked at Renny, who gave the tiniest of nods. "All right," he said. "Deal."

Ross clapped his hands once, sharply. "Excellent. Why don't we go over to your place right now and pick them up?"

* * *

Unlocking his apartment door, Dex felt almost giddy. There was a full moon tonight, and he'd be rid of Frank Serge before the next one. He imagined the mournful interviews he would give, lamenting the great man's demise

81

and offering *Merchant!* as an opportunity for the public to pay tribute. Stars would line up, hoping to play the part, and this time *he'd* be the one dictating terms.

"Don't mind the mess," he said, opening the door. "It's been a while since I had company." In fact, he'd never brought anyone here, too embarrassed by the small room and its secondhand furnishings.

He crossed the living room to the mantel and picked up one of the goblets. "We should wrap these in newspaper, find a bag you can use," he said. He turned.

Ross, Leona, and Renny were standing just inside the front door. All three had guns in their hands, and there was nothing jovial in any of their faces.

"Wait," Dex said. "I don't understand."

"Shall I tell him, Cookie?" Leona asked.

"Go right ahead, Sugar," Ross said.

"Frank Serge is sick of your stupid musical, and he sobered up long enough to read his contract," she said, raising her gun. "It says the show doesn't happen if the writer and director dies. And he pays a lot better than you do. Up front, in cash. He didn't even try to haggle."

The goblet fell from Dex's fingers as he threw his hands up, looking desperately from side to side for anything that might save him. But in this final moment, in this shabby room surrounded by shabby things, Dexter Wakefield had absolutely nothing to bargain with.

Evening Primrose
broadcast November 16, 1966, on the ABC Television series Stage 67

"If You Can Find Me, I'm Here"
"Charles Meets Mrs. Monday"
"Charles and Ella"
"Check List"
"The Basement"
"I Remember"
"When"
"Take Me to the World"
"The Ball"
"Roscoe and the Guard"
"The Ball, Part 2"
"Escape"
"Take Me to the World" (reprise)
"Final Credits"

Music and lyrics by Stephen Sondheim.
Book by John Collier and James Goldman.

If You Can Find Me, I'm Here

by Jeffrey Sweet

Toni Bates did not anticipate that getting hired to play a criminal on a true-crime TV show would lead to her being kidnapped. By the real-life criminal she'd been hired to play.

Well, technically, by the guy the real-life criminal sent to kidnap her.

But she had to concede that, if you *had* to be kidnapped, it was a plus to be kidnapped by someone who, as he was putting a hood over your head, said in a soothing tone, "Don't worry, she just wants to talk to you." Toni would have asked "Who?" if he hadn't also put duct tape over her mouth.

Careful, she said to herself. *Mustn't get excited.*

As she was trying to will her pulse rate back to normal, it occurred to her that what was happening was probably connected with her appearance in an episode of the TV show *Perps*.

Other reactions to her performance had been less extreme.

"Wow!" said Viv, who usually sat next to her in acting class. "You come across so nice in session, but I turn on the tube and—wow! You are an unadulterated genius!"

Others were similarly complimentary, and Toni was pleased. It meant that she had caught something of the essence of Charmian Collier, something of her unpredictability, her danger, her humor. It meant she had created the illusion that she was somebody else, somebody radically different from herself—which is the whole point of acting, yes?

And playing the part had been fun. Fun to wear the outfit Collier wore—a copy, anyway, of the tweed jacket and Peter Falk mask—during the re-enactment of the robbery. And fun to make the defiant gesture—blurred when it ran on broadcast, but clear and in focus on streaming—as she disappeared into the perfectly timed getaway car with no license plates.

And as if the fun weren't enough, there was the check, which would cover her rent for the next few months. So all told, Toni's experience with the project had been a happy one.

Until, that is, she was duct-taped, hooded, and abducted.

As she was being spirited away, Toni remembered a text message she had received shortly after the broadcast. Three words: "Not good enough," the sender identified only by the initials "C.C." At the time, she'd thought it was a lame joke perpetrated by a friend. Now she had cause to reevaluate that assumption.

As it happened, the Charmian Collier episode had generated more than the usual buzz. The target of the theft dramatized on *Perps* had been a pharmaceutical company in a small West Virginia town that was in the process of closing its factory, throwing a significant percentage of the local population out of work. Few people had sympathy for the company. Add to that the fact that Collier had left an envelope of cash at Goldman's Grill, specifically to buy drinks for the laid-off workers. It was rumored she had been in Goldman's in disguise, had enjoyed the informal party with them. That was only a rumor, but it hadn't kept the producers of *Perps* from shooting a sequence with Toni-as-Charmian wearing the Peter Falk mask and dancing with a lot of roistering extras.

The only part of the filming that had been less than a joy was the show's technical advisor, the West Virginia cop who'd caught the case—but had *not* caught Charmian Collier, had not gotten over it, and had retired soon after. His name was Robinson Hubbell, and he had not appreciated the fact that Toni was very evidently enjoying playing the woman he'd failed to bring to justice.

"She's a sociopath, damn it!" he'd shouted, and he'd stomped away, cursing and slamming the wall with his fist. A minute later, he'd returned to say, "Sorry. I realize this doesn't mean as much to you as it would to a normal person. I mean, you're just an actress." Not looking to fight with a cop, even one collecting his pension, Toni had nodded to indicate she accepted what he'd thought was an apology.

The numbers on the episode when it was broadcast were sufficient for the network to suggest to the producers of *Perps* that another Charmian Collier episode would be welcome. There were certainly other of her escapades more than suitable for filming: Charmian's adventures had long made news editors happy. They appreciated that, while her primary objective was to relieve rich targets of their goodies, a significant secondary objective was to do so with a flair that would play well on television. Collier generally saw to it that there was vivid security camera footage of her in one of the many masks she employed during the commission of her crimes, almost as if she were a performance artist who chose to perform in unconventional venues.

Toni's abductor drove maybe half an hour before he pulled over, opened the door, guided her down some stairs and through what she guessed was a doorway, and then steered her to a comfy armchair. He removed the zip tie from her wrists, but before she could take off the hood and see what he looked like, her kidnapper had left the room, closing the door behind him. She worked the duct tape from her mouth, and then the door opened again, and Madonna came in.

Actually, it was a woman wearing a Madonna mask. She was carrying a grande-sized coffee. "You take it with almond milk, right?"

Toni nodded, and Charmian Collier handed her the cup. "I'd join you, but it's murder drinking through a mask."

Toni took a sip. "You sent me that message," she said. *"Not good enough?"*

"Oh, so you did get it."

"I did the best I could with what's available," said Toni. "You're not exactly easy to research. For one thing, nobody knows for sure what you look like, much less your real name. I'm assuming it's not Charmian Collier."

"Not even close. And I suppose the message wasn't fair. Probably nobody who's been played by an actor ever agreed with how they did it. I mean, do you think Queen Elizabeth told Helen Mirren, 'Ooooh, you nailed me!'?"

"She *was* great, though."

"One time the Oscars got it right," said Charmian, the sides of her mask wobbling a little as she nodded. "And, yeah, you had less to work with. I did like your dance in the bar."

"Did you actually do that?"

"Too risky. If I'd shown up in the Peter Falk mask, *someone* would have called the cops. Even if they were glad I did what I did, they would have been tempted by the reward. But I watched a little through the window. That was a kick. Coffee okay?"

"It's fine," said Toni.

"I hear you're going to play me again."

"How do you know that?"

"I have sources. Which of my jobs are they doing?"

"The diamond theft."

"It's going to look awful familiar to anyone who's been watching *Lupin*. Did you see the first episode of season three?"

"Afraid not."

"Netflix. French show. Pretty good, but that episode was a total rip-off. I mean, you can copyright a song, right? Seems to me you should be able to copyright—"

"—a heist?"

"The whole logic of it was something I put together. And then they go make money off what I worked out."

"You want royalties?"

"Well," said Charmian, "a line crediting me in the end titles, at least."

"You could sue them for plagiarism."

"There you go."

Toni took a sip of her coffee. "So," she asked, "why am I here?"

"If you're going to play me again, I thought we should talk. Actors like to research, right? Oh, I saw on the first one that Hubby was a technical advisor."

"Hubby?"

"My pet name for Mr. Hubbell. He hates it. Is he going to advise on this one, too?"

"I hope not."

"Didn't get along with him?" said Charmian, a laugh bubbling behind Madonna's unmoving lips.

"I don't know how much you know about acting," said Toni, "but when you play a part, you try to play it from the inside. You try to get inside the perspective of the person you're playing, to merge your perspective as much as possible with the character's."

"What does that have to do with Hubby?"

"He loathes you," Toni said. "He wanted me to play you like evil personified. He thinks you're a sociopath."

"If I was a sociopath, would I have bothered getting almond milk for your coffee?"

"His negativity wasn't useful to me. I couldn't have done that scene in the bar—the dancing—if I thought of you like that. After all, nobody's a villain to themself."

"Poor Hubby. Yeah, he's obsessive. I think it's gotten worse since he retired. He doesn't get that it wasn't personal. I've tried to let him know there are no hard feelings on my side. I sent him a Christmas card filled with good cheer and glitter."

"You sent a Christmas card to the guy who tried to lock you up?"

"If you were me, would you have been able to resist?"

Yes, Toni thought, *I can incorporate this into the next episode.*

* * *

Hubbell was on set when they shot the second episode. It was a little awkward, since he wasn't on the payroll this time, and the story they were shooting hadn't happened in what had been his jurisdiction. But he seemed so morose, nobody wanted to tell him to go chase himself.

He was there the day Toni asked the director for a line change. When the director asked why, she replied, "Charmian wouldn't say that. She'd make a wisecrack. I mean, she's got a sense of humor."

"How do you know that?"

"Well, as it happens—"

And then she noticed Hubbell staring at her, so intently she could practically feel his eyeballs pressing against her face.

"As it happens *what?*" said the director.

"Never mind," Toni said, and she did the line as written.

* * *

After the take, Hubbell approached her before she could escape to her dressing room.

"Where?" he demanded. "When?"

Toni gave him a look that she hoped would radiate utter innocence. It didn't work.

"Ever heard of obstruction of justice?" said the retired cop. "It's a crime."

"What obstruction? I'm playing a character, and my sense of the character is that she would make a joke there."

"Based on what?"

"Like I said, my sense of the character."

"You didn't say, 'I don't *think* she would say that.' You said, 'She *wouldn't* say that.' Like you know her. Like you *know* what she would say."

"When I played Liesl in *The Sound of Music*, I knew what *she'd* say—and I never met *her.*"

"I'm not buying it."

"Listen, Hubby—"

His eyes opened, as if he'd been bitten in the ass by an alligator. "Hubby?" *Oops!*

She tried to mollify him. "You should be enjoying your retirement. Plant flowers in the garden. Take a Viking cruise through the Rhone Valley with your wife."

"We're divorced."

"I'm sorry."

"Don't change the subject. Where and when did you meet Charmian Collier?"

Ultimately, she did indeed tell him what she knew—which, of course, was nothing he could use, exactly as Charmian had intended. Toni had no idea where she'd been driven, who had driven her, or what Charmian looked like behind the Madonna mask. Her mention of the Christmas card didn't help.

"Goddamn glitter," Hubbell muttered. "Some of it fell into the dog's food bowl. When I took her out for a walk, I saw it in her poop. You think I enjoyed picking that up?"

* * *

"I assume that was a rhetorical question on Hubby's part," Charmian said, when she and Toni spoke next.

Because, yes, the second Charmian episode went over well, and the producers decided to shoot a third. And Charmian heard about it. Again the hood, again the drive—to what felt like a different location, this time—again a mask. This one of Leo G. Carroll as Mr. Waverly from *The Man from U.N.C.L.E.*

"Talk about obscure," said Toni.

"I always liked Leo G. You ever see the old series where he played a guy haunted by a couple of ghosts?"

"I can't say I did."

"And he was a killer in one of Hitchcock's movies."

"So, Charmian," said Toni patiently, "why am I here *this* time?"

"I heard you're doing another one, but I don't know which caper."

"The bank job."

"The tunnel from the department store basement into the vault?"

"That's the one. We'll shoot right there in Stickney's."

"Nice touch. Are you going to use the real bank vault, too?"

"No, we'll have to do that on a sound stage."

"The bank wouldn't let you film there?"

"For some reason," Toni said drily.

"Have they given you a script yet?"

90

"They're working on it."

"I hid from a security guard by pretending to be a mannequin in a wedding tableau. I was the groom. You can tell the writer that. Actually, you can tell anyone you like anything you want about our meetings. I've got it covered."

"It might not be all that safe to be over-confident."

Charmian handed her a pastry wrapped in waxed paper. "Nutella croissant. I hope you don't mind. I know you prefer chocolate, but they were out."

"See," said Toni, "that's the kind of mistake they could use to trace you."

"How?"

"If they canvas coffee shops looking for one where someone ordered a coffee with almond milk and a chocolate croissant but wound up taking a Nutella one and find the store, and then go through the security-camera footage...I'm assuming you weren't wearing Leo G. Carroll when you bought this?"

"Who said the place had a security camera? Or that I even went there myself?" said Charmian. "But I like the way you're thinking. Sharp as a tack. That's the kind of mind you need to have in my line of work. Figuring the angles. You're very *me*, if you don't mind my saying so. Besides which, are you planning on *telling* them I got you a coffee and a Nutella croissant?"

"I wasn't originally planning on telling them I met you at all, and you know how *that* turned out."

"Like I said, I've got it under control. You can tell whoever whatever. Nutella included. Don't worry."

"I don't want to be the reason you get caught," said Toni.

"Aww, you care! I'm touched."

And even though this was said through Leo G. Carroll's rubber face, Toni believed her.

* * *

As it turned out, the writer didn't put the mannequin gag into the script for the department store caper. "I'm sorry," she said, "I just don't believe it."

91

There was enough to work with to make the episode sparkle anyway, including a frantic chase down an up escalator and a disco ball that Charmian rigged to drop from the ceiling as speakers blared "Macho Man," a moment that so discombobulated the pursuing cops they stopped and stared as Charmian jumped out a second-story window, bounced off an awning, and disappeared into the night. Toni's mask this time was a copy of the one Charmian had worn of Angela Lansbury.

The day they were to shoot that climactic scene, Toni was heading to her dressing room in a corner of the department store when she had a sense of someone following her. She spun around and caught sight of Robinson Hubbell as he dove to the floor behind a perfume counter. "I saw you," she said. "Get up."

"I think I twisted something," came his voice from behind the counter.

She walked back and found him on the carpet, nursing his right ankle. He looked up at her.

"You're not supposed to be here," she said. "You were banned from the set after the last episode."

"Banned at your request."

"I don't appreciate being bullied."

"I apologized for yelling at you, didn't I?"

"It's like she says, you're obsessed. If you can't get your hands on her, you'll settle for me."

"I haven't touched you."

"You're stalking me. What do you imagine you'll see?"

"I have this feeling—"

"What feeling?"

"I think *she's* obsessed with *you*. She grabbed you again, didn't she?"

"Yes. The same deal—the hood, the car, the room, the coffee. So what?"

"I don't think she'll be content just to watch you on TV."

"You think she'll show up here?"

"Would that surprise you?"

"No," Toni said, "it wouldn't surprise me one bit. So you're watching me because you think you'll catch *her* watching me?"

"It's a theory."

"She'd have to be nuts."

"And she isn't?"

"I think you're both nuts," said Toni.

Hubbell managed to get to his feet. "Are you going to help me?"

"By doing what? My job is to play this part, not get involved in your revenge fantasy."

"Are you going to have them throw me off the set?"

"Just stay out of my damn way, okay? I don't want to be in the middle of whatever weird thing you two have going."

He winced a little as he limped away.

Toni went to her dressing room and sat in the makeup chair. "I don't see the point of getting made up for this scene," she told the makeup woman, a new one she hadn't seen before. "I'll be wearing a mask."

The makeup woman laughed.

* * *

The scene was shot as scripted—except for "Macho Man." (The copyright holders wanted too much money for permission, and a substitute track would be dubbed in post-production.) The disco ball descended, the guys playing the cops were suitably discombobulated, and the figure wearing the Angela Lansbury mask made her escape out the window, onto the awning, and into the street.

The director called cut. His assistant checked playback on the monitor and saw the camera briefly reflected in a mirror. "We can either take it out digitally or go for another take."

"We've got time," said the director. "Let's do another take. Toni, you ready?"

Toni didn't answer.

"Where the hell is Toni?"

Hubbell's stomach turned over. He hobbled to Toni's dressing room and heard a muffled noise from the closet. He opened the door.

93

Seated on a chair, encased in gaffer's tape with a gag in her mouth, sat a pissed-off Toni Bates. The retired cop removed the gag, and, before he could ask the question, Toni said, "Yes."

She pointed to the makeup mirror, on which was scrawled in lipstick, "Hey, kids, pardon while I disappear. Till next time."

* * *

Speeding away from the set in a yellow convertible with the top down and no license plates, Charmian Collier took off the Angela Lansbury mask and shook her long brown hair loose in the evening breeze.

Act III

The 1970s

Company

opened April 27, 1970, at the Alvin Theatre, New York

ACT I

"Company"

"The Little Things You Do Together"

"Sorry-Grateful"

"You Could Drive a Person Crazy"

"Have I Got a Girl for You"

"Someone Is Waiting"

"Another Hundred People"

"Getting Married Today"

"Marry Me a Little"

ACT II

"Side by Side by Side/What Would We Do Without You?"

"Poor Baby"

"Have I Got a Girl for You" (reprise)

"Tick-Tock"

"Barcelona"

"The Ladies Who Lunch"

"Being Alive"

"Finale"

Music and lyrics by Stephen Sondheim.

Book by George Furth.

Being Alive

by Brian Cox

The parcel in his PO box was unexpected, and Robert Dean Jones considered it with a curiosity approaching suspicion. The return address was for an out-of-state sporting-goods store he'd never heard of. Old mistrusts die hard, if ever, so he waited until he was in his truck before cautiously opening the package with a pocketknife. Atop the packing paper inside was an unsigned note in a familiar handwriting that read, "Robert, I heard you've taken up fishing. Now you just need bait."

He pulled away the packing paper to find an assortment of cheap lures and a box of slip bobbers, the kind he hadn't used since he was a kid. He gave the paper a once over, noticing nothing unusual, before turning his attention to the colorful spinners. He studied each one but didn't spot anything out of the ordinary. If there was something his old station chief wanted him to see, he was at a loss. He examined the orange-and-yellow bobbers next, but still found nothing of note. It wasn't until a second, closer examination that he noticed one bobber seemed ever so slightly heavier than the others. He gave it a gentle twist.

* * *

"Another vodka stinger, please," said Marta, pushing her empty glass forward. "Heavy on the sting."

She had thought when she walked into the Rock River Tavern that she might need to tell the bartender how to make her preferred cocktail. There were only two bars in this rural Upper Peninsula town, and she suspected a vodka stinger might be viewed as something exotic. Who even knew if they had crème de menthe this far from civilization? But she'd been mistaken. Joanne's past was portrayed in a gallery of tattoos up and down her right arm, and she clearly knew how to do more than pour pints of beer and shots of whiskey. Rock River seemed to attract people with all manner of personal histories—some they shared and some they didn't.

Joanne set the drink in front of her. "Extra sting," she said.

The only other person in the tavern was a guy in an orange hunting cap at the end of the bar, hunched over a draft. His name was Steve, but the locals called him Stove because he ran a fireplace-and-chimney repair business. He'd been eyeing Marta since she walked in but, so far, had said nothing, only plucked occasionally at a jaw harp pinched against his teeth, grinning when Marta looked his way at the sound of the instrument's twang.

In the window hung two four-leaf clovers cut from green cardboard—an unenthusiastic gesture to mark St. Patrick's Day—and between them, an orange neon sign that read ROUQIL. On one wall was a framed copy of the yellowing front page of the *Mining Journal* with the headline "Champs!" immortalizing the high school football team's Class C State Championship from almost fifty years ago. Outside, Main Street was deserted, the only traffic an occasional pickup sporting a gun rack.

Marta wasn't surprised that *this* was where Robert would arrange to meet.

"I expected it to be a lot colder," she said.

She'd taken off her parka when she came in and sat down. She wore jeans and an untucked red flannel shirt she'd chosen because she thought it would help her blend in. Her dark hair was shoulder length, with a sharp part on the left. Her black eyebrows were bold, defined, and swooping. When she smiled with closed, thin lips, her cheeks lifted as though filled with puffs of air. Men had told her that her cheeks made her look younger. Innocent, some said, which made her laugh.

"It's been a peculiar March," said Joanne. "Normally, we'd have four, five feet of snow. Even the old-timers say they can't remember it being so warm, this time of year."

Marta scanned the bar, the pool table, the dart board. The late-afternoon quiet seemed to slow time. "Not too good for business."

"No snow, no snowmobilers," said Joanne, shrugging. "They'd've had to cancel the outhouse race last week, if they hadn't trucked in snow from Chatham."

The jaw harp twanged from the end of the bar. "They race outhouses built on skis," Stove said. He flicked the jaw harp twice and grinned in delight. His voice was raspy from inhaling ash and chimney dust for decades and smoking weed daily. "There's a parade and everything."

"People come from all over," added Joanne. "Place was packed."

"Sounds fun," said Marta.

"Where you from, anyway?" asked Stove. "Not from downstate, I know that much. I got an ear for accents." He twanged the jaw harp to underscore his confidence. "If you want, I can give you a tour of the waterfalls 'round here."

Before Marta could decline the offer, a familiar voice from the past interrupted.

"She's not here to see the waterfalls, Stove."

Without a sound to mark his arrival, Robert Dean Jones stood by the dartboard, hands in his Carhartt coat pockets. It was as if he'd stepped out of a shadow where he'd been waiting all along. He must have entered from the back, which didn't surprise Marta. Of course, he would. She expected he'd been here since well before her arrival.

He hadn't changed much in seven years. He had the same brown eyes that resembled melted caramel. But the rough beard—with flecks of gray among the reddish-blond whiskers—was new. When he quit the Company, he'd been clean-shaven and kept his curly hair cut short. It was longer now, curling out like angel wings from under a faded green ball cap. His long form was still lean.

In the instant Marta first turned to look at him, his narrow face was set, his caramel eyes hard and expressionless, but then he said, "Hi, Marta," and turned on the legendary magic smile that ignited his eyes. They shone amber and transformed his face into a glowing welcome, producing a magnetic pull that most people found irresistible.

Robert Dean Jones could make people adore him. It was his special power, and he had learned to wield it well, whether to gain love, trust, loyalty, cooperation, or information. How many witless women—and men, for that matter—had that smile seduced? Marta couldn't hope to count. She was among the few who had not succumbed to its promise—*her* power was a deep skepticism of anything smelling even remotely of love.

"Happy birthday, Bobby," she said without rising from the barstool. "Are you surprised to see me?"

"I certainly am," said Robert, remaining still but continuing to smile broadly. "Very."

"Today's your birthday?" asked Stove. "Shit, I didn't know that, man. Happy birthday, Bobby bubby."

"Thanks, Stove. I don't make a big deal of it."

"How about a beer for the birthday boy?" said Joanne. "On the house."

"Shit, yeah, I'll drink to that," said Stove.

There was a beat of silence as Robert gauged Marta. She felt him trying to decipher her every muscle movement.

"Well," he said, concluding something. "I wasn't planning on it. Who wants to celebrate getting older? But, okay, sure. You're only thirty-five once. I'll have a Two Hearted." He took his hands from his pockets and spread his arms. If possible, his smile expanded, its illumination brightened. "But first, let me give an old friend a big hug."

* * *

"Tony's dead," she said. "I thought you'd want to know."

They were in his Ford F-250, headed to his place on the lake. Leafless sugar maple, basswood, and beech trees edged the two-lane highway. There was no snow, but the sky—which earlier had been a cold blue—was now gray with swirling cloud cover. It felt like the temperature had dropped ten degrees, and she was glad to have her parka.

In the tavern, Marta had refrained from telling Robert the reason she'd come, and he hadn't pressed her, content in the presence of Joanne and Stove to chat like old friends catching up on the years. They shared memories of their time at Yale—him studying Chinese history, her majoring in economics—and traded tales of onerous professors and oddball classmates.

"So, did you two ever, you know, become a thing?" Stove had asked, twanging his jaw harp suggestively.

"No," said Marta, laughing, "nothing like that."

"We ran in different circles," said Robert.

Neither mentioned the coincidence that they'd both been recruited the summer following graduation or brought up the few nights they'd spent together during their first year with the Company. Their time in Barcelona had been brief, after all, and two years later, when they reconnected in Singapore, any spark that remained was too faint to be rekindled. They'd learned that some things are better left unsaid, if not forgotten.

Now Marta looked at Robert, measuring his reaction to the news of their former station chief's death, but he kept his eyes on the road, revealing little.

"When?" he asked.

"Three days ago. A single-car accident near Arlington. Police say he hit a tree."

"Dangerous things, trees."

* * *

Tony Furth had been a good guy. He ran the Singapore office all three years Robert and Marta were posted there. He'd reminded Robert of a librarian with his slight frame, brushed-forward hair, round glasses, and unbuttoned tweed vest. His reputation for diligence and patience was renowned across the Company. After the Yao debacle, Furth had tried to get Robert to reconsider resigning, but even his substantial persuasive tactics couldn't convince Robert to stay on.

"We need people like you," Furth had said. "What are we going to do without you? This wasn't all your fault."

But Robert couldn't wave away the guilt he felt from failing Yao, who had begun as an asset but become a friend.

"That was your mistake," said Furth. "Becoming friends. Listen, every relationship you have is transactional. It's product, that's all it is—and that's how you avoid moral dilemmas. It's an important lesson. Learn from it and move on."

"I promised him I wouldn't let anything happen to his family," said Robert.

"I know, I know. Isn't this some world? It's a rotten world, Robert, but it's the world we've got. Is it shit that *we* have to be the ones who see things the way they are? Yes. But we do it so millions of people can live blissfully unaware of how perilously close our civilization is to descending into chaos. We are the defenders of dreams and illusions."

Robert slid the envelope containing his resignation letter across the desk. "My mind's made up," he said.

"I'll hang onto this," said Furth. "You take some time away. Go home, see your father. Fish. I know you like fishing. Give it some more thought, and you'll see I'm right. You were meant for this work, Robert."

That was the last time Robert and Tony had talked. He'd done as his station chief asked and gone home to stand on the shore of Lake Superior, listen to the rhythmic sigh of the waves, feel cool air pass across his face, consider the vastness of the horizon as the sun set and the sky became rinsed in reds and oranges.

His thoughts returned again and again to Lawrence Yao and his family. His elegant wife, Jingbai, had welcomed him into their home on many evenings for dinner. He recalled the Chinese bank executive's gentle smile and subtle humor, and the soft sound of Jingbai's laugh when he fumbled in Mandarin. He remembered days sailing with the family in Marina Bay, the children—an eight-year-old daughter and a six-year-old son—shouting with delight. When he eventually approached Larry about providing account and routing numbers for suspected Chinese arms dealers selling weapons to countries in West Africa, he convinced his friend that the information would make the world a safer place.

"If I do this, you must promise nothing will happen to my family," said

Larry.

"You have my word," he said. "I'll give my life to protect them."

Standing on the beach, Robert's mind was bombarded with flashes of Jingbai's bloodied body crumpled in the doorway to the children's room, her long black hair unpinned and strewn across her face. The children—in pajamas, their little feet bare—curled together in the closet where they'd tried to hide, dead from single shots to the head. The images came at him rapidly, like a choppily edited film, causing a stabbing pain behind his eyes, a tightening in his chest

When the sky was drained of color and pocked with a universe of remote stars, he located the light point that was Jupiter. He remembered stargazing on the beach with his father and marveling at the planet's distance and mass. Now, he was moved by the depth of its indifference.

In the end, Furth had been wrong: when he left the beach, he was more settled than ever that he was done deceiving himself about ideals being worthy of sacrifice. There was only the wonder of being alive. The miraculous fact of existence, *here* and *now*. Everything else, he concluded, was hubris.

His separation from the Company was processed, and he came home to Rock River, to the small cabin on the lake where his father still lived. He took up making and selling bent-twig furniture. He stripped the extraneous from his life and washed himself of the delusion that his engagement with the world was of consequence. He ignored all news outside the close circle of his reality.

That was almost seven years ago, and he hadn't heard from Furth since—until the package arrived in his post office box.

* * *

Robert turned off the state road onto a two-track that cut through the woods toward the lake. In the shadows, stubborn snow clung in clumps to the bases of trees.

"And you think what?" he asked Marta, who was gripping the grab handle as the truck jostled over ruts.

"I think somebody didn't want him looking back into Gunsmoke," she said.

"Gunsmoke was closed down after Yao was disappeared. No one cared what happened *then*, so why the hell would Tony care now?"

The official version was that Yao had killed his family and fled to Beijing after he came under suspicion for embezzlement. All bullshit, of course. Obviously, he'd been turned out to one of the arms syndicates the Company was working to disrupt, but how and by whom Robert hadn't been able to determine. As the economic analyst for Gunsmoke, Marta had spent three sleepless nights reviewing the transaction data collected over the life of the operation, but to no avail. After an investigation of less than a week, the deputy director had ordered Gunsmoke folded up and cleansed, despite Furth's objections. Two days later, Robert handed in his resignation.

"Because Stritch is being vetted for Secretary of State," answered Marta.

"Peter Stritch?" Robert threw her a surprised glance, his face clouded with distaste for the former deputy director. "Are you shitting me?"

The truck jounced, and Marta absorbed the shock straight up her spine and into her teeth.

"This road is awful," she complained. "I can't believe you live back here."

"We don't get many visitors. Tell me why Tony was looking at Stritch."

"Tony always suspected Stritch had something to do with Gunsmoke blowing up. You know he didn't like how quickly Stritch shut the investigation down. I think he was trying to connect Stritch with what happened, in order to scuttle his nomination."

"Why would you think that?"

"He sent me a letter. An honest-to-God *letter*." Marta shook her head in amazement. "Only Tony. It came two days before he died. Said he'd found evidence that Stritch was siphoning off a small percentage of every fund transfer we flagged. Came to millions, all redirected to an account in the Caymans."

Marta watched Robert mull that over. A vein throbbed in his temple, and she imagined it to be a manifestation of him calculating consequences and connections. She waited for him to piece together a scenario that held weight.

"You think," he said before long, "that Stritch was using Gunsmoke to line his own pockets, and when one of the syndicates found out, he let Yao take the fall."

"That's what Tony thought," said Marta. "And then Stritch ran for the Senate two years later."

"Hold on. You're saying this was all to launch a *campaign?*"

Marta shrugged. "Stritch has aspirations, and he had to get his starter money somewhere. The underfinanced don't become senators. Or presidents."

"Jesus Christ," muttered Robert, slapping the steering wheel. "God-damnit!"

The two-track came to a fork. To the left, it led west into the Hiawatha National Forest, nearly nine hundred thousand acres of wilderness populated with moose, black bear, bobcats, and timber wolves. It was a rare morning that Robert didn't consider taking the left fork and wandering off into the forest, never to be seen again, content to live the remainder of his life unleashed from popular culture's desperate search for significance in the form of likes and followers and retweets. Maybe when his father was gone....

He took the right fork, and a hundred yards later, a rustic cabin of red pine logs emerged, separated from Lake Superior by a patch of cleared land covered in pine needles and a narrow strip of wet sand. A small metal dock extended into the lake. Under a pair of jack pines was a large pile of split wood and an overturned canoe on sawhorses.

When he parked and shut off the truck, Robert didn't open his door. He stared out at the lake as the heater ticked down. The water was a gray-blue and flashed white when waves slapped against the beach. The sky was starting to turn a husky orange. It wasn't hard to think that this could be the end of the world.

"It's beautiful," said Marta.

"It's deceptive," said Robert. "It would just as soon kill you. Happens all the time."

A light came on in the cabin. His father was awake and had heard the truck pull up. An old man on oxygen after forty years of smoking Pall Malls, he spent his days yelling at the television or building hummingbird feeders at the kitchen table.

"It's down by the dock," said Robert.

"What is?"

"What you came for."

"Tony said in his letter that I was to get it from you."

"What are you going to do with it?" he asked, as they got out of the truck and started toward the dock.

"What Tony wanted me to do with it," she said, stumbling on an exposed root. "I'm going to double-check the data, and—if it's right—I'm going to get it to the director. Who, by the way, is no fan of Stritch."

"I don't know why he sent it to me in the first place," said Robert.

"Maybe he thought you still cared," said Marta. "You were always his favorite."

"He was wrong. I want nothing to do with it. That sonofabitch Stritch can rule the world, for all I care, as long as he leaves me alone."

"This new you is kind of sexy, in a disillusioned-hero sort of way," said Marta.

She followed him to the dock. It buoyed and clanked under their feet. At its far end, Robert knelt and reached into the icy water. He found the fishing line and pulled up a waterproof stash jar, untied the fishing line from its neck, and twisted off the lid.

From inside, he removed the bobber that had carried the mini-USB onto which Furth had copied all the accounts, routing numbers, transaction dates, and dollar amounts that traced the path of Stritch's theft.

"Whatever you do with this, I don't care, okay?" He handed Marta the bobber. "Just leave me out of it. I'm done, you understand? I'm a man on a lake in the woods. That's it. I'm out of the game."

He started down the dock toward the cabin.

"I'll give you a ride back to town," he called.

Marta slid the bobber into her coat pocket and drew the Glock from the small of her back. She sighted it on Robert as he walked away. She was astonished to find that she couldn't shoot him without saying goodbye. Who could imagine she would be sentimental? Maybe his superpower had gotten to her after all. Or maybe hers was failing.

"Oh, Robert," she said, "how did we ever become such good friends?"

He stopped and turned. The last rays of the sun captured the sadness and resignation on his face when he saw her holding the gun. He raised his hands.

"I was hoping you wouldn't do this," he sighed.

"I wish I didn't have to," she said, and she was surprised again to find that she meant it. "But there's no other choice."

"There's always a choice. My father, too? He knows absolutely nothing."

"I'm sorry. I really am."

Robert nodded, understanding that this was how the game was played. The innocent were of no consequence, merely impediments to be overcome on the way to a fleeting objective. He had wanted to be wrong, had wanted to think it could go another way. He had given it every opportunity to divert from the predicted path. Furth would have been disappointed in his foolishness. But now, it all seemed inevitable.

"So you were in on it with Stritch?" he said.

"No one was supposed to miss the money," said Marta. "It was pennies on the dollar."

"All just greed, then."

"It's the way of the world, Robert. You know that. Everybody wants theirs. You take, or you get taken. *You* want too little, and that's your problem."

"What about Yao and his family? Were you in on that, too?"

"No, that was all Stritch. I swear. They were supposed to have time to get out of the country, but it all went sideways. I felt sick about it."

"I'm sure," said Robert. "And Tony?"

"Stritch arranged that, too," said Marta, sounding regretful of the necessity. "That should have been the end of it. And then I got his goddamn letter."

"And he sent you for me."

"We have history, after all."

From the woods came the screech of an owl, as the forest's nocturnal life began to stir. A slicing wind moved in off the lake. A cold front was coming. Maybe even snow.

"Did I mention Tony wrote me a note?" said Robert. "It was in the bobber with the USB. It said, 'Here's the bait. Hook the fish that takes it.' I sure as hell didn't think he meant you."

"What do you—?" For the first time since arriving in Rock River, Marta sounded unsure.

"You all set?" Robert called into the descending darkness.

The jarring twang of a jaw harp came from close at hand.

"A lot of people aren't aware that Stove used to be Special Forces," said Robert. "Everybody's got a past, you know. He's probably high, but he won't miss."

Marta looked left and right but saw only shadows, shades of black merging and twisting where the lake met land. The jaw harp twanged again, and she twitched. How the hell had she allowed herself to be caught out here in the open on a goddamn dock? She was an idiot. She lowered her gun and swore softly.

"Was it that hug of yours that signaled him to follow us?"

"No," said Robert. "It was the phrase 'old friend.'"

"Hmm. 'Old' did seem a little insensitive."

Robert stepped to her, took her Glock, and turned it on her. He reached into her coat pocket and pulled out the bobber. What he would do with it, he had no idea. He'd figure that out later.

"You can go, Stove," he called. "I got this."

"You sure, Bobby? I don't mind staying."

"No, you go on," said Robert. "It's best."

A final twang sounded as a sign-off.

Robert stepped behind Marta and patted her down. She thought of turning on him, trying to shove him into the lake and running, but he was too big and close and had the Glock pressed against her ribs. He took her elbow and guided her back down the dock.

"It doesn't have to be this way," she said, working to control her breathing. "There's enough for both of us."

"There's always been enough," said Robert. "But you and Stritch are the kind who always want more and ruin it for everyone else."

At the end of the dock, he turned and led her toward the national forest, which was quickly growing darker.

"This won't solve anything, Robert. Please." The base of Marta's neck tingled with fear. "He won't let this be. He'll keep coming for you."

Robert looked out to where the indiscriminate lake met the impassive night sky. The first stars were emerging, billions of years old and still burning, with billions of years to go before they ultimately blinked out.

He shrugged. "Everybody dies," he said. "Seems the only choice we've got is how to be alive."

Follies

opened April 4, 1971, at the Winter Garden Theatre, New York

"Prologue"
"Overture"
"Beautiful Girls"
"Don't Look at Me"
"Waiting for the Girls Upstairs"
"Montage (Rain on the Roof/Ah, Paris!/Broadway Baby)"
"The Road You Didn't Take"
"Bolero d'Amour"
"In Buddy's Eyes"
"Who's That Woman?"
"I'm Still Here"
"Too Many Mornings"
"The Right Girl"
"One More Kiss"
"Could I Leave You?"
"Loveland"
"You're Gonna Love Tomorrow/Love Will See Us Through"
"The God-Why-Don't-You-Love-Me Blues"
"Losing My Mind"
"The Story of Lucy and Jessie"
"Live, Laugh, Love"
"Chaos"
"Finale"

Music and lyrics by Stephen Sondheim.
Book by James Goldman.

Losing My Mind

by Kristopher Zgorski

MORNING(S)

I arrived for my hellish work shift at five thirty-seven, shortly before the break of dawn. You'd be forgiven for assuming that "hellish" is a metaphor for a toxic workplace and that I hate my job as a barista at Infernal Grounds, but the truth is that my job is literally in Hell. At the corner of Broadway and Fleet Street in the center of the Underworld, to be exact.

Other than its unusual location, Infernal Grounds is your typical neighborhood coffee shop. Once we open our doors at six, we have a consistent queue for several hours, just like most coffeehouses from Seattle to Baltimore—except that many of our customers are the spirits of murderers, rapists, terrorists, and that ilk. Criminals paying the ultimate price for their crimes. But believe me, they still love themselves a tasty caramel macchiato.

Iced, of course. I mean, it's *hot* Down Here.

You might be asking yourself how one gets a job in Hell. I wish I had some fascinating answer for you. But the reality is that you just apply and interview, same as for any other job.

My name is Salvador Durante. I put both names on my badge, because I've spent too much of my life in rooms with multiple Salvadors. Totally cray-cray, when one wants to stand out. But in the end, people call you whatever they want to call you, and most everyone calls me Sal.

I live "upstairs." That's how most of us refer to the world of the living. It was someone in Management's brilliant idea to help curb the unemployment rate by allowing honest and willing citizens who are still alive to pick up shifts at some of the shops in Hell. Since I don't like most of my living brethren, this seemed like a no-brainer for me. So five days a week, I trek my ass "downstairs" and sling caffeine for the condemned.

I look good doing it, too. The uniforms at Infernal Grounds wouldn't be negatively clocked at any of the upstairs go-go bars. There's barely anything to them. (Again, the heat.) Our IG-branded short-shorts highlight the goods, both front and back—advertising, without giving the merchandise away for free—and I'm not complaining. I like the attention.

Anyway, my story really begins when I met Phillip Rogerson.

Normally, I like to be the one who's pursued. That's the way it works upstairs, but Down Here, the dead don't normally get to have relations with the living. That doesn't stop infatuation, though—in either direction.

Psychopaths rarely make good lovers, but the moment I saw Phillip, my heart skipped a beat. Or ten. He was effin' hot. Trim and muscular, oozing with masculinity.

I first spotted him about six months ago. I was too shy to interact much beyond batting my eyelashes, but I made sure it was me who served him his coffee that morning and every day thereafter. Grande Americano, no sug. I sensed that he wasn't offended by my interest—and might even be into it if our situation was different, so eventually, I started adding some hearts to the side of his coffee cup, surrounding his name. After all, the no-go rule doesn't forbid flirty conversation.

Which is how I found myself joining him at a small table in the back of the shop on the regular during my breaks. He would come in and start reading the newspapers some of us smuggled in from upstairs, and I would sit with him when there was a lull in customers.

Over the course of a few months, our meetups allowed us to get to know each other. As you can imagine, one of our first conversations revolved around the clichéd question, "What's a nice guy like you doing in a place like this? You know, *Hell*." And Phillip was nothing but honest, which I

113

appreciated. I rarely ever got honesty from the men I swiped right to meet upstairs.

"It's not that interesting a story," he said. Which is code for *get ready to pick your jaw up off the floor.*

"It was the spring of 1971," he went on, knowing full well that I hadn't at that time been born. At the time I'm telling you about, I was nineteen years old. Phillip was twenty-one, but only because aging halts when the heart stops beating. (Hey, don't shoot the messenger, but the damnation thing doesn't seem like too bad a gig to me. Not even a hint of crow's feet or sagging skin after half a century upstairs? Sign me up!)

Anyway, Phillip's intro reminded me of my history classes, to which I'd rarely paid attention. "Maybe a bit more detail," I hedged.

He gave me a look that made it clear he was disappointed but not surprised. "It was several years after the Stonewall Riots," he continued.

My face lit up. "That launched the gay rights movement, right?"

"So they say. Though I can tell you, many of us had been fighting that fight for far longer. Stonewall was when others began to notice." He sighed. "So, it was April 4, 1971, and my friend Carlotta Nerve and I had just been to the opening night of a new Broadway show playing at the Winter Garden. Carlotta loved musicals. He was—she was—a drag queen and loved any excuse to wear a fancy dress. On our walk home, some off-duty coppers confronted us."

I could see Phillip's hands getting fidgety. This was not an easy tale for him to tell. I wanted to comfort him, but I remained silent—equal parts respect and a desire to know more.

"The pigs were no more interested in conversing with a pair of queers— one of whom was dressed as a woman—than an alligator is willing to help out a frog. One of the cops— Benny Whiteman, I'll never forget his name— got really rough with Carlotta, tried to claim that she'd solicited him, which was completely made up. Meanwhile, the other bastard came for me. I was just defending myself"—he took a breath—"but when I pushed him, he must have slipped. He fell backwards, hitting his head on the curb, and I guess he died instantly."

"Oh, my God." As tears created tributaries down Phillip's face, I took his hand. He seemed not to mind—or maybe he was so caught up in his story that he didn't even notice.

"The first cop—Benny—pulled his gun, aimed directly at me, and pulled the trigger. As I bled out, he fired again, which I guess was the end of Carlotta." This revelation was tinged with sadness and regret. "She's in a better place now—the Pleasant Kingdom. And I'm happy for her. As for me, it turns out even an accidental killing will get you sent Down Here. And here I remain."

Not all of our chats went that deep, but over time, we shared details about our lives, our dreams, and desires, and I'll never forget how Phillip confided in me. It was as though each word he imparted was a verbal tattoo, inked on my psyche for eternity. His trust meant so much.

It was probably a month later when I told him my idea.

"Listen, Phillip," I said, "we have sat here too many mornings avoiding the elephant in the room. Do you know whatever became of Benny Whiteman?"

"I have no idea."

"Well, I'm going to find out. And I'm going to make sure he pays for what he did to you—and your friend."

Phillip took my hand in his. "I love you for that. I really do. But what's the point? The past is the past."

I heard what he was saying, but I could tell that the circumstances of his death still weighed on him in unimaginable ways.

I was a man with a mission, and I would see it through.

＊ ＊ ＊

MIDDAY(S)

When my shift ended at noon, I usually hung out with some of my upstairs friends before heading home. A confidentiality clause in my contract required that I keep my employment secret...or at least the truth about where exactly I worked. I guess Hell doesn't want any looky-loos. Anyway, I needed the job, and it kept me close to Phillip, so the NDA didn't cause me any angst.

On this particular day, I was supposed to meet Hal over at Yvonne's place. When I got there, I buzzed to let her know I'd arrived but lingered outside her apartment. It was a lovely day—and, frankly, after six hours in Hell's stifling heat, the breeze felt good.

I couldn't stop thinking about Phillip. Every little thing reminded me of him. The honeysuckle scent carried by the wind matched his. The blue of the front door across the street was identical to the shade of my favorite of his shirts, the one with the top few buttons undone. (And oh, what was underneath?) I knew that, if he could hear the birdsong, he would smile as I was doing right now.

"Bruh. What's the dealio?" Hal said, bounding around the corner. He was old-school in a weird way, but I could always count on him.

"Just waiting on the girls," I said, then added the stinger I knew would annoy him. "Yvonne's invited a friend to join us. Maybe you'll get lucky!"

He punched my shoulder. "From your mouth," he said. "And speaking of, what's the deets on the man-crush?"

I had confided in my friends about Phillip. In the abstract, of course. No point telling them I was lusting after yet another unattainable dude. I typically dated older guys, but there was an undeniable chasm between one foot in the grave and, well, already *dead*.

"Yeah, spill the tea about Mr. Smoking Hot," came a voice from above. I heard the girls' laughter before I saw them descending the stairs. Yvonne looked snatched, as always. And her friend caught Hal's immediate attention.

"What's this? Someone's got a hot bae?" said this new member of our clique. "I'm Alexis. It's so nice to meet y'all. Yvonne can't shut up about you."

I turned to Hal. "Sorry, dude. There goes any chance you had." We all laughed and headed for Greenwich Village and our favorite gastropub, the Folly.

As we were eating, my friends could tell my mind was elsewhere. My thoughts of Phillip were becoming increasingly common—and, truth be told, obsessive. I figured there was no harm in getting their input. "Remember I mentioned that this new guy comes with some baggage? Well, he's looking for an old friend of the family, a former policeman. But he's sort of hit a—a dead end. I want to help. As a good Samaritan—and because it will put the lock on my irresistibility."

Alexis leaned in. "Hash-tag lucky day. The law office where I intern uses lots of retired cops as expert witnesses. There's a database." She pulled a tablet from her bag. "What's the cop's name?"

"Benny Whiteman," I said. "I think he's probably ancient."

Alexis clicked away on her screen. "Found him," she announced. "Benjamin Whiteman, age eighty-one." She looked at me, and I nodded. "Says here he lives in the Loveland Nursing Home, over in Brooklyn."

Score!

I could tell Hal and Yvonne were getting bored, so I let the conversation shift to other topics, even as my thoughts returned to Phillip.

* * *

Pulling up in front of our house, I saw my grandfather digging up a bush on the side of our property. "Let me help with that, Poppy," I said, jumping from the car.

"No need, buddy. I'm just about done." He moved the bush onto a plastic tarp that was spread out on the grass. "I'm glad you've been hanging out with your friends. That's important. Those carefree days go by too quickly."

I'd heard this all before. Stephen Michael Durante was never one to deny folks their fun.

"Tell you what," he added. "Once I finish here, you could pull out the mower and tidy up the lawn."

Branches and dirt were everywhere. "What is all this, anyway? Looks like you're hunting armadillos."

As he straightened from his stooped position, I could hear bones cracking.

"I think you mean moles, Sal. But no. This is an oleander, and your grandmother's been nagging me to remove it. It's dangerous, and she's worried about the neighborhood pets nibbling on it."

"Dangerous?"

"Toxic. One of the deadliest plants around. Even the ground where it's planted becomes tainted, poisonous. We should have removed it years ago."

This gave me an idea.

"Let me get changed," I said, "and then I'll come out and help."

A quick Google search, I knew, was in my immediate future.

* * *

AFTERNOON(S)

The Loveland Nursing Home seemed like a decent facility. No one was going to mistake it for a boujee vacation getaway, but the patients looked to be getting the care they needed. All the staff I encountered were on the ball, strict about visiting hours but willing to help when needed.

Thanks to the tip from Alexis, I confirmed that Benjamin Whiteman— Benny—was in a ground-floor room. The receptionist told me that only family members were allowed to visit the residents without special authorization. So maybe I lied when I said I was researching the history of the NYPD and was hoping Mr. Whiteman would be willing to chat with me. Fortunately, Benny was as egotistical as I suspected he would be, and he agreed to add me to his list of approved visitors.

I tried to make my initial visits as authentic as possible—I didn't want anyone getting sus before I could complete my task. I brought my laptop and pretended to take notes as Benny and I chatted. He eagerly reminisced about his early life, what made him go into law enforcement, and his record, which included several commendations and retirement with a full pension. It was during my third or fourth visit that I asked about the aftermath of Stonewall.

"Those riots never needed to happen," he said, sitting on his blue plaid La-Z-Boy. "Back then, that kinky stuff was against the law. Still should be, you ask me."

I tried not to react to his vitriol. "Were you involved?"

Benny sucked his teeth before answering. "I joined the force just after, but I did my best to keep my part of the streets clear. You young'uns need to understand: all this 'woke' shit wasn't a thing back then. People just wanted to live wholesome lives."

"Don't you think 'those' people wanted to live *their* lives, too, as honestly as possible? What was the harm? What *is* the harm?"

That was when Benny began to get the sense that he might be entering tricky territory. "Look, I was just doing my job. The higher-ups issued orders, and we followed them."

I left it there that day, but I was pissed. How could this man believe he was just obeying orders? I *know* no one told him to entrap folks by making up accusations that weren't true.

With my anger rising, the beacon of Phillip illuminated my mind. *I'm doing this for you*, I told myself. *And for Carlotta.*

Anger is a great emotion when you need to get shit done. My chores that afternoon passed in a whirlwind. I cleaned the kitchen and bathroom, got through three loads of laundry, and pulled out the vacuum cleaner.

The house got cleaned, but my mind was so scattered I didn't know if I should go left or right. It was all so overwhelming. The realization that, half a century later, we're still fighting so many of the same battles really shook me to the core. I broke down in tears, not fully realizing why. I had to *do* something to right the wrongs of the past....

* * *

On my next visit to see Benny Whiteman at Loveland, I brought him a treat. I had told him that I worked at a popular coffee shop. Thankfully, he never asked the name, probably assuming it was one of those overpriced chains with no character.

"Benny, my man," I said, walking into his room, "I have a surprise for you. This is a classic Americano from my shop."

He looked at me, totally confused.

"It's coffee," I explained.

He waved his arm like he was swatting away a pesky insect. "Why the hell they got to make it sound like some Hispaniola thing? This is America!" He was on the verge of shouting, like he was at a Trump rally.

This was going to be easier than I thought.

"Let me just heat this up in the microwave for you," I said, crossing the room to his kitchenette. As the to-go cup circled, I broached a subject we'd been dancing around during my last few visits. "Tell me, Benny, did you ever do anything you shouldn't have, while you were on the force?"

"I lived a respectable life," he replied, without a trace of hesitation. "I contributed more than my share, and I can go with the knowledge that I leave this world better than it was when I started."

I had to be careful not to drop the coffee as I removed it from the microwave. Not because it was hot, but because the bullshit this man was spewing was so infuriating. As I carried the drink across the room, I felt no regret for what I was about to do.

"I'll miss my friends, of course. We had some great times." As he took the cup, he seemed to drift off into a memory. "Well, no point dwelling on the road not taken. All life must end, sooner or later."

"True dat," I said.

I watched him take his first sip. Little did he know that the water in which I had allowed the oleander root to steep would cut his pitiful life short in the twilight of his years.

* * *

EVENING(S)

After I did it, time crawled. Not that I felt any guilt, but because of all the wasted hours, time when I *could* have been with Phillip.

At the end of every sleepless night, I'd roll out of my new bed and head for Infernal Grounds.

Now, though, I stood in the queue, not behind the counter. To a spectator from upstairs, we'd probably resemble a chorus line waiting to start our high kicks.

You may wonder why I was on the customer side of the service counter. I won't say it's a long story—that would be a lie.

After Benny Whiteman drank from the tainted cup, see, I did the same.

Don't act so surprised. Didn't you understand that my goal was to be condemned, so I could be with Phillip forever? Consumed with lust, I strategized on how to make it happen—and then Phillip served up the answer on a golden platter.

Sure, it was nice to avenge Phillip's and Carlotta's deaths, but let's be honest. I'd wanted to bone Phillip from the moment we met, and that couldn't happen unless I was dead. Dead and sentenced to eternity in Hell.

So for almost a week, I showed up at the coffee shop I'd once worked at, certain that love would see us through.

The way it turned out, though, the joke was on me.

Once I got Down Here to stay, I looked everywhere for Phillip, eager to explain what I had done and why. But he ghosted me. (Pretty ironic, getting ghosted by a ghost when you *are* a ghost.)

It's not easy to just *bump into* someone in the Underworld, so I simply began living my afterlife, going about my business, hoping for a chance to plead my case.

I wasn't sure exactly what I'd say when, at last, we met. "Hey, I killed a man for you" didn't seem like an ideal pick-up line, but I supposed it'd be a start.

As for Benny, I was sure he had to be Down Here somewhere. I didn't fancy seeing him again. He was bound to be pissed. But he knew what he'd done to earn eternal punishment. All *I* did was speed things up a bit. From the looks of things at the Loveland, I don't think he would have lasted much longer, anyway.

* * *

One evening, with the primrose-scented perfume of the woman in line ahead of me assaulting my senses, I heard the door of Infernal Grounds squeak and turned—and there he was. Phillip Rogerson stood there in the dim light, like a vision manifesting from the ether. With a simple gesture of his chin, he let me know we should meet at our usual corner table. Our reunion would occur at the same location where our love affair began.

When I brought over our coffees, I wanted to go in for a hug, but Phillip seemed salty.

"Fancy meeting you here," I said, trying his own line on him to no good effect. "I'm glad to see you. I don't know if you heard that I live here now—or whatever you call it."

"I heard. And I think I owe you some honesty." He pulled out a chair and sat. "I know you went after Benny for my sake, and that really means a lot."

He understood!

"I did it for us," I said, my heart soaring. "So we could be together."

"Listen, kid, that would never work out. Age is just a number, but we're from completely different generations. I could say I was being friendly out of kindness, but the truth is I led you on for another reason."

His words didn't register at first. Was I delulu? Did this specter just say what I thought he said? After all I'd done for him?

"Phillip," I began.

"No, let me finish. When I told you about that night in 1971, I didn't tell you everything. It was true that Carlotta and I were assaulted—killed—by two off-duty police officers. But they weren't alone. They had a buddy with them."

I was confused. "What does that matter?"

"Well, you see, he did nothing, just stood there and watched as two human beings were gunned down before his eyes. His name was Stephen Michael Durante."

And my world came crashing down around me.

"Poppy?" I said, the shock obvious in both the tenor of my voice and the look on my face.

"When I saw your last name on your work badge, I figured you two must be related. And when you told me about your family, I knew. That was when I let my worst self guide me. I wanted *him* to experience the same kind of loss *we* felt."

Tears rolled down my face. "You *played* me?"

He didn't need to answer, just got up and walked out the door. Out of my life—well, technically, out of my death—forever. I had fated myself to Hell for a man who had no true feelings for me. A man who had crushed my idealized vision of my family, shattered it forever.

I picked up the Americano in front of me and took a sip, then tossed it in the nearest trash can.

"Okay, boomer," I said, "there are other fish in the sea. Game *on.*"

I went up to the counter, focusing my attention on the sexy barista twink skillfully serving customers.

I mean, you know what they say: after all is said and done, hope springs infernal….

A Little Night Music

opened February 25, 1973, at the Shubert Theatre, New York

ACT I

"Overture"
"Night Waltz"
"Now"
"Later"
"Soon"
"Soon/Later/Now"
"The Glamorous Life"
"Remember?"
"You Must Meet My Wife"
"Liaisons"
"In Praise of Women"
"Every Day a Little Death"
"A Weekend in the Country"

ACT II

"Entr'acte"
"Night Waltz I (The Sun Won't Set)"
"Night Waltz II (The Sun Sits Low)"
"It Would Have Been Wonderful"
"Perpetual Anticipation"
"Dinner Table Scene"

"Send in the Clowns"
"The Miller's Son"
"The World Won't End/Every Day a Little Death (reprise)"
"Reprises"
"Send in the Clowns" (reprise)
"Last Waltz"

Music and lyrics by Stephen Sondheim.
Book by Hugh Wheeler.

Every Day a Little Death

by Josh Pachter

"Sugar?" asked Anne Bergman, carefully setting her lovely Meissen Zwiebelmuster teapot back on the oval-topped faux-marble table at her side and reaching for the matching bowl and scalloped spoon without waiting for a reply. She and Charlotte Simmons had been best friends since they were schoolgirls at the Wallinska Flickskolan in Stockholm in the last years of the Nineteenth Century, and she was quite well aware that Charlotte took precisely three-quarters of a spoonful of sugar in her tea.

"Thank you, dear," said Charlotte, waiting patiently while Anne's hand hovered over the creamer and plate of lemon slices before selecting a slice of lemon and floating it on the surface of her own cup. "No milk?" she asked, as she always did, though she knew quite well that citric acid would cause milk to curdle.

"Not today," Anne replied with a smile. "I feel perhaps more lemony than milky today."

"Nothing wrong, I trust?" Charlotte took a small sip of her tea. "Oh, my, this is lovely. Something new?"

"Fredrik brought it back from his last trip to Paris. Orange pekoe, I believe, from Mariage Frères."

Charlotte patted her rouged lips with a lace handkerchief she then returned to her sleeve. "Speaking of *mariage* and Fredrik," she said, "how *is* your charming husband? I haven't seen him since the *fête* at Madame Armfeldt's estate last month."

126

Anne pouted. "I've barely seen him myself. He's been so busy this summer. When he isn't off to Paris or London to oversee his business interests, he meets with bankers and stockbrokers and suppliers and heaven *knows* who else until all hours of the night. Then he comes home exhausted and more often than not goes directly to bed."

"And should I assume that you continue to maintain separate bedrooms?"

"*Ja självklart!* The man *snores* like a hibernating bear."

Charlotte giggled. "And what do you know of hibernating bears, my dear?"

Anne blushed prettily. "Well, as I *imagine* a hibernating bear would sound."

Charlotte finished her tea and pushed her porcelain cup forward for a refill. As Anne poured and spooned sugar, she said, "But you haven't answered my question, Anne. What is it that has you feeling lemony on this lovely summer afternoon?"

Anne lowered her eyelids, revealing the slightest hint of a cosmetic imported from Helena Rubenstein's new enterprise in the United States. "I'm afraid," she acknowledged demurely, "that it *is* my hibernating bear."

Charlotte set down her cup with a clatter. "Fredrik? Why, Anne, dear, what is it that concerns you?"

The tip of Anne's pink tongue drew a line across her upper lip as she considered how to put her worry into words. "He tells me that he has 'meetings' most evenings," she said at last, "and I'm certain that at least *some* of them must indeed be connected with his various professional enterprises."

"But...?" her friend prodded.

Anne drew a deep breath and sighed it out. Stalling for time, she refilled Charlotte's cup yet again and added three-quarters of a teaspoon from the sugar bowl, then poured more tea for herself and dropped in another slice of lemon. "But," she confessed, "I have begun to believe that other of his assignations are...how shall I say this?...dishonorable."

Charlotte leaned back in shock. "You suspect him of infidelity, Anne? Surely not."

Anne laced her fingers together and pressed a knuckle to the tip of her retroussé nose, hiding her mouth from view. "I think so," she murmured. "I am very much afraid that certain of his 'meetings' are mere camouflage for a liaison of the heart."

Charlotte laughed. "A liaison? *Fredrik?* How very amusing, dearest."

"It's not a joke, Charlotte. I am quite serious."

"But—but the idea is absurd! And who do you suspect? Elizabeth? Margaret? Not poor Diana, please!"

Anne allowed herself the hint of a smile. "No, not Diana."

"Who, then? You must—"

"What does it matter *who*, Charlotte? What matters is that my husband is deceiving me with another woman. I've been sure of it for weeks now—I've suspected it for almost a month—and every day has been for me a little death."

Charlotte leaned forward and placed a comforting hand atop that of her friend. "I am shattered to receive this news, my unhappy girl. Has he asked you for a divorce? Have *you* asked *him?*"

"Not yet," came the whispered response. "Not now. But soon, perhaps—or, if not soon, then later. Oh, I don't know! My mind whirls with confusion. But I can't go on like this much longer." For something to do with her hands, she lifted the Meissen teapot and emptied the last of its contents into Charlotte's cup. "You and I have always shared our darkest thoughts with each other, my oldest friend. Remember how we sat together as children, plotting revenge on those of our playmates we imagined had somehow wronged us?"

Charlotte nodded soberly.

"Well, I haven't dared say this to anyone else," Anne confided, as she moved the scalloped spoon from sugar bowl to cup, "but you, dear companion of my youth, I will tell you this: I have even entertained thoughts of...of murder."

"Murder! *Min kära Gud!*" Charlotte exclaimed. "Truly, Anne, you mustn't say such things!"

"I've thought of using a gun," Anne continued, now icily calm, "but where would I get one? And besides, I'm sure I would be so nervous I would merely shoot myself in the ear."

Charlotte reached for her cup, but her hand trembled from the shock of her friend's confidences, and a bit of her tea splashed over the rim and pooled in the saucer. "Anne, you frighten me. I hardly know what to say. But this talk of murder? I fear for your sanity."

"I am quite sane," said Anne. "But as that Englishman Congreve wrote, *'Helvetet har ingen vrede som en kvinna som föraktas.'*" She raised her own cup and sipped appreciatively.

"'Hell hath no fury,'" Charlotte repeated slowly, "'like a woman scorned.'" She forced her hand to remain steady and drank the last of her tea.

A moment later, the clock on the parlor's mantlepiece chimed three times. "*Min Gud!*" Charlotte exclaimed. "Is it three o'clock already? I must fly."

"So soon?" said Anne. "I thought we might allow ourselves a small glass of akvavit, now that we've finished our tea."

"Not today, darling, forgive me. I have an engagement this evening, and I have to bathe and dress. And as delicious as your *Mariage Frères* orange pekoe is, it seems to have given me a bit of a tummy-ache."

"Oh, no! I'll have Petra throw the rest of it away. But what about your engagement? Anyone I know?"

Charlotte's auburn curls danced around her lovely face as she shook her head. "I don't think so, no. He's a politician, of all things, and sure to be frightfully boring. But he's got pots of money and promised me the best supper I've ever eaten."

"Den Gyldene Freden?" guessed Anne.

"No idea, sweet. All I know is that I am to wear my finest frock." She gathered her things and jumped to her feet. "No need to show me out, dearest. I know the way. Next time at my house, agreed?"

"Yes, of course," said Anne. "Next time."

As she crossed to the door, Charlotte's heel seemed to catch on a corner of the Rollakan parlor rug, and she stumbled slightly before regaining her balance and her composure.

"All right, dear Charlotte?" Anne called after her.

"Quite all right, love," her friend called back. "I just came over dizzy for a moment. I must have gotten up too quickly."

"A tummy ache *and* dizzy? How terrible for you. I hope it all passes before your engagement."

"I'm sure it will!" Charlotte blew her friend a kiss and was gone.

When she heard the front door close, Anne rang for Petra, her maid, who had served her parents since Anne was a child and had moved with the young mistress to Fredrik's stately Östermalm townhouse on the occasion of their marriage.

"You can clear away the tea things," she said, when the old woman had shuffled into the parlor in her flowered apron and incongruously dainty lace cap.

"Yes, Fru Bergman. I'll just go and fetch a tray, ma'am."

As Petra left the room, Anne rose and picked up the sugar bowl and spoon and Charlotte's cup. She took them to the kitchen, emptied the bowl's contents into the sink and spooled the remaining white crystals down the drain, then carefully washed and dried the bowl, spoon, and cup and put them away in their proper places.

She crossed back through the parlor—where Petra was stacking the remaining tea things on a lacquered tray that had been a wedding gift from her brother Carl-Magnus and his French wife Desiree—and into the foyer.

As she ascended the broad oak staircase to her bedroom, she was humming a merry tune.

The Frogs

opened May 24, 1974, in the Yale University swimming pool,
New Haven (CT)

ACT I
"Opening Fanfare"
"Invocation and Instructions to the Audience"
"I Love to Travel"
"Dress Big"
"I Love to Travel" (reprise)
"All Aboard"
"Ariadne"
"The Frogs"

ACT II
"Hymn to Dionysos"
"Hades"
"It's Only a Play"
"Shaw"
"Fear No More"
"All Aboard" (reprise)
"Hymn to Dionysos" (reprise)
"Final Instructions to the Audience"

Music and lyrics by Stephen Sondheim.
Book by Burt Shevelove and Nathan Lane.

I Love to Travel

by John M. Floyd

Dion Duran climbed out of the rowboat, slogged across the muddy creekbank, and leaned against the hood of his car to light a cigarette. Through a cloud of blue smoke, he watched his old friend Zanthy Blyden pull their boat onto dry land, cursing and slapping mosquitoes at every step. Both men were shiny with sweat. This vast bottomland they'd known since their childhood was infamous, and not only for its summertime heat and humidity. Old-timers said DeLavallade Parish led the South in gator-related deaths.

"You thought any more about what I said?" Zanthy called.

Dion rubbed his eyes with his free hand. "Do I usually?"

"Well, this time you should. Them Poole stores is easy targets." Zanthy trudged over to join him, holding their fishing rods and a stringer heavy with catfish. "I told you, D, they been hit so often they're thinking about giving robbers their own parking spots."

Dion snorted. "What *I'm* thinking is you're dreaming too small. Like always."

"How *should* I be dreaming, smart guy?"

Dion flipped ashes into the mud. "Tell me something, Zan. You like to travel?"

Zanthy grinned. "I love to travel."

"You know the name Lincoln Shaw?"

"No. Should I?"

"He's the owner of all them Poole stores."

"So?"

Dion studied his friend's face. It was almost dark now; a chorus of bullfrogs' voices rose from the marsh around them. "He's the one we oughta rob. *Him*, not his stores."

"And how would we do that? You know where he lives?"

"No," Dion acknowledged. "But I know somebody who does."

* * *

They spent most of that evening eating fried catfish and discussing the possibility of unexpected wealth. They spent most of the following morning driving northeast to Brentford, just south of Baton Rouge, to the rural home of one Moses Burke. According to Dion, Mose could not only point them in the right direction; he could singlehandedly break into almost any safe manufactured in the free world. The fact that he was retired from all that was beside the point. Everybody needs money, Dion said, including ex-cons.

They found Mose sitting on a pond bank behind his shack, his graying hair riffling in the wind as he puffed on a pipe and gazed into the murky water.

"This is your expert?" Zanthy whispered. Dion made no reply, just kept walking until they stood beside the older man's lawn chair.

Mose never looked up until Dion mentioned Lincoln Shaw and their hope to relieve him of part of his fortune. At that, the former inmate raised his head.

Dion grinned. "You've thought about it yourself," he said. "Haven't you?"

"I've considered it," Mose said in word-sized chunks of smoke. Somewhere in the distance, a fish jumped and splashed.

At that point, Zanthy spoke up. "I gotta ask. If this man's as rich as you two think he is, how much security does he have? And how in the hell could we—?"

"Shaw's different," Mose said. "I got a feeling your compadre here knows that already." After a glance at Dion, he continued. "Lincoln Shaw's old

133

school, in more ways than one. Sorta like they say that Walmart dude was. Lives in a regular house, drives hisself to the gas station and grocery store in a beat-up old pickup, just like everbody else."

"And you know where he lives," Dion said. "Right?"

"Yeah, I know. He's in Florida, just outside Tampa."

"What about his security?" Zanthy asked again.

"Last I heard, he *has* guards, yes—they call themselves the Frogs, after military units like the Seals—but not many *of* 'em, and honestly, I doubt they ever been tested."

Dion leaned closer. "How do you know all that?"

"'Cause I knew one of 'em, them Frogs. They're mostly country bumpkins like you two—no offense—and they mostly just keep an eye on his house. Shaw don't allow 'em to follow him around."

"So you're saying it could be done."

Mose focused again on the pond. The wind had died down, and the water was still as glass. "Oh, yeah, it can be done." He looked up. "But I'd want half."

"A third," Dion said. "That's still a lot."

Mose nodded. "A third'd suit me. But I'll want to add another member to the team."

"Why?"

"One reason is, she can pick locks. Any lock, and fast."

"She?" Dion said.

"That's right."

"I thought *you* was the safecracker," Zanthy said.

"There's a difference."

"Well, where do we find her?"

"We pick her up on the way."

Dion took a moment, thinking that over. "Her pay comes out of your third," he said at last.

"Agreed."

"Okay, then."

The three men shook on it.

"When can you leave?" Dion asked.

"For Florida? Anytime you want."

"Right now, okay?"

Mose smiled. "I love to travel," he said.

* * *

The fact that the fourth member of their team would be female wouldn't normally have bothered two red-blooded Southern boys.

Except for her age.

"Fifty?" Dion said, when Mose informed them of that fact. "Hell, she's an old woman."

"To you two, maybe." Mose was sprawled in the back seat of Dion's ancient Ford as they roared east on I-10 just north of Biloxi. "Not to me, though—or to Lincoln Shaw, neither."

"You sayin' this friend a yours is gonna try to romance a reclusive multimillionaire she never laid eyes on before?"

"Not romance," Mose said. "Distract. And my buddy Suzie can sho nuff do that."

"Huh," Dion said. "We'll see."

* * *

Turned out the ex-con was right. As soon as the three travelers parked in Mose's friend's suburban Pensacola driveway and she strolled out in a T-shirt and jeans to greet them, all doubt vanished. Susan Siberry—fifty or not—could've been a fashion model. Hell, she could've been a Bond Girl, if she lived in Hollywood instead of the Florida Panhandle.

"Moses Burke," she said, wrapping him in a hug. "As I live and breathe."

"My fair lady," Mose replied.

He introduced her to Dion and Zan, and the four of them took seats in cane rockers on Suzie's porch. It took Mose less than twenty minutes to recruit her. The men sat and smoked and watched a fat frog hop across her front yard while she went inside to pack, and at half past seven, with the sun setting in his rearview mirror, Dion aimed the big Ford toward Tallahassee and points south.

Less than twenty-four hours had passed since Dion and Zanthy had stood at the edge of a Louisiana swamp with their day's catch and little else to their names, and now—lo and behold—they were on their way to riches and leisure.

Or so they hoped.

Not much had actually been *accomplished* as yet, except a lot of talk. And there was more of that to be done. Around midnight, in a ground-floor room in a roadside motel in the middle of nowhere, the team worked out the beginnings of a plan, which everyone understood would be fine-tuned when they reached their destination and saw the lay of the land.

"I love a challenge," Dion said.

"I love money," Mose replied. "If we got to march, trudge, tramp, slog, and plod to get it, then so be it."

When they adjourned for the night, Suzie and Mose headed for their separate rooms.

"I figured you two might be bunking together," Zanthy said.

"I heard that," Suzie called from the hallway. "Tell him, Mose."

"This trip's all business," Mose said. "What Suzie and me do after we're done, that's *our* business."

Suzie came back into the room. "Moses and me always been good together," she said. "Ain't we, Mosey?" To Dion and Zanthy, she added, "Where you think Clyde woulda been, if not for Bonnie?"

Maybe alive, Dion thought, but he didn't say so. If she could help them pull this caper off, he'd be a Suzie Siberry fan forever.

When the others were gone and the lights were out and he and Zanthy were tucked away in their motel beds, he said, "You think we're doing the right thing, Zan, my man?"

"What's the problem, D? You homesick?"

"Oh, yeah. Gnats, wasps, snakes, mosquitoes. I miss 'em already."

Zanthy stayed quiet for a moment. "Are we doin' the right thing?" he echoed at last. "I dunno, partner. I'm trying to remember whose idea this was. If it was mine, it'll probably work. If it was yours, I ain't so sure."

Dion chuckled. "Me, neither. But it's too late to back out now."

* * *

Lincoln Shaw's residence turned out to be even more "regular" than Mose had described: a white frame house with green shutters and a two-car garage on a half-acre of land just outside the Tampa city limits. There were neighboring houses around, but only one within shouting distance.

According to Mose, Shaw had a Frog living in the second bedroom of the main house and two more of them—a male/female team—in the house nearby. Other security measures seemed lax. There were no obvious surveillance cameras on the property, and Mose's latest info said Shaw still insisted on his independence while offsite. Widowed and mostly retired, he grudgingly took several Frogs with him on business trips, but when in town, the seventy-year-old drove solo in an old manual-transmission Chevy pickup with a huge metal toolbox bolted on behind the cab. He even dressed the part, usually wearing jeans or coveralls and a Texas Christian University ball cap, and his eccentric nature wasn't limited to his appearance. The bulk of his wealth wasn't tucked away in banks or offshore accounts. It was in cash and bearer bonds, hidden in the kitchen of his home—in a safe inside his unused dishwasher.

"*What?*" Dion said. They were sitting in a corner booth at Doolittle's, a diner not far from Shaw's place. "You're kidding, right?"

Mose shook his head. "I shit you not. My contact swears it's there."

"I wonder if the Frog-in-residence ever pushed the start button by mistake," Suzie said, grinning.

"He ever did," Zanthy said, "I bet it was only once."

Shaw's old-timey and bullheaded ways, Mose went on, caused the Frogs nightmares. For one thing, he'd been known to give away large sums of money on his outings, endearing himself to the townsfolk but drawing a target on his plaid-shirted back for those who saw all that flaunted money and yearned to grab a piece of it for themselves.

"So he carries piles of cash around in his truck?" Zan asked.

Mose shrugged. "Maybe it's stuffed in the glovebox or under the driver's seat. I'm just tellin' you what I been told."

"It occurs to me," Dion said, "that we're basing pretty much our whole plan on what you been told. I damn sure hope you been told right."

"If I ain't," Mose said, standing, "I guess we're up Shit Creek."

Dion and Zanthy watched the older man limp off to the restroom, chuckling to himself. Suzie was staring into her cup, as if trying to read the tea leaves.

Dion hoped she was seeing good things and not the absence of a paddle.

* * *

The team's base of operations was another motel, this one on the main highway two miles south of Chez Shaw. Once again, they took separate rooms for Mose and Suzie and one for Dion and Zan to share. Mose wound up renting a second car, a Honda, so Suzie could have freedom of mobility. Her involvement was key to their plan, because they needed to know Shaw's whereabouts at all times.

"This friendship you mean to strike up," Zanthy said, as they huddled in the motel restaurant that night. "What if he's not interested?"

Suzie chewed her chicken-fried steak—change of venue, change of menu—and smirked. "He'd be the first," she said. Beside her, Mose let out a laugh.

Dion didn't see the humor. "If he *is* the first," he said, remembering Han Solo's tractor-beam comment, "this is gonna be a real short trip."

Still smiling, she patted his hand. "Don't worry, honey. You do your part, and I'll do mine."

Later, in their room, Zanthy said, "Remember *Mission: Impossible*? The TV version?"

"Before my time," Dion said.

"Mine, too, but I streamed the first couple seasons. Better than the movies, you ask me."

Dion circled a hand impatiently.

"My *point* is," Zan went on, "all that preparation they did, every week, right down to the last detail—and yet things never *ever* went as planned."

"That's a *show*, Zan. If everything went as planned, there'd be no suspense. This is real life."

"Oh, right," Zanthy said. "Thank God."

* * *

The following morning, they were parked in the rented Honda, watching Shaw's house from up the road, when the tycoon's blue pickup pulled out of his driveway and headed the other way. Even from a distance, they could see that he was alone in the truck, and no other vehicle followed him. So *they* did.

Two miles up the road, Shaw turned into a shopping center lot, parked in front of a hardware store, and went inside. Mose parked the Honda some distance away and let Suzie out.

Inside the store, she browsed the garden tools section and watched Shaw from the corner of her eye as he picked up two rolls of duct tape and got in line behind a middle-aged woman at the checkout counter.

When the woman left with a bucket of white paint, Shaw stepped up to the register and exchanged greetings with the clerk. Suzie edged closer.

"Tell me, Willy," Shaw said, "you got anything to keep deer out of the garden? They're eating my peas and beans faster'n I can pick 'em."

"Ain't much that'll stop that, Mr. Shaw, 'cept a tall fence. And sometimes *that* don't. Since you ain't got many close neighbors, you might just get you a little .22 rifle."

"That won't work. Can't have my brother's granddaughter finding out I shot Bambi." Shaw paid for his tape and said, "How about Tabasco sauce? Maybe sprinkle it on my plants?"

"That don't work, either. Besides, I know you like your Tabasco. Can't be wastin' that stuff."

They laughed at that, which gave Suzie the opening she needed. "Try a

BB gun," she said. "I got a Daisy I use on all kinds a varmints."

Shaw and the sales clerk turned toward her, and she saw the familiar blink as they focused. Suzie had long ago stopped being surprised at the effect she had on men.

"I was serious about Bambi and my niece," Shaw said. "Wouldn't a BB gun hurt the deer?"

"It would've, when we were kids," she said. "Mine could punch holes in a Campbell Soup can. But not anymore—they're not as powerful. These days, a BB'd just sting for a second."

Shaw nodded. "That might work, then."

"We don't sell 'em here, though," the clerk said. "You might try Walmart."

Lincoln Shaw made a face. "Don't use that word around me, Willy."

Again, both men chuckled. Suzie put a confused look on her face, which she figured might be the way to go. And, sure enough, Shaw seemed to like the fact that she didn't appear to know he was famous.

"Thanks for the tip," he said, still smiling.

She gave him a thousand-watt grin in return. "My pleasure." Then, after a pause, "You could pay me back, actually, if you're headed north."

"I'm not, but I could be. Where you need to go?"

"The library, up the road a ways. My sister was supposed to meet me here, but she's been delayed, and—"

"Enough said. That'd be *my* pleasure. You take care, Willy."

He offered Suzie his arm, and they left together, chatting away.

* * *

From that point on, things fell into place. Dion and company put faces to Shaw's three Frogs and got a feel for everyone's routine, while Suzie met up with Shaw for several daytime outings. Though she treated their relationship as an enjoyable friendship, he was clearly infatuated. In any case, the two of them grew pleasantly comfortable together, and the team now had eyes on Shaw almost every time he left the house.

Mose came up with the idea of outfitting a local teenager with a camo vest and half a dozen *Field & Stream* magazines from Dion's trunk to take to Shaw's front door. Sure enough, the live-in Frog—a hefty guy with a buzz cut—answered the doorbell, and the hired kid pretended to try to sell him a subscription. That planted an important seed.

Zanthy bought an archery set and half a dozen tennis balls from the local Walmart—"Don't tell Shaw," Suzie said—and spent an hour puncturing the balls with a screwdriver, packing the hollow insides with strips of alcohol-soaked cloth, tucking a cloth wick halfway into each hole, and stoppering it with a cork.

By their fifth day in Florida, they were ready. That night, the foursome gathered as usual in Dion and Zanthy's room to go over their plan, complete with drawings and diagrams and timelines. Dion was reminded of Lee Marvin standing with pointer in hand, telling the Dirty Dozen how to storm the castle and win the battle that would help win the war.

I love a challenge, he'd said to Zanthy, four nights ago.

Well, the challenge was coming.

* * *

The following evening at precisely seven, Suzie drove the rental car to a local steakhouse, where she'd agreed to meet Lincoln Shaw for dinner. At seven-twenty, she phoned Dion from her car and reported that Shaw's truck was pulling into the lot.

All systems were go.

Fifteen seconds later, Dion, Zanthy, and Mose gathered their gear and climbed out of Dion's car, which they'd parked in a grove of trees near Shaw's home. The two friends headed for the strip of woods that bordered the back of Shaw's property, while Mose strolled down the darkening road toward the house itself, the hunting magazines under his arm and an empty duffel bag over his shoulder.

"Mud, dirt, thorns, and vines," Zanthy grumbled. "Just like home."

"Quit your bellyachin'," Dion said, trudging on.

At seven-forty, they took a position just inside the woods behind the house

141

occupied by the two Frog guards. It was almost full dark. They couldn't see Mose from there, but Dion knew the older man was at Shaw's front door by now, first telling the third Frog he was following up on the sales call his young trainee'd made previously to put the man off his guard, then tasing him and pulling his unconscious body inside.

Dion and Zanthy's job was to mount a diversion, just in case one of the two Frogs in the neighboring house had caught sight of Mose approaching Shaw's home or picked the wrong time to wander over there. They also didn't want to chance the guards seeing Mose leave Shaw's house with a full duffel bag.

Working fast, Dion punched the tip of a wooden Walmart arrow into one of the six tennis balls and handed it to Zan, who notched the arrow into his bow and took aim. Dion lit the wick with a pocket lighter, and Zanthy fired the mini Molotov cocktail in a long arc into the dry grass behind the Frog couple's house. Flames leaped head-high within seconds.

The two Frogs burst from the house, one carrying a fire extinguisher, the other a blanket. Dion and Zan stayed hidden, watching. As expected, the fire wasn't easily handled, and when Zan was sure both guards were looking the other way, he shot another flaming arrow into the weeds behind them.

Surely Mose had by now been able to pop the safe in Shaw's dishwasher and was on his way out with as much cash as he could carry. It was time to skedaddle. Working together, Dion and Zan sent two more arrows into the field to keep the firefighters occupied, then made their way back through the woods to their car.

Mose wasn't there. They waited ten minutes for him, and by then, the fire department had arrived, and the fires were out.

It was time to git gone, Mose or no Mose. They drove back to the motel and called Mose's cell. No answer. They tried to contact Suzie, but there was no response from her, either.

They waited by their phones until midnight, and when there was still no word from either of their teammates, the hard truth set in. They'd been screwed, and royally.

Who was the asshole who said there was honor among thieves?

* * *

Suzie Siberry didn't check the newspapers or watch TV the next morning. She just sat back and enjoyed the flight south. St. Lucia was hot this time of year, but who cared? That's what hotel pools were for, and colorful drinks with little parasols in them. Exotic *and* erotic.

She wondered what Lincoln Shaw was thinking about the events of last night. She hadn't seen him since she'd left him at their table in the steakhouse to go to the powder room. Where she went, of course, was out the back door and around to his truck, which he'd parked beside her car in a dark corner of the lot. She hopped into the truck bed and, within a minute, picked the padlock on the steel toolbox attached to the back of the cab. Inside the box was more money than she had ever seen.

It took five full minutes to transfer the cash to the trunk of the rental car and would've taken longer if Mose hadn't arrived to help her. He'd taken a cab, having never gone to Shaw's house at all. Suzie had found out from a lovesick Lincoln Shaw two days earlier that the money her team had come to Florida to steal was hidden in his truck, not his kitchen. And since Suzie knew, Mose knew.

That's why he was sitting beside her now. She wasn't sure Mose was the right man for her—she wasn't sure *any* man could keep her happy for long—but she could stand him for a while, at least until they decided where they wanted to go next with the cash packed into their bulging suitcases. Her next trip, she might be alone or she might not—that remained to be seen.

But one thing she knew for sure.

"I love to travel," she said to her current partner in crime.

143

Pacific Overtures

opened January 11, 1976, at the Winter Garden Theatre, New York

ACT I

"Prologue"

"The Advantages of Floating in the Middle of the Sea"

"There Is No Other Way"

"Four Black Dragons"

"Chrysanthemum Tea"

"Poems"

"Welcome to Kanagawa"

"March to the Treaty House"

"Someone in a Tree"

"Lion Dance"

ACT II

"Please Hello"

"A Bowler Hat"

"Pretty Lady"

"Next"

Music and lyrics by Stephen Sondheim.
Book by John Weidman.

The Advantages of Floating in the Middle of the Sea

by David Spencer

"Open wide for me, *querido*," Teaser whispered. "You know you want to."

His comb pick made its way to the end of the shear line, and the last of the stack moved into its cylinder. He felt the satisfying

snick

—soft as a lover's exhale—

as the display-case lock disengaged.

Seventeen minutes left before the mansion's security system would detect the hack. If Teaser wasn't off the private island by then, he'd wind up on a state-run island, in a much larger house than this one, with many more doors. Doors that would glide aside like metal screens and clang shut behind him like the end of the world.

He swung open the much quieter glass panel fronting the individual-item display case.

"Object within reach," Teaser said. Knowing the biggest danger now would be overconfidence.

"You hope." Pran's voice. Earbuds. Bluetooth. Budget smartphone burner. "Let's find out."

Teaser lifted the phone off the floor with his free hand, the other still clutching the pick. Thumb-tapped to reverse the cam angle. Activated the flashlight. Began panning the dark-veined Brazilian wood interior for any hint of battery-powered infrared or even filament-tension apparatus; hidden speed-trap-style photo capture was becoming increasingly popular as off-grid backup.

"Top looks clean to me. You?"

"Same. Sixteen minute. Pressure plate?"

Upon the satin of a tapered lavender cushion, the object lay angled for view. Removing its weight might spring-release a security trap. Teaser prodded the cushion-front with his lockpick's blunt end, up-wedging as much as he dared. "Solid wood finish all I can see. You?"

"Same. You certain 'bout surface? No break in vein? No outline you miss, blend into pattern?"

"Not to the naked I. Pun intended."

"Be sure. Nice pun. Fifteen minute."

Teaser wasn't *precisely* naked. His bulkware—scuba suit and accessories—lay outside in the bushes, at a vantage overlooking the Pacific Ocean, whence he had emerged. Not deeply hidden, but no one was on site to find them: occupants were overseas, staff had the weekend off. Left there because he couldn't afford to have free movement encumbered by a Diver Dan ensemble during the break-in overtures and the full score. He had donned a whole 'nother designer wardrobe for that: most of his full glory was now enveloped in a transparent ultra-thin full-body poncho; in essence, a disposable hazmat suit, with elastic bands tight around his face and wrists. Actual nudity would leave behind skin cells, hair follicles. True, Teaser had never been jailed, but he'd been investigated. And no one lived to be thirty-two years old in These United States without leaving traces. A clean police record didn't mean there was no medical record of his cross-matchable DNA out there somewhere.

On the floor within reach were the likewise bare essentials he'd entered with: underwater-safe toolbelt and double oxygen tank. Next to those: crumpled single-use gloves he'd peeled off, needing naked access to the most valuable tools of all.

His hands.

He'd wipe away prints later. There wouldn't be many.

He tapped off the flashlight app, returned the phone to the floor, stood again. Mulled. Frowned. *How* to be sure?

"*¡Diablos!* If I had a solid flat-edge—long enough, slim enough, light enough—I could slide it underneath. I'd feel any seam."

He wasn't overestimating his prowess. A half-Jewish orphan from the barrio, adopted by a family named de Falla, he had become Teaser because he could tease anything he touched into letting him inside. Better than a legal tag, your handle was your rep; it saved on explanations. In civilian life, he had become freelance travel writer C.O. Quetez—not quite the spelling of Teaser in Spanish—and because he *went* places, he *knew* places. Knew their vulnerabilities. And had stolen things from half of them. Free fares and accommodations; world-class souvenirs. But this was his first swimmer, and a watertight utility belt could only hold so many tools.

"Boo-hoo, no flat-edge," said Pran the Merciless. "Find one."

Teaser scanned the library.

"Too well-appointed. Nothing out of place."

"How 'bout what *in* place? Check windows. If Venetian blind, then slat."

He did. And sure enough.

"Always a little learning," he half-whispered.

"You decent pupil. Fourteen minute."

Ji-Yeong Pran, Korean émigré, a generation older than Teaser, sometime-partner/sometime-mentor, was currently operating electronics in the back of a command-post minivan on the mainland, approximately three miles away. In the legit world, Pran was an importer of exotic fruits from international suppliers: Pran's Plantains. In the underworld, Pran was a gatherer of exotic info from international connections, the industry-preferred repository for classified documentation: blueprints, schematics, maps. His handle was atypical: his actual surname. Pran's Plantains had led naturally to Pran's Plans (with its brilliantly explicit/deniable motto: "Never so many; never like these") and ultimately to just Pran, a Bamboo English pun. After many years in America, he could speak almost perfect English, but he clung rebelliously to the no-nonsense efficiency of eliminating already-implicit articles, conjunctions, and irregular verbs. Extra syllables added time to a transaction—or a crime, especially when he himself was involved as strategist, timekeeper, and guide.

Teaser snipped a length from the bottom of the blinds and returned to the display case.

Holding his improvised probe with only fingertips, he wedged it under the lavender cushion and pushed it…slowly…slowly…forward…

"Thirteen minute."

…feeling nothing until it touched backboard. Performed the extraction as painstakingly. Dropped slat to carpet.

"Smooth," he reported, and heard Pran exhale.

"Good! But handle care. I keep looking at photos. I still no idea what hell thing is. Client say 'purely dec'rative.' Not so sure. Shape too odd. Twelve minute."

Teaser had seen the client-supplied pix: old, low-rez black-and-white scans from an unidentified source. Pran's photo-restoration software had revealed no useful details, making the image only smoother, not crisper. Moot now. The authentic article was vividly before him, crisp as could be… seeming to possess a living power. *Cruel beauty,* he thought, not knowing why.

What he *did* know was that Pran's client was a curator on the board of Tokyo's Ancient Orient Museum, represented by a shadier, deadlier intermediary; that she aimed to restore this missing piece to the so-called Manjiro Collection; and that she was willing to pay *boku* yen for its retrieval.

Other realities remained remote, save minimal history: the item's name, translated, was Kayama's Pride, and Kayama—whoever or whatever he'd been—had commissioned it for himself around 1862, a decade or so after the West invaded Japan.

Teaser lifted it out caressingly, like a potentially explosive newborn.

"Feels sturdier than it looks. And it looks like, well, like a medieval remote control."

Evoking a manufacturer's logo, the silhouette of a dragon's head faced the top, mouth open as if to spit fire. Calligraphy ran along one side, its brushstrokes violent slashes. Reputed translation: *The Change is Everything.*

Two feet in length, oblong, curved edges. Swirls of filigreed metal engraving dancing around but never entering a smooth oval under the midpoint of one side. The Pride settled into Teaser's palm, as if it *belonged* there.

"What about jewels? If settings done with glue tack, may be brittle, so much age, break off."

The Pride's ovoid circumference was highlighted all around by a ring of small gems in a repeating green-to-pink-to-gold pattern.

"Examining. But these baubles ain't goin' anywhere. Embedded. The last time I saw fittings this flush was in a tea ceremony *hentai* on—whoa."

"Whoa?"

"Three jewels in succession have a hair's-breadth perimeter around 'em. Right where my thumb might go. *In,* but not like the others. Different technique."

"Weird. What you think?"

"That I've been stealing too many things for too long not to recognize mechanism buttons. But for what? Is this thing a...canister? An ancient thermos? Are they a release to—I don't know what—lift off the top?"

"No press, no open! What inside maybe perishable. If air expose—"

"—could expire," finished Teaser. "Got it."

Expiration might compromise the payday. Or nuke it altogether. Okay, then: no press, no open.

"Eleven minute."

Teaser gingerly placed the Pride back on its cushion—trusting its passivity less than before—and reached for his double oxygen tanks. One of which was a phony, doctored up by the third member of the team.

Gadge.

As if on cue, Teaser heard him say, "Did you tell Tease I said how ya doin'?"

"I tell! I tell!" Pran replied testily.

"Ask him how's the tank workin' out?"

"Say I'll let him know in a minute," said Teaser, grateful for a reason to smile.

Gadge, also in the minivan. In about two hours, when Teaser (theoret-

149

ically) emerged onto the beach from the ocean, Gadge would drive him, Pran, and the Pride back to the city. Little guy, chattery energy, he'd at first conjured for Teaser those oh-*him* actors who played stoolies in 1940s noir, an image quickly transmuted to that of eccentric genius, for, in fact, Gadge was a former aerospace engineer (a veteran of Lockheed, no less) who one day decided he wanted less corporate grief, more tax-free dough, and the freedom to invent things that made a tangible difference. *His* handle was short for "gadget"—and was he ever good at building things. Things mechanical, electronic, practical, handy. Specialty items for specialty work, like the phony tank.

Teaser unscrewed its top, tilted the tank downward, and out slid a waterproof casing. He opened it, exposing two halves of foam-padded interior. One half provided a recess, molded to the Pride's approximate dimensions. He lowered the Pride into it, jewel-buttons face up.

"Ten minute."

Poking through either side of the recess, top and bottom, were paired plastic bands—the kind fastened by snapping stubs into perforations— cannibalized from cheap Chinese watchbands. Teaser secured the Pride, its berth now jostle-proofed. He closed the casing and returned it to its metal cocoon.

"Tell Gadge *excellente,* as always! A *mitzvah!*" Likely Pran showed a thumbs up, because Teaser heard Gadge yip with delight.

"Everybody happy. Nine minute."

Keep it moving. Next. All about acceleration now, checklisting backwards, managing pressure, the whispered jazz of random fast-brush-scatting his shield against endgame fog.

Fresh pair of gloves—*scatty-wa-doo*—close the display case—*deet'n-dat'n-ditty*—reintegrate slat and obliterate prints—*duwee'ah-duwee'ah*—leave the illusion of an undisturbed room—*undisturbed room, undisturbed room*—delay their noticing the Pride's gone *zoom,* arrange tomorrow like it's yesterday, *let's hear it for the bandit in the boys.*

Still scatting, he returned to his toolbelt, secured its watertight pouches. Clicked the lockpick into its berth within a Craftsman-branded, credit-card-shaped variety pack of six, cheap at Amazon. Not storing *that* one away yet; he'd need it again soon.

"Eight minute."

Quick-striding with toolbelt and tanks, Teaser exited the mansion to the landing, palmed out the six-pack o' picks—and stopped scatting. Mental stillness required now. Background sound only: the gulls, gliding and diving quickly through the air—*Hai! Hai! Hai!*

"I'm out. Re-engaging door locks." Trickier than breaking in, but if he didn't, the re-activated system would detect the breach.

Pran kept counting down. Seven. Six. Five. Four. "Three min—"

"Done! Done! Do your thing! Your turn!"

Heard Pran tappity-tapping on his hackity laptop. And then: "Electricity restore. Alarm re-verify. One minute spare."

Teaser exhaled hugely. "Copy that."

Now he could relax. Sort of.

He trotted to the bushes shading his diving gear. Divested himself of thinware, zipped into the scuba suit's skintight fit. Crumpled the disposables into a tight ball, save for one glove into which he crammed the ball, then that into a back pocket. He'd release it into the ocean, where it would sink and dissolve. All biodegradable sheepskin, another Gadge flourish.

"Off the grid for about a minute."

"Copy."

He shut down the phone, removed and stored his earbuds, and shrugged into the double tank unit, conscious of the altered weight distribution now that he was carrying the Pride. Onto the toolbelt he slipped a watertight set: holster containing flare gun and tube-holder containing spares, all branded Kingzar, all bright orange. Risky last resort, but if return-swim misadventure forced him to diverge from the rendezvous point sans audio contact, shooting up a flare would be near as good as sending new coordinates. And snug around his waist went the toolbelt.

Penultimately, Teaser donned the full-face hood, which housed its own built-in transmitter-receiver. Powerful, sophisticated—and again all Gadge. He signed on.

"Back. Copy?"

"Copy. Maybe ninety minute before Coast Guard area patrol. You come home now."

Nice, safe margin. Nothing left but an easy swim to the mainland.

Neither one said so. The Pride was not yet delivered to the client. It all but vibrated with secrets they hadn't cracked. And the Crime Gods liked nothing better than to reward hubris with a lesson in irony.

Finally, Teaser lifted his fins off the ground and waded into the water, sending ripples to the shore. At waist depth, where the fins' wide webbing wouldn't send him tumbling, he slipped them on, secured their clips, executed a graceful backward roll, and slid under the surface.

Where the Crime Gods would have fun with him anyway.

* * *

Gadge kicked back in the passenger seat, knees up against the dashboard, rewarding himself with an episode of *Perry Mason* on his Android folding phone. Not one of the new-ass color eps exploring some multi-part, post-woke origin myth that wasn't worth the cable bill his bit-torrenting nature circumvented anyway, but one of the B&W classics starring Raymond Burr.

The soundtrack streamed into wireless earbuds so as not to bother bespectacled Pran, who was riveted on Teaser's progress via laptop and other electronics. Nonetheless, Gadge let out a "He-*heeee!*" Then: "Sorry, Pran." Then: "He-*heeee!*" once more.

Pran exhaled ruefully, looked up from his tracking screen, moved a headset earcup slightly off its enclosed pinna.

"Commodore Perry working endgame again?" asked Pran.

Gadge paused the video. "He's about to get a confession out of somebody who ain't even on the stand! He's some lawyer, I tellya."

Gadge had been on a *Perry Mason* kick for almost a month, making his way through the episodes from the beginning. His enthusiasm could be a lot to tolerate sometimes. There were two hundred and seventy-one of them.

"It fantasy," insisted Pran.

"Oh, yeah? Well, if I ever got make-believe caught, my fantasy mouthpiece would be Mason, hands down."

Pran grabbed a banana—soft food; no crunch to interfere with hearing Teaser's audio—snapped off the top, peeled it halfway. "Bad idea," he said, taking a bite.

"Whyzat?"

"Because you be *guilty!* He all time defend *innocent!* Look where you are! Look what we doing! We doing *wrong*doing! What advantages you give him work with, hah?" Pran swallowed decisively and reached for a bottle of the Chrysanthemum-brand green tea he imported for Asian-mart soft-drink refrigerators.

Gadge frowned. "'Titled to a defense. 'Titled to hire a pro."

"You say *now,* but what happen *court?*" Pran put down his tea, squared his shoulders like Raymond Burr, scanned the imaginary jury box, witnesses, gallery. "I'm Perr' Mason!" he said haughtily. "I connect dots!" He suddenly jabbed his banana at an imaginary offender. "And *you! You* did it!" He looked at Gadge. "And person not you. *Client* get off, someone *else* take fall. That be Mason defense, all time."

Gadge's frowny-face tightened into a mask of determination. "I'm gonna get back to you on that, Pran."

"Good. Get back. I look forward."

Something caught Gadge's eye. "You should look at your tracking screen," he said.

Pran returned his attention to it, adjusted his glasses, unplugged the headphones so Gadge could hear.

"Teaser! You moving off course! You in trouble?"

"No, just temporarily waylaid. I've kind of met up with this dolphin. I think *she's* in trouble. She's been swimming with me for a while and—"

"Wait. Dolphin? You say: *dolphin?*"

"She's re-routing me. I'm assuming it's a she. Hard to be sure. Males have their peeners in a pouch or something."

"I no care dolphin peener. Why you wasting time with fish?"

"Dolphins are intelligent mammals, Pran, like us."

"Come home. Buy dolphin-safe tuna. You conscience clean as whistle."

"She's being very insistent. Something's put her in a temper. I couldn't circumvent her if I tried. What the hell d'you expect me to do?"

Pran looked at Gadge and gestured vehemently. Gadge shrugged, thought for a moment, said: "Tease! Ask if she has a sister!"

Pran growled. "What hell I 'spect? You carry ancient payday! I 'spect you be ruteless criminal!"

"I can't be ruthless to a *dolphin*, Pran. Come on! If what she needs looks too involved, I'll...I'll break her heart then, promise. I'll keep you posted."

* * *

The dolphin led him to a small fishing trawler in a secluded cove. Approaching it from below, he saw three shallow-water cages hanging over the side, a dolphin in each of them.

Prisoners.

Teaser didn't know much about dolphin poaching, but he knew the victims always ended up dead, and what else was there *to* know? He'd been conscripted into rescue service, and—since reporting the matter to the cops wasn't an option—

—he found himself, for the second time that day, picking the lock on an enclosure.

The cage in which his recruiter showed a special interest had the smallest, youngest occupant. Teaser immediately intuited that this was her offspring, randomly decided it was male, and named mother dolphin Mom-Doll and the baby, in homage to the Pride's ultimate destination, Li'l Man-jiro. The baby poked its snout between two bars, studying him avidly until

snick

—soft as a bubble's pop—

the cage door swung open, and Li'l Man-jiro was able to escape. The reunion with his mother was happy but quiet. Sophisticated animals, the dolphins sensed they were still in danger, though Mom-Doll nuzzled Teaser with emphatic affection.

"I think I have a new best friend," Teaser grinned.

"Yeah, I sure she Chick' of Sea. Hurry up."

The locks were rudimentary, and he released the remaining dolphins quickly, having every intention of swimming off with them and getting back on course.

A net gun fired from above scuttled that expectation in less time than it took him to grok what was happening. Flailing reflexively, before logical assessment could kick in, he became hopelessly enmeshed, and as he felt himself being dragged up, he had just enough time to say, "Pran! I'm caught! I'm caught! You'll have to be—"

* * *

The poachers dumped him out of the net onto the deck. There were two of them. Both formidable.

One had a barrel chest and a square jaw out of *Terry and the Pirates.* Thick Popeye forearms. Dull blueish neckerchief complementing dull blueish stubble. Tanned skin like leather.

The other: taller, leaner muscle mass, like he aspired to be a tree and was having some success. Black beard, ebony skin. Wearing an incongruous striped woolly cap with a cardboard brim like a bowler hat and topped with a beanie. Training an evil-looking speargun at Teaser's chest.

With only gestures—why waste words on a head encased in rubber?—they made him shrug out of tank and toolbelt, lower them to the deck. He followed the speargun's request to move away from the gear and get onto his knees without removing his fins, which would make getting to his feet unassisted a cloddish sideshow and forced his feet to bend backward painfully.

His captors gestured for Teaser to remove his hood and drop it near his toolbelt. He tossed it clumsily, as if too nervous for coordination, keeping it near enough that Pran might hear as much as possible. He couldn't count on voices being raised.

Squarejaw's was the voice of a murderous leprechaun. "Humanitarian, are ye, boyo? Aquatic savior? Your priest never teach you what happens to saviors?" A crack about having a Korean rabbi popped into Teaser's head, but he kept it off his tongue.

Woolcap raised the speargun to a more concerning angle, sighting down the barrel, but Squarejaw held up a palm to belay the shot.

Woolcap frowned. His voice was a melodious, exotic basso, Trinidad cadences predominant. "Whynwe juz keel him, mon? Chum for de sharks?"

Great, Teaser thought. *These guys have keeled before.*

"He ope'ed our cages with a lockpick. Look over 't yon gear belt. See that metal yoke like a credit card, half out its pocket?"

"Look like multitool survival card. *We* gots doze. Sumtin' special, his?"

"Oh, aye. *His* be a multitool *lockpick* card. Holds a whole set o' jimmies. Perfessional-like."

"And is we wond'rin' why Scuba-Man have pro lockpicks?"

"We *is.* I'm t'inkin'… our lad here be no more law-abidin' den *we* are. Yet indulged himself a dolphin detour because…I dunno. He's a softie. And an eejit."

Woolcap took a moment to parse that. "You figger he *goan* someplace to steal sumtin'?"

Teaser kept his eyes from flicking to the oxygen tanks but took too quick an inhale. Squarejaw noticed, slow-smiled.

"I figger…he just *came* from stealin' somethin'. Mebbe we got us a bigger haul than what he set free." Squarejaw went silent for a moment, putting more pieces together. Then, to Teaser: "Well, now…your ecologics has cost us a lot of money, son. And you just *know* we're bound to seek some restitution for that."

"Shouldn't we get out of here first?" urged Teaser. "Coast Guard patrol will be here. *Soon.*"

"Them never comes inta this cove. Y'must know that if y'ken their schedjool. Points fer tryin', but don't waste any more of our time."

Squarejaw shifted his gaze to Teaser's gear.

* * *

Pran wrestled with the question of what to do next. Teaser had as good as asked him to call the cavalry, but even if the Water Cops got to him in time, they'd find the Pride. The heist would go south, the deal would go south, Teaser would go up the river, the advance payment would need to be returned east…and Pran no longer had enough of it for a full refund. Which meant the deadly intermediary from the east would return for *him.*

But if he did nothing, Teaser's chances of survival started south. *What hell best?*

Seeing Pran's distress, Gadge said, "If someone *else* worryin' a quick-solve puzzler called for your Zen from the Orient to orient their Zen, what woudja say?"

Pran closed his eyes. "I say…I say…when many moving part, can be variable you no foresee. Live in moment, not complexity. Each problem separate, in order priority." He opened his eyes.

Gadge said, "Well, there you go."

Pran nodded, then called the Coast Guard on a burner phone, giving them—with unaccented, Oxford English precision—an anonymous tip about dolphin poachers just beyond their normal patrol area.

* * *

Squarejaw chinned toward Teaser's equipment. "Nice touch, the spare tank. Open it."

There was no point in playing stupid. *They* weren't stupid. Not sufficiently.

But he had two secret advantages.

The first was theoretical and its ultimate value fraught: Pran might have alerted the Coast Guard. They would not be far away. Could he stall long enough?

The second was how good his hands were. How sensitive. And, when necessary, how fast. The poachers knew he was a thief, but not that he was a virtuoso.

Teaser angled his view to look at his gear, memorize distances, calibrate physics. One of the tanks rested atop the end of his toolbelt. Instinctively, he wanted the toolbelt closer.

He faced forward again and, holding Squarejaw's gaze, leaned sideways… stretching…mindful of being scrutinized. Gripped a harness strap, looped and lifted, gauging the gradient. *Feeling* how the tank's balance transmitted the give in the toolbelt's material, how much pressure he'd have to apply.

He made the tank pull his toolbelt nearer. Nine inches. As much as he dared, lest it seem purposeful. Then rotated his wrist, taking tank-weight off the belt, both tanks now touching only deck. Pulled them in, metal scraping wood. Positioned them upright in front of him, like scrolls of the Torah.

"Open it."

Teaser took his time unscrewing the cap, tilting out the protective case.

"Ye can open that fella, too."

Teaser laid the case flat. Undid its seals.

"Point 'er toward me. Bottom first."

Teaser did.

"Hands behind yer head. Keep 'em there."

Teaser complied.

Squarejaw stepped forward just enough to touch the case. Pulled it toward him without lifting. Down on one knee, he flipped it open.

And stared at the Pride.

He unsnapped the security straps. Stared some more.

"This," he said with genuine awe. "This."

He lifted it out tenderly—as Teaser had, not an hour before. "Desmond, me lad, will y'look at this."

Woolcap sighted down the speargun at Teaser again. "Used my name, Keegan." The irony, appreciated by his partner, was very deliberate.

"Momentary lapse. Still, don't lance his nature-lovin' heart just yet."

"Why? You tink he know sumtin'?"

"Oh, aye! He c'n name the purchaser."

Teaser cut in dramatically. "You'll never sell it without me to front the deal! My buyers even *smell* you coming, they'll disappear faster than your buddy's anonymity."

Squarejaw smirked. "Somehow I'm feelin' that's dissin' generous. Threat of exposure, mayhap they even buys at twice the former price."

Teaser paused to affect a desperate adjustment. "If I tell you who they are, they'll kill me."

"If y'don't, we'll torture it out of ye, an' ye'll be dead, anyway."

Teaser's stall repertoire was running thin. "Is there no other way?"

"Hmm. We'll hang that'n on a hook fer later."

But Teaser knew the poacher would sooner hang *him* on a hook.

He needed a distraction.

And then one was delivered.

For Squarejaw was pivoting the Pride upright. As the artifact rotated on its axis, sunlight reflected off its top—and Teaser knew its secret.

It wasn't the mansion's display case that had a hidden seam—*You certain 'bout surface? No break in vein? No outline you miss, blend into pattern?*—it was the *Pride* that had one!

What sunflash revealed—hitting the Pride's metalwork top just so, just now—was the way its filigree articulated a protective stopper-guard over a thin slot.

The Pride wasn't a canister. But there sure was something inside.

Squarejaw delicately kneaded the now-vertical object in opposing palms. A little to. A little fro. In thrall to it. "This," he repeated.

Teaser mentally reran the sensation of gripping the controller-like contour one-handed...what Pran had warned about the settings...the configuration of the jewel buttons...the jewel that would have been easiest for his thumb to trigger, had he positioned the Pride for battle.

The Change is Everything, said the Pride's lettering. And now Teaser knew why. Knew what it was. Knew what Kayama's station must have been. And understood the Pride's cruel beauty, its black dragon spitting fire.

"*Please* steady the pink jewel near your middle finger," he begged. "The glue is old and brittle. If the gem falls out, the value drops."

He braced himself to move.

Squarejaw stopped kneading the Pride. His finger rested on *that* jewel. He looked at it. Said, "What, this little wond—?"

as he pressed it in

and Teaser heard

snick

—soft as an unfolding verdict—

the sound of the slot-guard *snapping* open!

Whereupon the spring-loaded samurai blade within the Pride, having waited nearly two centuries for release, *shot* out of its scabbard with such propulsive force that it bisected Squarejaw's forehead as if slicing through a kiwi, stabbing bloodlessly out the back of his skull and—

—Squarejaw staggered backward, already dead, and—

—Teaser hit the deck, rolling toward his toolbelt before Squarejaw's body fell, as—

—the jolt of Squarejaw's self-assassination made Woolcap's forearms fling outward, whipping spear-trajectory off Teaser—

—who, reverse-rolling, yanked the orange flare gun out of its holster with one hand, palmed away its waterproof sheath with the other and fired upwards—

—*vhoosh!*—

—a perfect gutshot below Woolcap's sternum—

—which made the big man's trigger finger jerk spasmodically, launching the spear into the deck eighteen inches from Teaser, with a *thunk* that had the resonance of tympanic punctuation.

A brief moment of stillness.

Then Woolcap looked down in growing fascination at the big new hole in him...at what had *made* it...at the sparking Kingzar, burning somewhere incomprehensible, burrowing further—

—and then he *felt* its agonizing preview of Hell, his eyes going wider—

—and emitting a soft, balloon-leak obbligato, two octaves higher than his speaking voice, flailed backward until the deck abandoned him, somersaulted long legs over the railing, and was gone.

The sound of the splash was lost on Teaser, who could hear literally nothing but his own thundering heartbeat. It took him a full minute—half of it spent trying to stop hyperventilating—to recover a working simulacrum of his senses...which started to become aware of Pran, who was flipping his banana-loving cookies via spillover from the two-way in the scuba hood.

"What going on? What going on? *Teaser! Please, hello!* What going on?"

Teaser stood, scooped up the hood, held it to his ear.

"I'm here, Pran. It's okay. The Pride is safe, and"—he made himself look at Squarejaw's corpse—"and the poachers are dead."

"Dead? But—*Coast Guard* coming! I call *Coast Guard!"*

"When?"

"When? When you *tell!* What, I 'pose wait see if you kill poaches first?"

"Valid point," Teaser conceded, already calculating what he had to do next and how fast. "Radio silence for a minute or two—wars are being won—hang tight."

He gently dropped the hood and, fins still on his feet, frog-walked to Squarejaw's final harbor: head against the cabin wall, where the point of the blade had hit first and been pushed forward, a congealing blood-dribble along the poacher's nose connoting the reverse slice.

With both hands, Teaser grabbed the Pride—the hilt of the sword—and felt unexpected resistance. The tip had apparently embedded itself into the wood behind the head. "Loverly," sighed the thief. Then, putting a webbed foot on the poacher's chest, he gently rocked his Excalibur until its point was freed, and the full blade, honing itself along bone with a disquietingly keen *zzzzing*, slid out of the poacher's skull. Blood that had been stoppered at the skull's parietal wound dripped down the cabin wall, pooling onto the deck.

Teaser swiped the bandana from Squarejaw's neck and wiped the blade, which seemed as resistant to raw pathological detritus as Teflon. He tossed the rag over the railing, wondering how much pressure against the Pride's inner spring it would take to reload the sword, and if he could push its tip against a flat, hardwood surface without breaking it, warping it or embedding it again.

161

Or—wait. There were those two additional jewels. They had to have useful functions, didn't they?

He pressed green, felt something unlock. Pressed gold—and the blade retracted as zippily and startlingly as it had appeared, the stopper-guard snapping closed with an ancestral haptic he could feel up to his elbow. Very *Lost Ark.* He wasn't Gadge, didn't need to know how it worked. *Works for me* was all that mattered.

Teaser flip-flopped back to his gear, reloaded the Pride into its watertight sheath, belted up, masked up, and before shrugging into the tank harness, checked the air gauge—

—which indicated that he didn't have enough to make it back to shore. The release valve had been banged loose in the fracas.

Teaser thought he could hear the motor of a patrol boat in the distance. Game over.

And then he heard a loud chittering from below. He looked over the railing—and there was Mom-Doll, Li'l Man-jiro swimming in excited circles around her. When she saw Teaser, her chittering became more emphatic. "What the—?"

She redoubled her efforts to communicate, fairly dancing above the water, as if to say, "For the love of Neptune, come *on!*"

"*¿En serio?*" he whispered. And then, louder: "Pran, you reading?"

"'Course I reading! I losing hair and reading!"

"Don't toss your combs just yet. I have a feeling I'll see you in a few minutes. Count 'em down!"

"*Minutes?* How?"

"Looks like I'm hitching a ride with my new best friend!"

Teaser secured the tanks on his back and jumped, hit the water, and dog-paddled until Mom-Doll was near enough to offer her dorsal fin. Li'l Man-jiro nudged him closer and kept him from slipping off his mother's smooth skin. Teaser took double-grip hold of the fin, and then they were churning white foam, slicing through the water at jetski speed.

Mom-Doll seemed to know exactly where to go.

Maybe it was his touch.

* * *

The skyline was poking above the horizon as the minivan approached the city. Pran emailed the client that all was well, then migrated to the front passenger seat. Beside him, Gadge was driving as if road safety was his alibi.

In the back, Teaser—wrapped in a thick bathrobe—finished filling them in on the blanks of his misadventure. The narrative wasn't as long as the return trip, but he'd first needed time to decompress. To sit inside himself and contemplate the view.

His stirring denouement was followed by a few minutes of thoughtful silence, broken suddenly by Gadge exclaiming: "Well, *there's* my Mason defense, Pran!"

"Whatchoo mean?"

"How Perry would *defend* me. Teaser just laid out the angle."

"And is what?"

"Perry would say to the court, 'It's *true,* Ladies, Gents, and Yerronna, that my client is a thieving bum. But this other guy is a killer! Give *him* the lethal hot shot!' See?"

Pran pondered this.

"So, you think it to Commodore Perry advantage that you guilty—just not guilty *enough.*"

"Sure, it's an advantage. Whattaya think, Tease? Ain't it an advantage?"

"Ohhh," sighed Teaser, abstractedly. "The advantages go on and on, Gadge. As long as you don't lose your edge, they go on and on."

With that, he pulled up on the recline-adjustment handle, leaned back two levels, closed his eyes…and slept the sleep of the justifiable, more beautiful than true.…

Sweeney Todd: The Demon Barber of Fleet Street
opened March 1, 1979, at the Uris Theatre, New York

PROLOGUE
"Prelude: The Ballad of Sweeney Todd"

ACT I
"No Place Like London"
"The Barber and His Wife"
"The Worst Pies in London"
"Poor Thing"
"My Friends"
"The Ballad of Sweeney Todd" (reprise 1)
"Green Finch and Linnet Bird"
"Ah, Miss"
"Johanna"
"Pirelli's Miracle Elixir"
"The Contest (Part 1): Shaving Scene"
"The Contest (Part 2): Tooth-Pulling Scene"
"The Ballad of Sweeney Todd" (reprise 2)
"Wait"
"Pirelli's Death"
"The Ballad of Sweeney Todd" (reprise 3)

"Johanna (Mea Culpa)"
"Kiss Me"
"Ladies in Their Sensitivities/Kiss Me (Quartet)"
"Pretty Women"
"Epiphany"
"A Little Priest"

ACT II
"God, That's Good!"
"Johanna (Quartet)"
"I Am a Lass"
"By the Sea"
"Wigmaker Sequence/The Ballad of Sweeney Todd
(reprise 4)/The Letter"
"Not While I'm Around"
"Parlour Songs (Part 1): Sweet Polly Plunkett"
"Parlour Songs (Part 2): The Twelve Bells in Tower of Bray"
"Parlour Songs (Part 3): Sweet Polly Plunkett" (reprise)
"Final Sequence"

EPILOGUE
"The Ballad of Sweeney Todd" (reprise 7)

Music and lyrics by Stephen Sondheim.
Book by Hugh Wheeler.

No Place Like London

by Joseph Goodrich

It was just before five in the morning when Dahlia abandoned the notion of sleep and kicked the sheets aside. Downstairs, she pulled on her hiking boots, zipped up her parka, and set out for the Old Forge Trail. She'd always found pleasure in movement and solace in the numinous early light of day; this frigid October morning was no exception.

Later, walking home through the still-empty streets of Cold Spring, she felt deliciously sleepy and hungry. The prospect of coffee, scrambled eggs, and toast with apricot jam followed by blissful unconsciousness was deeply satisfying.

Inside the house, she draped her parka over the back of a kitchen chair and checked her messages. She never took her phone when she was hiking, preferring to be in the world by herself, accompanied by nothing but her thoughts flying free and the sound of her boots on the trail. The first three messages were all related to car insurance. The fourth pushed any idea of breakfast and sleep out of her mind.

The voice was low, precise, trained, but urgent: "It's Annabel. Call me."

She glanced at the clock on kitchen wall. Twelve minutes after seven. Twelve past noon in the UK. Frowning, she dialed her old friend's number.

Annabel picked up on the first ring. "Dahlia?"

"I got your message. You okay? Family's okay?"

"We're fine, but I have some horrible news. Brace yourself."

Dahlia's fingers tightened around her phone.

"Ian killed himself last night."

Dahlia gasped as if she'd been punched. *"No."*

"I'm sorry, darling. I hate having to call you with news like this. But you had to know."

"What happened? Where are you?"

"In London," Annabel said. "A conference at the National. We'd planned to meet for breakfast. When he didn't show up, I called him. No answer. I went to his house and pounded on the door. Still no answer. I was getting worried, so I went to the back, broke a window, and climbed in. And found him."

"How did he—?"

"A combination of alcohol and painkillers. The house was filled with empty booze and pill bottles. Margot says he'd been on a downward spiral since the *Sweeney Todd* catastrophe. He had to leave the production. Did you know that? It must have happened right around the time of your trip."

Dahlia hesitated. "We weren't on speaking terms by then."

Annabel sighed. "I wish you two had settled your differences. When I called to say I'd be in London, he said he hoped you could be friends again. Did he ever call you?"

"No, he never did. But tell me—how are *you?*"

"Devastated. Completely devastated. Will you come for the funeral?"

"When is it?"

"Wednesday."

"I'll be there."

"I'm so glad," Annabel said in a rush of emotion. "I couldn't bear this by myself. You need to be here. This is one of the *important* deaths, you know? When a part of you dies, too."

After they disconnected, Dahlia searched for a flight. Everything was hideously expensive, especially given the short notice, but she had no choice in the matter. Annabel was right: she had to be at Ian's funeral. Of course, she did.

Doesn't a killer always return to the scene of the crime?

167

* * *

Dahlia wandered absently through the house to the living room. She pulled aside the ivory silk drapes and stared out the front window.

She didn't see the shifting tree branches, leaves mostly gone now, or the gray sky over Stone Street. Instead, she was looking out the window of #9, Coronation Court, Brewster Gardens, West London. And the year was 1983.

That was Dahlia's year abroad. She was studying at one of the smaller drama schools, and #9 Coronation Court was her home. Her flatmate was Joey Pirelli, the daughter of a minor mob boss. On her first day at drama school, Joey met Mustafa, a would-be thespian from the Dardanelles, and moved in with him that same night. Dahlia didn't mind. She got to have #9 to herself, and Joey went on paying her half of the rent. "Daddy will kill me if he finds out about Mustafa," she said. "He *hates* actors. You won't tell anyone, will you?"

Dahlia promised she wouldn't let anyone know about Mustafa.

On *her* first day at drama school, Dahlia encountered Ian Maxwell and Annabel Lewis. They were in their final year and were clearly the stars of the school, as adept at Jacobean revenge tragedies as they were at Aldwych farce, moving with ease from Ben Jonson to Ben Travers.

Annabel was from Cardiff, strikingly tall and thin, and possessed of a dark-eyed intensity she shared with Ian, who was a dyed-in-the-wool Londoner. They wore only black and might have stepped out of a Beardsley print. Both of them smoked Dunhill Reds at an alarming rate.

Dahlia admired their effortless elegance. They admired her blunt sense of humor and "American enthusiasm," as Ian put it. The three of them were soon inseparable, a self-contained unit other students envied or jealously dismissed. Ian and Annabel were a couple, and Dahlia was happy to be their cherished third wheel. She freely admitted to herself that she had a gigantic crush on both of them. If they hadn't befriended her, she might have drowned in the ocean that was London, overwhelmed by it all.

It was a glorious time. London glowed, and her days seemed enchanted.

To be young in the theater, caught up in the making of art and the discovery of one's true self, is a powerful intoxicant. It forges a bond that may attenuate but never breaks.

But now Ian Maxwell was dead, and the bond had been broken.

* * *

Ian and Annabel, the golden couple, had gone their separate ways after graduation but remained friends. Both had done well over the years. Annabel ran a respected theater for youth in Edinburgh. Ian, possessed of aquiline features, a twenty-eight-inch waist, and that indefinable but always recognizable quality called charm, built a successful career on stage and screen.

As he entered middle age, however, Ian's charm receded. ("Like his hairline," Annabel said, "but never tell him I said so.") His figure thickened, his complexion reddened. Grave's disease made his eyes bulge. This affected the roles he was offered and nettled his vanity. His complaints were bitter and continual.

The last time Dahlia saw him, he'd run true to form. It was in early April, six months before his death, and she'd gone to London for a week's vacation, to revisit old haunts and see some shows in the West End. Ian owned a house in South Hill Park Gardens, a quick walk from the Hampstead Heath railway station. They met for lunch at an Indian restaurant not far from John Keats' house. Dahlia picked at a blazingly hot curry as Ian downed one icy Kingfisher after another.

Early in the conversation, he told her he'd been offered the role of Judge Turpin in an upcoming revival of *Sweeney Todd*. Dahlia was pleased for him, but Ian was less than thrilled by the prospect. He should have been cast as Sweeney, he complained, not the judge. The actor playing the demon barber of Fleet Street was obviously having it off with the show's producer, Ernest Berkeley. "He once put the moves on *me*, you know, when I was better-looking and thirty pounds lighter. I turned old Ernie down. I can't help feeling this is his revenge. Vindictive bastard. Producers are nothing but vermin."

As beer followed beer, resentment gushed out of him. Margot—the actress he'd been living with for the past decade—had walked away from their relationship and showed little inclination to return. Kate Mackintosh, his agent, wasn't worth a packet of piss. His professional life was stalled, a lost cause, a train wreck, a plane crash, a catastrophe beyond description—a veritable Vesuvius of volcanic vicissitudes.

Dahlia listened patiently, trying to withhold judgment. She'd never willingly hurt an old friend—and she sympathized with him, of course she did. But all the same, she found herself saying: "*Shut up.*"

Ian blinked, as if waking from a trance. "What?"

"You've spent the last forty-five minutes complaining, do you realize that? You haven't asked one single thing about me. Which is fine, I'm used to it by now. I just think you should realize there are other people in the world. People who'd be *happy* to have your problems."

Ian was petulant. "How dare you say that? It's my *life* we're talking about. My *career.*"

"And what exactly is wrong with your career?"

"It hasn't worked out the way I envisioned."

"Ian, who gets what they want in this world? You do the best you can with what you've been given—and you've been given a great deal."

He made a scoffing noise.

"You *have*! Add it up. You'll see." Dahlia counted the points on her fingers. "You've worked steadily for more than four decades. You're a well-known and respected figure in the arts. You've been cast in a major revival of one of the greatest musicals of all time. You own a home in one of the loveliest cities in the world."

"London's a pit," Ian said, voice throbbing. "A dark and dangerous pit. I no longer recognize the place. I no longer feel safe here. I walk in shadows and fear what's lurking in the dark."

Dahlia couldn't help but laugh. "The only thing you're scared of is the Inland Revenue Service. Be grateful for what you've accomplished. That's all I'm saying."

Ian polished off his Kingfisher and signaled for another. "I should be grateful, yes. To the outside observer, I must appear to be the jammiest of bastards. But inside?" He tapped his sternum. "It's something else. As good as it is—and yes, it's very good, I fully and freely admit that—it's still not the *dream*. I was going to be the next Olivier. Didn't happen. I've done something worse than destroy my talent. I've degraded it."

And that was the moment when, looking back, Dahlia realized she blew it.

"No wonder Margot left you," she said.

She saw Ian flinch, saw the arrow strike him in the heart. She saw it—and kept talking.

"I don't blame her. Who could put up with your eternal pissing and moaning, your litany of grudges and jealousies and petty rivalries? All it does is drive people away."

Ian ignored the fresh beer their waiter placed on the table. His face was very red, his eyes very dark. His tone was exceptionally polished and polite, which meant he was absolutely livid.

"I accept the fact that the vagaries of my career matter less to you than they do to me," he began. "Perhaps I am rather too concerned with my own lot in life. It's certainly true, as you've so kindly pointed out, that I've not asked you anything about yourself. What you've been up to. What's going on in *la vie de Dahlia*.

"But you see, that's the problem. For the life of me, I can't name a single thing you've accomplished—anything worth asking *about*. That's nothing new, though, is it? You were never really interested in *doing*, were you, Dahlia? You'd rather dream and sigh and fantasize. You'd rather *teach* theater history than risk being a *part* of it." He took a long swallow of beer and set the glass aside. "I think that's why you were never any good as an actress. Characters *want* things, don't they? They *do* things to get what they want. And what have *you* ever wanted? Except me, of course. Or Annabel. I could never really tell which of us you were more obsessed with. We didn't mind. We thought of you as our child." His smile gleamed with malice. "Or our pet." He pointed his fork at her plate. "Are you going to finish that?"

* * *

The flowers Ian sent to her hotel suite did nothing to ease the anguish caused by his attack, and she ignored the flurry of messages he left at the front desk. They didn't meet again before she flew back to the States. They *never* met again.

On the morning of her flight home, she woke up at four. *The Goldberg Variations* was playing on BBC Radio 3. The music evoked in her a sorrow so deep it seemed fathomless. Unable to get back to sleep, she reviewed the scorched terrain of her life.

Ian was wrong—she'd very much wanted to be an actor, but gave it up because it was too uncertain, too provisional an existence. One had to love it above all other things to withstand its indignities. Instead, she'd made a saner, safer decision: she would teach. Grad school was the opposite of theater. The steps to an academic career had been reassuringly unambiguous.

Now, though, her decision seemed nothing but the action of a coward. Why hadn't she stayed in London? Who would she be today if she'd taken that chance? A parallel, unlived ghost life haunted her. A life that didn't exist and could never be realized, the sum of all the things she hadn't done.

What had Ian said?

Characters want *things. They* do *things to get them.*

Well, Dahlia wanted something badly: to sabotage his career. And she did something to get it, too.

Before leaving the hotel for Heathrow, she made a telephone call.

Once the plane was in the air, there was no turning back—and no escaping the enormity of what she'd done. It was a source of great and bitter pleasure, all the way across the Atlantic.

* * *

Back in London for Ian's funeral, Dahlia took a room in a hotel on the north side of Hyde Park, near Marble Arch. Annabel met her there at noon and drove them to Highgate Cemetery. After the funeral, they went to the Cape and Crown, a public house in Soho favored by theatricals, where Ian's friends and loved ones bade him a liquid farewell.

Late in the afternoon, when gin and emotion had taken their toll, an exhausted Dahlia sat alone in a booth in a dark corner of the pub. Too much Tanqueray and too little to eat had left her light-headed and queasy. If she drank enough, she'd pass out—and, for a blessed if far too brief period of time, she'd be able to stop thinking of what she'd done.

"There you are," Annabel said. "I've been looking all over for you." She sat down with a groan in the chair opposite Dahlia. "Christ, am I wrung out. How are you holding up? You must be ready for the knackers' yard by now."

Dahlia mumbled something.

Annabel studied her closely. "You okay?"

"I'm fine."

"I hope so." She placed a hand on one of Dahlia's and squeezed. "Thank you for being here, darling. For Ian. And for me."

"For the Three."

Annabel's eyes widened, and she laughed with delight. "Oh, my God, that's what we called ourselves, wasn't it? I'd completely forgotten. What a pretentious lot of tossers we must have been. Well, we were young, that's all. And time took care of that." Annabel raised her glass. "To the Three. Who are now Two. In memory of the One."

They drank.

"I'll always remember when he got his first big break," Annabel said. "I can still hear him pounding on the door of my dreadful little flat in White City." She rapped furiously on the table. "'Annie, open up! I've made it! I've made it!' Champagne at nine-thirty in the morning." She laughed again. "*How* he went on about it. I was tempted to puncture his balloon and tell him he might have had the *slightest* bit of help landing the role."

"What do you mean?"

"That Mafia daughter you shared the flat with? Jody? Judy?"

"Joey. Joey Pirelli."

"I ran into her once at the Old Vic," Annabel said. "It would have been the first autumn after you went home. We had a natter in the bar. She saw I was looking down in the mouth and asked me why. I told her that Ian had recently auditioned for a play but hadn't been cast, and he was taking it hard. It was a shame, because he'd have been perfect for the role. She wanted to know who'd been cast instead. I said it was someone she'd remember from school—Clive Elders.

"She asked if I ever heard from you. I said, of course, I hear from her all the time. And she said: 'Next time you do, let her know I'm grateful to her. I asked her to keep Mustafa a secret from my father, and she did.' Then she said: 'Dahlia's a good person. She never made fun of me. Other people at school did, people like Clive. They thought I was too stupid to notice. But they were wrong. I notice everything, just like my father.'

"Two days later, Clive was mugged on his way to rehearsal. His right leg and elbow were broken. That afternoon, Ian took over his part—and the rest is history." Annabel studied her glass. "I feel sorry for Clive, getting smashed up like that. But then I remember he's a sniveling shit who doesn't need my sympathy. And he's had quite a nice career. I hate to admit it, but he was tremendous in the *Sweeney Todd* revival. It just closed last week."

"Who'd he play?"

"The judge. Why do you ask?"

"It's—" Dahlia paused. "It's about the falling out Ian and I had."

"Ah, yes," Annabel said, "the infamous falling out. The one neither of you ever explained."

"I couldn't. It was too painful."

"Can you tell me about it now?"

Dahlia shuddered. "Not now. Not ever."

Annabel touched her friend's forearm. "Whatever happened is in the past. It's over and done with. Tell me."

"You'll hate me."

"That's ridiculous, and you know it. I could never hate you."

"You say that now. But remember, I warned you." Dahlia fiddled with a drink coaster, turned it over and over and over. "When I was here in April," she said at last, "we had lunch near his house. All he did, from the moment he sat down to the time he left, was bitch about his career. Finally, I couldn't take it anymore, and I lashed out. Then he attacked me." She looked at Annabel. "He savaged me. He cut the heart out of me. I was filled with such—"

"Annabel!"

Ian's sister Clara and his mother approached. Both were tall, both were dressed in stylish black, both were overwhelmed with grief and trying very hard to present the proper front.

Annabel embraced them.

"You remember Dahlia," Clara said to her mother. "She was at the Academy with Ian and Annabel."

"Dahlia came from New York to be here today," Annabel said.

"All this way for Ian?" Mrs. Maxwell placed a blue-veined hand over her heart. "Oh, you wonderful girl. You marvelous, wonderful girl. You must have loved him very much." The old woman's composure cracked, and she began to cry.

Fighting to keep her own composure, Clara moved in to comfort her mother.

Annabel watched, feeling helpless, pierced to the heart by the depth of Mrs. Maxwell's sorrow.

Dahlia rose unsteadily and fled the pub. Down the street from the Cape and Crown, she was seized with nausea, came to a ragged halt, and, clinging to a parking sign, vomited in the gutter. At the sound of her name—a worried Annabel had followed her from the pub—she hurled herself off the sidewalk and into the path of a Lovett's Bakery van.

* * *

Annabel sat beside Dahlia's hospital bed. Cold autumn rain pelted the window. Dahlia, pallid as the English sky, spoke from an opioid cloud high above Harley Street.

"After our lunch, I planned my revenge. I came up with something I thought was really clever. I'd call the producer of *Sweeney Todd* and pretend

I was Ian's agent. I'd tell him that Ian was leaving the show. That Ian loathed him. That he was going to tell the world how the producer had tried to molest him—and not only him but others, too, some of them underage." She cleared her throat harshly, licked dry lips. "Could I have some water?"

Annabel brought a glass to the bedside, helped Dahlia drink, returned to her chair.

"I wanted to hurt him the way he'd hurt me. No—I wanted to hurt him *more*. I wanted him *dead*. I got him fired from the show, Annabel. I sent him into that spiral. My wish came true. I killed him. And you know what? I couldn't have been happier. Until I realized what I'd done. I'm the one who really deserves to die."

* * *

The following afternoon, shortly after a nurse checked Dahlia's vitals and gave her another dose of pain medicine, Annabel returned, this time in the company of a slim, silver-haired woman, who she brought to Dahlia's bedside. "Darling, this is Kate Mackintosh, Ian's agent. You've met before, I think."

"At one of Ian's opening night bacchanalias," the agent said. "Annabel tells me you've had a bit of a rough time. I do hope you're feeling better."

"I am," Dahlia said. "Thank you." She didn't sound very convincing.

"After I left you yesterday, Kate and I met for a drink," Annabel said. "We talked about how good Clive Elders was in the *Sweeney* revival."

"Splendid, wasn't he?" the agent said. "I've never seen a Judge Turpin to match him. He positively *radiated* malevolence."

"How would Ian have been in the part?" asked Dahlia.

"Magnificent. We were all terribly upset when he had to drop out of the show. These things happen, you know, and there's nothing one can do about it. But I still think he deserved a good thrashing."

"Why?" Dahlia said. "For what?"

"For being an exceptionally naughty boy. He'd taken a tumble with a skinful of scotch and aggravated an old back injury. Not only did he leave

176

the show, he refused to accept the fact that he'd been injured. He should've had surgery, but he kept putting it off and putting it off. I gather the pain was excruciating near the end, and that's what led to…well, what happened. Heaven rest his poxy soul."

The first eight notes of Beethoven's *Fifth* sounded. Kate pulled out her mobile and checked the number. "Must take this, I'm afraid. I'll just step into the hall."

* * *

"You see, darling?" Annabel said, when Kate Mackintosh had wished Dahlia well and left the hospital. "It's not your fault. You didn't kill Ian. You see that, don't you?"

"But I called the producer." The pain pill was kicking in, and Dahlia was fading fast. "I said terrible things about him."

"Did you actually *talk* to the producer, or did you just leave a message?"

"I—" She hesitated, thinking back through an opioid fog. "He wasn't in, so I left a message on his machine."

"He must not have heard it. Kate obviously didn't. She'd have said something if she had, believe me."

The rain beating against the glass was the last thing Dahlia heard before she slept.

* * *

The first snow of the year had fallen on Cold Spring the day before. The house on Stone Street was so quiet Dahlia could hear tree branches creaking with the weight of the fresh snow. She got out of bed and went downstairs, where she awkwardly prepared coffee with one hand—her right arm was still in a sling and would be for a while yet—and sat numbly at the kitchen table, waiting for it to brew.

The painful and humiliating conclusion of her trip to London still rankled. It ran in a perpetually embarrassing loop, impossible to ignore, and only stopped when she was asleep.

She'd slept a great deal in the three days she'd been home.

The shame she felt was corrosive, the sense of loss and waste heavy as concrete.

She poured coffee into a *New Yorker* mug and hobbled into the living room, favoring her right leg; it hadn't been broken in the accident but was one long bruise. The glare of the snow-covered world outside bit into her like a headache, and she closed the drapes.

She had to get on with the day, no matter how reluctant she felt. The pile of mail on the end table, for instance. It had accumulated like the snow on her unshoveled sidewalk, and she'd paid it just as much attention. Most of it was junk, fit for nothing but the shredder. The letter with the English stamp was another matter.

Dearest Dahlia—

These codeine cocktails pack a punch, so I'll dash off a few lines before my handwriting deteriorates completely.

I came so close to calling you just now. But I was afraid you wouldn't want to talk to me. I don't blame you. I've been no one's definition of a good friend. I've been selfish and egotistical and monstrous.

I can't tell you how often I wish you and Annabel and I were together again, and we could talk and laugh and be silly like we were in les années perdues.

I ache for those days when we were young and dreaming so fervently of the future. When nothing had happened yet—but everything might. When there was no place like London.

Oh, darling, what happened to us? How did we wind up like this?

Whatever happens, remember: You're not to blame.

I love you, Dahlia Louise Silverman. But I suspect you already know that.

IAN

Dahlia drew a sheet of her favorite blue stationery toward her and uncapped her Sheaffer.

Ian,

What am I to do with your letter? What am I to do with you? You pose a problem I don't know how to solve.

I tried to hurt you. I failed, but that doesn't invalidate my evil wish to see you hurt. How does one apologize to a dead man?

I wanted you to suffer because you made me suffer. Which leads me to ask: how do you forgive a ghost?

I honestly don't know.

All I can say is: Ian Peter George Maxwell, I love you, too. For whatever good that does—or doesn't—do.

I'll never send this letter. You'll never receive it. But at least one of us will know I wrote it.

* * *

The morning slipped past in a myriad of trivial but necessary tasks. After lunch, she carefully picked her way over the snowy sidewalks to Cold Spring's Main Street. The bookstore had just received a volume she'd ordered before her journey to London, a study of British theatrical fiction; research, perhaps, for a paper of some kind. After picking up a few Silvine notebooks at the stationery store, she popped into the wine bar for a cheerful word with its owner. She spoke to friends and accepted their good wishes for a speedy recovery.

The murderer had been paroled, and life went on, almost—but not quite—the same.

Act IV

The 1980s

Merrily We Roll Along

opened November 16, 1981, at the Alvin Theatre, New York

ACT I

"The Hills of Tomorrow"
"Merrily We Roll Along"
"Rich and Happy"
"Merrily We Roll Along"
"Old Friends"
"Like It Was"
"Franklin Shepard, Inc."
"Merrily We Roll Along" (reprise)
"Old Friends" (reprise)
"Merrily We Roll Along" (reprise)
"Not a Day Goes By"
"Now You Know"

ACT II

"It's a Hit!"
"Merrily We Roll Along" (reprise)
"Good Thing Going"
"Merrily We Roll Along" (reprise)

"Bobby and Jackie and Jack"
"Not a Day Goes By" (reprise)
"Opening Doors"
"Our Time"
"The Hills of Tomorrow" (reprise)

Music and lyrics by Stephen Sondheim.
Book by George Furth.

Not a Day Goes By

by J.A. Hennrikus

My ex-husband turned when I opened the door to the cabin. He was sorting through paintings and looked at us, startled.

"It's not what you think," he said, straightening and raising his hands.

"With you, Charles," said Franklin, stepping in beside me, "it never is."

* * *

Six Weeks Earlier

"Not a day goes by. Not a single effing day that he isn't somehow still part of my life," I said, wiping my eyes. We both stared at the small painting of two elderly men sitting side by side on a park bench.

"You haven't seen him recently, have you?" Franklin asked, his blue eyes searching my face over the rim of his black readers. He usually looked like a mischievous elf, but not today.

"Not since that time he showed up on my doorstep quoting Keats," I said. "What's that look? You believe me, don't you?"

"You've lied to me before, Mary, when it comes to Charles."

My gut reaction was to deny it, but he was right. I'd lied to Franklin about my erstwhile ex-husband going straight. Almost as many times as I'd lied to myself.

Charming men have always been my kryptonite. And Charles Tremain was as charming as they came. When we first met, he told me he was an art collector who owned a gallery. Since I was an art historian who worked in museum acquisitions, I felt as though I'd finally met someone who not only shared my passions but understood how they consumed me. Charles was also handsome, intelligent, charming, straight, witty, and sexy as hell.

So I started calling him Charlie and let myself fall. Hard. Thing was, he didn't tell me he "collected" art by *stealing* it or switching it out for forgeries—or that his "gallery" was a huge fencing operation he ran in New York, San Diego, Washington, London, and my hometown of Boston. By the time his stories stopped lining up, it was too late: I'd fallen in love, so in love that I believed him about going straight.

He did try. I have to believe that. I *do* believe he loved me. Problem was, he loved the con more. I deluded myself for a few more months before the final betrayal. Then he was arrested. The case was so solid even *he* couldn't wriggle out from under.

One thing I had to say for Charlie: he'd been careful to make sure I was blameless. Try as they might, no charges could be brought against me. Which wasn't to say that I wasn't tainted by my relationship with him. My career as I knew it was over.

I went to work in the small private museum our mutual friend Franklin ran. Charlie was sentenced to fifteen years but barely served three. When he got out, he tracked me down and came to my door quoting Keats, bearing flowers, and begging forgiveness. I showed him the restraining order I'd obtained. He didn't take it well, but he left. That was six months ago.

When Franklin called me into the museum that Monday, he showed me the painting and the note that came with it. Both had been addressed to me. *You might prefer to display the original*, the printed note said.

"I apologize for opening your mail, but I thought it was the lithograph we were waiting for. This painting, Mary, is authentic," Franklin said.

"But—how can it be? Niles Richards' 'Old Friends' is hanging upstairs. We're not shipping it to Chicago until next week."

"It appears that our entire Romley collection has been replaced with forgeries," Franklin said. "This package arrived on Friday. I had a friend come in over the weekend to authenticate—"

"The entire collection? How is that—"

"I called Dennis Romley this morning and asked what made his parents decide to loan their collection to us. As you know, several patrons have made generous gifts to the museum over the years, pleased by the attention we give to restoration and storage. They also enjoy seeing their collections loaned out."

"Franklin," I snapped. "What did Dennis *say?*" Of late, the museum had become more of a lending library, with deals brokered by Franklin. I didn't love the change, but I kept my head down and did my work.

"Apologies, Mary. He said that, ten years ago, a gallery owner named Chuck Tremont—"

"Oh, no," I said, feeling as though I was going to throw up.

"—befriended the family after discreetly helping them get rid of a few problematic paintings with dubious provenances. The man he described was Charles. Of that, there is no doubt."

"Of course it was," I said. "Chuck Tremont, Charlie Tream, Chaz Treadwill. The first name's always a variant of Charles, and the last name becomes a squiggle after the T-R-E. That made it easier for him to keep his various personas straight." I'd learned a lot—too much—about con artists over the past three years. I'd also kept the business cards bearing Charlie's many names as mementos of our marriage.

"So that means this particular scam started ten years ago," said Franklin.

"Meeting you must have been a goldmine for Charlie." I shook my head sadly. "A small museum with an eclectic collection would be a perfect cover for switching out paintings. But how did he pull it off? You had our 'Old Friends' authenticated when you purchased it, I assume?"

"All was in order, I promise. You aren't the only person who believed that Charles had turned over a new leaf, Mary. Our trust was obviously misplaced."

I've always thought that covering one's face and sobbing is melodramatic, but there I was, doing both. Franklin moved his chair closer to mine and put his arm around my shoulder.

"Weep, my dear friend. Get it out of your system—"

"When will it end, Franklin? When will I be able to start forgetting?"

"I don't know," he said, resting his cheek against my head and hugging me closer. "But here's my question for you: are you ready to stop cursing and crying and finally get him out of your life?"

"Absolutely," I said, looking up and flinching as I saw the steel in his eyes. "What do you think we should do? Call the police?"

"We've no proof it's Charles who sent us the original—though he may have. No, no, don't look at me like that. Loaning 'Old Friends' to the Art Institute of Chicago would be a coup for us and a feather in your cap, since you negotiated the loan. Perhaps he didn't want you to suffer the embarrassment of having our painting revealed to be a forgery."

"Or he didn't want questions to be raised. Kindness was never Charlie's primary motive." My mind wandered to the flowers and gifts he'd bring me, the meals he'd have ready when I came home, the hot baths….

"Apparently, he named a few names to get his sentence reduced. Did you know that?"

I shook my head.

"I've been on the telephone all weekend. From what I've gleaned from some of my less scrupulous sources, Charles has crossed a number of people. To protect himself—and his future—he's holding many of them hostage with his forgeries. There's going to be hell to pay."

"Explain," I said.

"The reputations of galleries, auction houses, and dealers rest on how they value the work they display and sell. Remember, artwork is frequently used as collateral, and fortunes have been lost when fakes have been discovered. It's in everyone's best interest to get the originals back."

"Why wouldn't Charlie *sell* them, if he needs money?"

"He's apparently decided that blackmail is more lucrative. In any case, it's a certainty that Charles Tremain has a cache of stolen art hidden somewhere."

"That son of a—!"

"Agreed," Franklin said. "But perhaps you can help stop him."

"How?"

"We'll figure that out."

"Charlie is my biggest regret, Franklin. I lost my heart to him. And my soul. And my reputation. And my self-confidence. As long as he's in this world, I die, day after day after day. What do you need me to do?"

* * *

Charlie and I had a system for sending each other messages that I thought, back in the day, was romantic—we'd log into a shared email account and leave a message in drafts—until I realized that he was merely loath to leave any sort of trail.

I attempted to log in now and was surprised to find that the password hadn't changed. The message I left was simple:

Someone sent me a lovely picture of some old friends of yours. We need to talk.

I signed off with the number of the burner phone I'd bought.

Three days later, I got a text from an unknown number:

You needed to know. I hope my message was clear. I'd rather explain in person, if you're willing.

I hesitated for a long time before replying:

I need your help to get my reputation back.

* * *

I shouldn't have been surprised when I came home two nights later and found Charlie sitting in my living room, drinking a glass of wine. He held his fingers to his lips and mimed turning off my phone. Which I did.

"I checked for listening devices," he said, "but they're so easy to hide these days. Damnable nuisance. It's just as well I'm out of the game. Technology takes all the fun away."

"Out of the game? From what I hear, you've now moved up to blackmail. Where's the fun in *that*, Charlie?"

"Without you, my darling, fun isn't part of my life."

189

"Oh, stop," I said.

"Would you believe I'm trying to protect precious artworks?"

"Not for a minute," I said.

He quirked a smile and gazed at me. It took all my willpower not to react.

"What do you know about this sordid affair?" he asked.

"I know you're blackmailing people with stolen artwork."

"Would you believe me if I said that wasn't true? That I've actually got honorable intentions?"

"I wish I could," I said. "But you can't blame *me* for hesitating to trust you."

"I suppose I can't. Would that we could go back in time. Do you remember the weekend we went to that cabin, the one with the shed—"

And at that moment, the world crashed in—"the world" being the front door of my townhouse. A bunch of people in FBI vests and helmets rushed in, armed to the teeth, and surrounded Charlie, shouting all the while. They made us both lie down on the floor, and I stayed there until they took him away. One of the officers, who introduced himself as Special Agent Allen, told me he'd be in touch.

I called Franklin and told him what had happened.

"I'm not surprised you've been under surveillance. Did Charles tell you anything?"

"Not a thing," I said.

* * *

A week later, Special Agent Allen came to my office while I was meeting with Franklin, who stayed with me for moral support.

"Have you heard from your husband lately?" Allen asked.

"He's in jail. I haven't been to visit him, but of course, you know that."

"He *was* in jail," Allen said. "But he escaped from custody earlier today."

"What? How?"

"A complicated sleight of hand having to do with a rest stop, a bathroom break, and a fire alarm. He hasn't reached out to you?"

"Of course not," I said.

190

"Let me know if he does, okay? The sooner we get him back in custody, the safer he'll be." He handed me his card and left.

"An imposing young man," Franklin said. "It must have been frightening, having him burst through your door."

"At least he helped me fix it."

"And you have no idea where Charlie is?"

I closed my office door. "Just before he was arrested, he mentioned a cabin we used to go to."

"Cabin? Where?"

"The Adirondacks," I said. "His family owned it. He liked the remoteness of it, in the middle of the mountains, nothing around for miles."

"Sounds like a wonderful place to hide out. Perhaps I should go up there and try to talk some sense into him—if he's there."

I shook my head. "I'll take you. I need to see this to the end."

"I'll drive," Franklin said.

* * *

We made the trip in just under four hours. The black velvet of country dark never soothed my city-girl spirits, and tonight was no different. There was a moon, which helped. We snaked our way down the dirt lane. I saw the glow of the windows before our headlights caught the cabin. Franklin turned off the engine and let the car merrily roll along the last few feet.

Charlie always hid an emergency key to his houses, and I found it. He'd used a fake hide-a-key rock as a decoy, but I knew to go three rocks to the left and two up to find the real hiding place. Three-two, his favorite code.

My ex-husband turned when I opened the door to the cabin and looked at us guiltily. The room was filled with crates, excelsior, padded blankets, and artwork. So much artwork. I recognized a few pieces, one of which I'd seen hanging in our museum that morning.

"It's not what you think," he said, straightening and raising his hands.

"With you, Charles," said Franklin, stepping in beside me, "it never is."

"Franklin, ah. So you two are working together. That's a mistake, my darling Mary. Our friend is not to be trusted."

"Charles," Franklin began, "don't you dare—"

"You know, Franklin, prison does wonders for clearing one's mind. I spent months trying to figure out who was in charge of the ring, who was pulling the strings. Who set me up."

"You were the mastermind," Franklin said.

"No, no. I've always been a middleman—a soldier, never a general. I didn't want that responsibility. No, the person in charge knew too much about the art world, cared too much about the paintings, understood how their value could be leveraged in ways I'd never imagined. I knew forgers and could plan a theft. But I didn't have the calculating vision this operation required. I've got to admit, it took me a long time to realize it was you, Franklin. You surprised me, old friend."

"I don't know what you're talking about," Franklin snarled. "Mary, he's out of his mind."

"Darling," Charlie addressed me, "ask yourself this: how did I get caught?"

"How did you?"

"What was the scheme that undid my life of crime, as you understood it?"

I shook my head. "The Georges Seurat forgeries."

"Found in a collection owned by a close friend of Franklin's. Did you never ask yourself, what tipped the authorities off? Or what happened to the originals? I'll bet you a million dollars they're in the museum's vaults."

"Don't listen to him," Franklin said. "He's a desperate, dangerous man, making up stories. Thank God I'm here with you, Mary. If not, he might get you to believe his ridiculous lies."

I stepped to the middle of the room and eyed them both. Franklin, my friend and savior. Charlie, my—my what?

I turned to him. "Charlie, I—"

"Think, Mary. You've been his secret weapon for all these years. You've been able to authenticate work, give him ideas, build a reputation, some of which even managed to survive a con artist husband. He vouched for you, but why? Don't you see? He used your relationship with me to leverage different clients and different sorts of transactions. He used me, and then

192

he used you."

I looked at Franklin, and my eyes filled with tears as I reconsidered all that had happened over the past ten years. What a waste. I took a step toward Charlie.

"Mary, don't," Franklin said. He pulled a gun from his pocket. "I wish you hadn't insisted on coming up here with me. I dread having to dispose of you, too. But what must be done must be done, and time is of the essence. Charles, I need those forgeries now. You know the ones I mean. My client is getting antsy. Fortunately, he's an idiot and won't know the difference."

Charlie grabbed a handful of excelsior and tossed it in Franklin's face, then tackled the older man. They fell to the floor, Franklin still holding the gun and moving it toward Charlie's head. I grabbed Franklin's arm, and the gun went off. Charlie screamed. I held on to Franklin's hand, and then the door crashed open. Suddenly, the room was full of people.

"You took your time," I said to Special Agent Allen.

"We wanted to get as much evidence as possible," he said, helping me up. "You okay?"

"I'm fine. Charlie?"

"Alive," he said, holding his shoulder. Blood flowed down his arm and dripped on the floor. I looked around and saw Franklin—my mentor, my friend—lying on the floor, blood streaming from his nose. He glared at me, then quickly looked away.

"Take these two outside and have them checked out by the medic. We'll debrief in a bit," Allen said.

A little while later, Charlie joined me in the back of an SUV.

"Are you hurt?" he asked.

"Bruised." I noted his sling and bandage but didn't ask for more details. "How long have you known about Franklin?"

"As I mentioned, prison was a mind-clearing exercise. It took me a while to convince anyone else."

"That's how you got out of jail early? By naming Franklin?"

"That was not sufficient, my darling. I had to *prove* that I'd turned over a new leaf, so—believe it or not—I helped the authorities set a trap.

They're hoping Franklin will point them in the direction of several unsavory characters."

"Was sending me the original Richards painting part of the trap?"

He nodded. "I knew Franklin would panic. He'd never have agreed to loaning out a forgery."

"How did you get the original?" I asked.

"I didn't. I knew the person who'd forged it for Franklin. He created a second copy as a favor to me."

"But why have it forged in the first place?"

"The Romleys—who were in on the trap—were making noises about recalling their loan to the museum."

"And Franklin was having artworks forged and then blackmailing their owners."

"Yes. I'd like to believe that he started the operation to help *save* the artwork. He was storing stolen pieces that were seen as collateral, not art. But greed must have taken over at some point, as it is wont to do. Did it never strike you as odd that such a small museum had so many pieces in storage?"

"Of course it did."

Charlie glanced at me sideways.

I shrugged. "Do you really think I'm that stupid? Special Agent Allen and I spent a lot of time in offsite storage this week. He had me carry a tracker, just in case I got into trouble. Which, tonight, I did."

"A nice touch, Mary, letting Franklin think of you as a useful idiot. Which, tonight and always, you have never been."

"Not useful?"

"Not an idiot, darling."

I turned away. "I still thought *you* were the mastermind, Charlie, and Special Agent Allen didn't disabuse me of that notion. He told me that my helping him would—"

He raised his eyebrows. "Would what?"

"Would help you get a lesser sentence," I said, turning toward the window to hide the flush rising on my cheeks.

"How noble of you, darling." He reached for my hand but thought better of it. "When you came in the door with Franklin, my heart stopped. That wasn't part of the plan."

"It would have been easier if we hadn't been keeping each other in the dark."

"Let's never do that again. 'Transparency at all times' will be our motto. A cellophane couple. What do you say? Should we give it another go?"

I shook my head. "I tried to forget you, Charlie. To move on. But you're a part of my life, and I suppose you always will be."

"My darling," he said.

"God help me," I sighed, taking his hand and giving it a squeeze.

Sunday in the Park with George
opened May 2, 1984, at the Booth Theatre, New York

ACT I
"Sunday in the Park with George"
"No Life"
"Color and Light"
"Gossip"
"The Day Off"
"Everybody Loves Louis"
"The One on the Left"
"Finishing the Hat"
"The Day Off" (reprise)
"We Do Not Belong Together"
"Beautiful"
"Sunday"

ACT II
"It's Hot Up Here"
"Chromolume #7"
"Gossip" (reprise)
"Putting It Together"
"Children and Art"
"Lesson #8"
"Move On"
"Sunday" (reprise)

Music and lyrics by Stephen Sondheim.
Book by James Lapine.

Sunday in the Park with George

by Fleur Bradley

Dorothy Peters arrived at the nursing home five minutes early for her shift, because she'd only been at Broad Horizons for a week and still wanted to make a good impression on her coworkers. She was earning ten cents an hour over minimum wage, but she wasn't there for the money.

That brisk Sunday, her first assignment was to take George Patinkin, a resident in the memory-care unit, to the park. She'd been looking forward to this and had been given specific instructions by the nursing assistants on how to manage the man, as if he was some sort of movie star. *He likes to sit by the river*, they'd told her.

Of course he does, she thought.

In Dot's opinion, Broad Horizons felt like heaven's waiting room—and from what she'd been told, George's number might be called any day now.

She found him in the dining hall, an empty cup of coffee in front of him. His wheelchair was wedged tightly under the table.

She put a smile on her face. "Good morning, George!" she called, approaching his table. Her scrubs were still new and uncomfortable. "Are you ready to go to the park?"

He looked up with a mixture of curiosity and irritation. "You're new."

"I am." Her smile felt like it was painted on, like a thin layer of ice, ready to crack. "My name's Dorothy," she introduced herself, "but you can call me Dot."

"Hmmm." George had his arms crossed on his lap. Arthritis had ravaged his hands, which he hid under a blanket. He frowned. "Did you clear it with my agent?"

She had been warned he might ask this question: Alzheimer's had taken up shop inside his brain. "Your agent should've let you know that I'm on your schedule for this morning," she said. "Come on, let's go to the park."

She pulled his wheelchair away from the table and rolled the old man out of the dining hall, her badge swinging back and forth in front of her like a pendulum.

Hunched under his blanket, George was a shadow of his former self. Once upon a time, he'd been an eccentric but successful painter with lots of abrasive opinions, mostly about women. His art had made it possible for him to afford the ten thousand dollars a month for a private room at Broad Horizons.

The front-desk attendant buzzed Dot out of the building. She felt a cool breeze on her face and hoped that George was warm enough. She didn't want to cut this walk short.

"Chilly," George muttered. He wrapped his blanket tightly around his shriveled torso with fingers like a bird's talons.

"It'll get the blood flowing," Dot said, in her perkiest Activities Assistant voice.

The nursing home was a block from the park, which ran for miles along the wide river, and Dot pushed the wheelchair as fast as she could.

"Are we on the clock or something, Missy?" George asked. It was a valid question, because, of course, they *were*. One hour, that was all the time they had. Otherwise, she'd have to wait until her rotation put her back with George again, which might not be for weeks.

"I think I see the sun making an appearance," Dot said, as they waited at the crosswalk. It took forever for the light to change, and she stood there with her hands tight around the wheelchair's handles.

The clouds parted, and sunshine warmed her face. "There it is," she said brightly.

George muttered a sound of agreement as the light changed. Dot hurried him across the street, smoothly navigating the curb and sidewalk.

Inside the park's entrance, a group of kids kicked a soccer ball back and forth across the grass.

"I always loved this park," George said, as Dot pushed his chair along the blacktop path toward the woods. "It wasn't this nice, though, back in my day."

"Is that so?" Dot murmured. She had walked this path several times in preparation for today. The sun didn't penetrate the forest canopy, and it was quiet between the trees. A lone jogger passed them and disappeared around a bend.

When they reached the river, the sun bounced off the smooth water like a reflection in a mirror. They came to a bench—to *the* bench, the one she knew George had sat on so often during his prime.

The old man didn't let on that he recognized it. Perhaps, given the state of his memory, he didn't. But Dot thought he straightened up a bit in his wheelchair. Didn't he, just a bit?

She pushed down the lever to engage the brakes and sat on the bench. "A lovely spot, isn't it?"

George gave her a side-eye, then let his gaze drift to the water. "Indeed. But you know very well this was *my* spot."

Dot felt a chill go down her spine. "Would you like to tell me about it?" she asked.

There was a long pause, and then, at last, he nodded. "Very well," he said, taking a beat to inhale the cool air. "I was a nobody when I first came here."

George geared up to tell the story he'd told so many times to the press, after his art became famous. His paintings sold for millions of dollars and hung in galleries all over the world. People lined up around the block to see them.

"Back then, the park was overrun with homeless. A lot of parks were, in those days. Economic downturn, drugs, blah blah." He waved an arthritic hand in dismissal, and his blanket fell from his lap, landing at his feet. Dot picked it up and tucked it back around him. "All I had was a twenty-dollar bill," he went on, "some paints and brushes, and a few blank canvasses."

The air was still, as if Mother Nature was listening in.

George smiled. "Thirty-One was the first. She looked like she was in her late fifties, but that's what the homeless life did—it aged them." He hesitated a moment, remembering. "She sat right there, where you're sitting."

"Was she asleep?"

George shrugged. "Eventually. First, we shared a drink and made friends."

Dot remembered those very words from an in-depth, decades-old *New Yorker* interview she'd found in the magazine's online archive. It was the first thing that popped up when you dropped the name George Patinkin into a search engine. She had read the piece several times.

"You never forget your first," George said, a little louder than necessary. There was no one around to hear him, but Dot, who felt the wooden bench radiate the remnants of winter, running up her spine and spreading like ink in a glass of water. She wondered if his Thirty-One had felt this cold, or if the alcohol had warmed her from inside.

"How did you come up with the idea to number the paintings?" she asked.

George glared at her, a sharp look, his teeth clenched. "Didn't you do your homework, girl? My agent said you did."

"Of course." Dot tried to smile, but her face was frozen. "I just want to hear you tell it."

She waited for him to continue. She knew from her research that he loved to talk about himself; she just had to be patient.

The breeze was stronger now, and George let his eyes drift back to the river.

"Thirty-One gave me the idea." He spoke softly, his voice clearer than his age would suggest. "To paint homeless women and name each canvas after the subject's age."

"And the missing faces? Where did *that* come from?"

George was silent for a moment, and Dot held her breath.

"They *were* faceless," George said, at last, an edge to his voice. "No one cared about them, no one saw them. When I sat here and talked with them, anyone who happened to walk by pretended not to see them. They were invisible."

He exhaled, his breath making a cloud in the cold air.

"*Invisible,*" he said again, almost spitting the word.

Dot knew all this from the *New Yorker* article and others she'd found, but she wanted more. She had to wait, though, for George to get there on his own.

"That first one, Thirty-One, was a disaster," he whispered. "She moved too much, and I was still just a student. I didn't know how to work with moving subjects. I had to get her to *pose.*"

"For your art," Dot said, as if agreeing with him.

The old man shifted position in his wheelchair, pulled up his blanket to cover his frail body. "Is the hour up yet?" he asked.

"Not yet," Dot said. The sun had disappeared behind gathering clouds. "Tell me more about your process."

George sat up a little, a lost look in his eyes. He'd drifted into the past, exactly what Dot had hoped for.

"Tell me how you got those women to sit still for your paintings."

"I started with wine or cheap vodka." He shook his head and laughed at himself.

"Started?" Dot asked.

He looked up at her, a devilish grin on his face. "Then I found this tranquilizer. That made it easy. I could position them the way I wanted them, and they'd pose for hours." He let his gaze drift back to the water.

Dot felt bile rise from her stomach at the thought of young women unable to move while George painted them. Without faces, because their identities didn't matter to him—or to the world.

George cleared his throat. "I didn't know it would go wrong." He sounded like he was about to cry. "The third session with Nineteen...that was an accident. I gave her the drink with the pills crushed up in it, and she started to nod off. But then she realized what I'd done and panicked. She jumped up and ran—into the river."

A bird flew across the water, its reflection on the surface making it seem as if it was flowing with the current. Dot tried to imagine what it had been like: Nineteen, just a girl, drugged, plunging into the river and drowning.

"It was terrible," George said. "But the world had given up on her, anyway."

He licked his lips and stared straight ahead. "I kept waiting for the police to show up on my doorstep, but they never did."

"Tell me about Twenty-Five," Dot said. The park was quiet. Not even the birds were singing. The world was frozen in time.

George didn't say anything for a while. Dot worried he would return from the past to the present, but she needed him to remember.

"Twenty-Five was injecting herself between her toes when I found her back there." He waved at the dense woods behind them.

A woman walking hand in hand with a young girl passed, giving Dot a friendly nod.

"You offered to paint her," Dot said, when the woman and child were out of earshot. "You said you'd pay her to pose for you."

George shrugged. "Money and attention—that was all they wanted. So I gave it to them. Well, not the money. There was no need to pay them." He turned back to the river. The water was like a Post-Impressionist painting, with dozens of dots in shades of gray blending into each other.

He resumed his story, his voice almost robotic now. "By the time I got to Twenty-Five, I had a system. And I was painting much faster. That one only took me a few hours."

Dot remembered the client who'd walked into her office three weeks ago. An elderly woman, close to George's age, searching for answers about the sister—Michelle, her name was—who'd gone missing decades before.

Homeless and a drug addict, Michelle had fallen off the family's radar. Until she called home out of the blue, proudly announcing that she was getting clean, that a painter had offered to pay her enough to go to rehab.

But Michelle ran out of coins at the payphone, the conversation ended abruptly, and they'd never heard from her again.

Until Dot's client, an art aficionado, took in an exhibition of George Patinkin's "Numbered Women" series...and recognized the tattoo on Twenty-Five's leg, a tattoo of a sun with a smiling face, a tattoo her sister Michelle had gotten on the occasion of her twenty-first birthday.

So Michelle had been George's Twenty-Five, and now—all these years later—her sister at last had a clue as to her disappearance.

"The park was like a black hole at night," George said. "No one around but the homeless, and even they were hidden in the dark. We sat right here." He turned to Dot. "Right where we are now."

He smiled, a lustful melancholy smile that turned Dot's blood to ice. "And when I finished painting, I gave her a little more of my magic medicine, and then I took her swimming."

There were nineteen paintings in the "Numbered Women" series, and the art world had paid George increasingly well for each new canvas, until early-onset Alzheimer's put a stop to his career.

"Twenty-Five was easy," George said with a laugh. "They're so naïve at that age. Now Forty-Eight was a lot harder." He laughed louder. "Oh, I could tell you some stories...."

Please don't, Dot thought. She closed her eyes, then opened them to the view of the wide river that had been the graveyard of so many poor women.

Her watch beeped, signaling that their hour was up.

"It's cold," George said, burrowing deeper into his blanket.

Dot roughly pulled it from his grasp and dropped it on the bench. "Nonsense, George. Look, the sun's coming out!"

The old man tucked his arthritic hands into his armpits. "I want to go home," he whined.

Dot gazed out across the river. She would have to report back to her client and take her tape of George's story to the police. The bodies were surely long gone, washed out to sea by the river's current. But a few Jane Doe cases would be solved at long last, and the paintings would be the nails in George's coffin. His art and his confession would be all the evidence they'd need.

"All right," Dot said softly, "let's go."

Before they left the tree line, she stopped and asked, "What about the little girl?"

"What little girl?" George said, obviously confused.

Dot didn't trust her voice, so she cleared her throat. There were families, she saw, picnicking on the grass.

"What *girl*?" George asked again.

Dot gripped the wheelchair, her knuckles white. "Twenty-Five's daughter, George. Tell me about Six."

Into the Woods

opened November 5, 1987, at the Martin Beck Theatre, New York

ACT I

"Prologue: Into the Woods"
"Cinderella at the Grave"
"Hello, Little Girl"
"I Guess This Is Goodbye"
"Maybe They're Magic"
"Maybe They're Magic" (reprise)
"I Know Things Now"
"A Very Nice Prince"
"First Midnight"
"Giants in the Sky"
"Agony"
"A Very Nice Prince" (reprise)
"It Takes Two"
"Second Midnight"
"Stay With Me"
"On the Steps of the Palace"
"Careful My Toe"
"So Happy (Prelude)"
"Ever After"

ACT II
"Prologue: So Happy"
"Prologue: Into the Woods" (reprise)
"Agony" (reprise)
"Lament"
"Any Moment"
"Moments in the Woods"
"Your Fault"
"Last Midnight"
"No More"
"No One Is Alone"
"Finale: Children Will Listen"

Music and lyrics by Stephen Sondheim.
Book by James Lapine.

Hello, Little Girl

by Rebecca K. Jones

The first time you hear Chip Baker's name, you will be fifteen years old, sitting across the chessboard from your grandfather Geležinis in his tiny sixth-floor walk-up in Williamsburg. He will be winning, because the only time you will ever beat him will be shortly before his death, when you are twenty-three and he is over ninety, and his vision is mostly gone. But when you are fifteen, your grandfather will beat you in two games every Sunday morning when you accompany your mother to return his clean laundry.

"Vilkas," he will say, because until he dies, he will refuse to call you by your Americanized name of William, "have you heard of the British Guiana 1-Cent Magenta?"

You'll roll your eyes, because you will have told the old man a million times that you don't care about his stupid stamps, but he will pretend not to see and tell you about it anyway.

"It's the most expensive stamp in the world," he will say, and at *this* you will perk up. You will dream of being rich your whole childhood and into adulthood. You will wish for Air Jordan sneakers and the latest videogames and Italian sportscars, and you will be disgusted every time you look down at your second-hand jeans that your mother keeps patching instead of replacing.

"How much is it worth?" You'll try—and fail—to keep the eagerness out of your voice. Even at fifteen, you will know that you should always play it cool. He will judge you if he knows that you're more interested in money than your Torah studies.

He will examine the board, and you'll watch him purse his lips. In and out. In and out. You will tamp down your impatience and wait quietly. "It's coming up for auction next month," he will say. "They expect the winning bid to be over eight million dollars, although I think it will bring in more than nine, perhaps as high as nine and a half."

You'll whistle. Even *one* million dollars will feel like more money than you have any right to hope for. In your mind, you will hear the echoed jeers of your classmates. "Anchor baby," they call you. "Trash." They say that you stink like cabbage and onions, and you resist the urge to defend your mother and her parents, who fled to the United States before glasnost and rebuilt their lives from scratch without knowing any English. You won't even be able to imagine what nine and a half million dollars would be like.

From that moment on, you will not rest until you own that stamp.

* * *

Six months later, you will be sixteen and helping your grandfather stock the shelves of his tiny corner store.

"Senelis," you will say, and he will look up from the packages of powdered milk, "did that stamp ever sell? The guinea whatever?"

He'll smile, and you will realize how much you look like him. "It did, Vilkas. I was right: the winning bid was almost ten million dollars!"

"Who won?" You'll try to sound casual, bored even, but the glint in his eyes will reflect the glint in your own. You will know, then, for the first time, that maybe he has spent his whole life dreaming of wealth, just like you.

"Chip Baker."

You won't recognize the name, but an image of the Monopoly man will come to mind. You'll think Chip Baker must be portly from expensive food, tanned from time on his private yacht. You will compare that image to your grandfather, shrunken under his cardigan and stooped with arthritis.

You will repeat the name under your breath, committing it to memory.

"Come," your grandfather will say. "I'll show you my own meager collection. This can wait."

You will spend the next two hours paging through his albums, full of images from the Soviet Union and the United States and Israel—the two places your grandfather spent his life and the one place he never got to see. They won't be worth very much, but you will fall in love with the birds and the flowers and the quiet satisfaction that comes from the collecting of a complete series of stamps.

A month later, he will fall and break his hip. He'll sell the store, and Jamba Juice will wind up moving in, and you will shake your head in disbelief at the thought of a six-dollar smoothie. But neither of you knows that yet.

* * *

When your grandfather dies, you will inherit his stamp albums, and you won't know what to do with them. You won't be homeless, exactly: you'll mostly be couch-surfing, and your mother will always let you sleep at home if you show up unannounced and looking pathetic. Your tuition at Baruch will be (mostly) covered by grants and scholarships and loans, but your own required contribution will still be high enough that paying for housing will be out of your reach.

Your mother will keep the albums safe for you in a banker's box full of odds and ends from your grandfather's house. You'll sift through them one Saturday night, wishing you had the money to join your classmates at the bars and clubs and parties you know they frequent each weekend. You will look down at your threadbare khaki pants—they will be used when you buy them, not from a fancy consignment or vintage shop, but from a Salvation Army store—and shake your head. There won't be any point in trying to get past the doormen in those.

In the box, you will find a stack of news clippings about Chip Baker, and you'll be surprised to see that he doesn't look like Mr. Monopoly at all. Instead, he will look like every other old white man you see going to and from their Wall Street offices every day. You will find the *New York*

Times wedding section clipping announcing the marriage of Chip's son Robert to his high-school sweetheart and then the birth announcement for their daughter Cindy. You will study their photos, the way Robert stands awkwardly behind his wife, the way he does not touch his daughter. You will note her birthday, see that she is only a few years younger than you. You will pause a long time, your mind racing, trying to catch up to the idea that is beginning to form, until your mother calls you for dinner.

"Yes, Mama," you will say. Dinner will be quiet, your mother tired from another long day of backbreaking work, cleaning apartments on the Upper West Side. Her employers will tell her how much they enjoy having someone around with skin as white as milk, instead of, well....

They won't ever finish that thought, but your mother will burn with embarrassment all the same. You'll be tired, too, still puzzling over the contents of Senelis' box.

* * *

In the library, you will use a public computer and find that Cindy Baker is a senior at Spence, way uptown. You won't want to get too deeply into the weeds, but you will do a thorough enough job for your purposes. Her Instagram will be a treasure trove, and you'll see what coffee shops she patronizes and what she does on weekends. You will find pictures of her boyfriends, all dark-haired, slender young men wearing broken-in chinos and ancient—no, *vintage*—Polo shirts. You will find Chip's obituary, dated the year before, which will tell you in its dry, impersonal way that Chip was survived by his wife Joanna, his son Robert, and his granddaughter. Cindy's Facebook account will show you that she has moved in with her grandmother, who lives close to school, and that her parents have decamped for a long-overdue trip to their second home in some town you won't recognize the name of.

The last vital piece of information will present itself with little fanfare. You won't realize what you're looking at until you're halfway down the page of *The American Philatelist* and find a photo of Joanna holding a display box with a caption indicating that it contains the British Guiana 1-Cent Magenta, the highlight of her late husband's magnificent collection.

It will be easy to mold yourself in Cindy's boyfriends' image. You will simply take photos of them to your barber, and ten minutes later, you'll have the same fade and pushed-back curls. The clothes will be more difficult, but you'll open another credit card in your mother's name, hoping she won't notice, and you'll swear to pay it off before a collection agency comes calling. It will take a full day of shopping before you have everything you need, and you'll spend hours aging the boat shoes until they look just right. Finally, you'll sit back and look in the mirror and smile. You'll be ready.

It won't take long, just a few days, timing your visits to Levain Bakery to coincide with what you will have seen on Cindy's Instagram. You'll bump into her one morning—literally, although you'll make her think that she was the clumsy one—and grip her arm to keep her from spilling her drink all over her corn-gold jacket. You'll smile the way you have practiced in the mirror, one side of your mouth curling up slowly, and *her* mouth will drop open when she looks at you. You won't know this until she tells you, weeks later and only days before the end, but she will think God dropped you in her path. The perfect man, sent as a gift.

"Hello, little girl," you'll say, your voice intentionally low and raspy.

She'll nod, speechless.

"I'm William. And who are you?"

Her blush will make you smile, for real, this time, and you'll be shocked at how *easy* the whole thing is. She'll start to leave, but you'll stop her by asking, "What's your rush?" You will have walked into the bakery thinking that swooning only happens in movies, and it will take you a second to realize that she will, in fact, have swooned for you.

You'll offer to walk her wherever she's headed, and she'll accept, taking your proffered arm and finally finding her voice. Her auburn hair will shine brightly in the sun, and you'll resist the urge to run your hand over it. When you get to Spence's front door, she will hesitate, obviously not wanting to leave you, and you'll ask if you can call her sometime. She'll say yes and give you her cell number—which you'll already know, having found it online on one of those websites where you pay ten dollars and learn everything about a person except for their shoe size. You will text her right then and there, asking if she wants to go to the Guggenheim that weekend.

You won't be surprised when she says yes—you already know she goes to the museum every Saturday. But you will be mildly surprised by how much you genuinely come to like her as the next month passes and the two of you grow closer. She will be tender, blushing pink at the slightest provocation, and her plump curves will excite you more than you will have expected. You won't have been attracted to this kind of all-American girl before, but she will drive you wild when she pulls away from your eager kisses. It will almost be a shame, you think sometimes, when this is over and you've moved on, whisking your mother to Paris to live the life you both deserve. Cindy will never know what hit her, but it will have to be done.

* * *

It will take six weeks for Cindy to invite you to Joanna's apartment high above Central Park. You won't push it—you will have seen early on how fiercely protective the girl is of her grandmother.

"Poppy took care of everything," she'll tell you. "Grams never had to fend for herself, and she still doesn't know how to do things like pay the Spectrum bill. I don't know what she'd do, if I wasn't there."

You'll nod sympathetically and pull her closer, murmuring into her ear how hard it must be. She will melt deeper into your embrace.

At last, on a Thursday night as you do homework together at the library— she won't know that you stopped going to classes weeks ago, that soon you won't have any need of further education—she will put down her pen and glance at you hesitantly.

"Do you want to come meet Grams?" she'll ask.

You won't respond at first, busy congratulating yourself on having survived the agony of waiting. Nothing is half so intriguing as what's out of reach.

"It's okay," she'll say, immediately backpedaling, mistaking your silence for disinterest. "She just said I should invite you, because she wants to see who I've been spending so much time with, but if you don't want to come it's fine, because I—"

You will lean over the table and kiss her gently, cutting off her explanation.

"I'd love to," you'll say, and it will be the first honest thing you have said to her.

* * *

You'll be nervous as you slip the gun into your pocket in your mother's tiny bathroom. You will have bought the small black revolver that morning from a guy on the street in Harlem who will seem taken aback when you tell him you're looking, not for drugs, but for a piece. You will spend the afternoon learning how to use it, loading the ammunition, aiming and firing. You will practice until you can do it without thinking, careful to keep your gloves on. You will know—everyone will know, by then, from twenty years of *Law & Order*—that fingerprints on a spent cartridge could give the whole thing away. If you're going to make this look like a break-in, you will need to be careful.

Your mother will ask you where you're going, all dressed up.

"*Niekur*, Mama," you'll respond, stooping to kiss her cheek. "Just to dinner at a friend's house. I'll be back in a few hours."

She will pat your back. "*Mano gražuolis sūnus.*"

She's been calling you her handsome son since before you can remember, but that night, you will look in the mirror and believe her.

Standing outside Joanna's door, the plastic wrapper of the bouquet you've brought slick with sweat from your palm, you will have second thoughts for the first time. *Can you really do this?* you'll wonder. *Can you really kill two people in cold blood, for nothing more than a bit of paper?*

You will take a deep breath and remind yourself that it isn't for one stamp, it is for Chip Baker's entire collection, which—based on the meticulous research you will have conducted—is worth over fifty million dollars. You will have helped your mother file her taxes since you were in the sixth grade, so you will know that the most money she has ever made in a single year is just shy of thirty thousand.

Fifty millions…. You won't even know how to *think* about that much money.

The door will open, and you will see Joanna and Cindy standing in the foyer of Joanna's airy apartment. Joanna will be slender and frail beneath her caftan, and Cindy will look unexpectedly childlike in her Spence uniform and pigtails. You will thrust the bouquet toward Joanna and cringe at your own awkwardness, but she will accept the flowers gracefully and invite you in before breezing past you to find a vase. The smell of her perfume will linger in the air after she's gone, and you will struggle to identify its earthy, herbaceous scent.

Dinner will test your patience. Small talk about the crunch of the vegetables and the smoothness of the pot roast will make you drink more than you will have intended. You will know that you need to keep your wits about you, will need to bring up the stamp collection organically, and your heart will jump when Joanna gives you an opening.

"Tell me about your family, William," she will say, and you will see the path appear before you.

"I was mostly raised by my grandparents," you will respond. That won't be true, but you will be past the point of caring about the truth by then, and you will weave a thrilling story about their flight from Lithuania with only the clothes on their backs and your grandfather's stamp collection.

"I didn't know your grandfather collected stamps," Cindy will say. "Poppy has—well, had—a wonderful stamp collection! Oh, Grams, can we show Will?"

You will look up from your plate and flash a bashful smile you will have spent hours perfecting. "Please, Mrs. Baker," you'll say. "That would be great—I'd love to feel connected to my *senelis* again."

Joanna will purse her lips, but she will eventually nod. She will lead you and Cindy into her late husband's study, where she will open a safe, hidden behind a large painting of a snow-white cow outside a small cottage, and you will catch a glimpse of the treasures inside—including the display box. Your mouth will start to water, and you will focus on your breathing. You will ask Cindy to show you to the restroom.

She will kiss you up against the wall in the hallway, and you will hope she'll think you're fumbling with her skirt as you wrench the revolver from your pocket. She will push away from you when she feels the barrel of the gun against her side.

"Goodbye, little girl," you'll say, and her eyes will widen involuntarily as you pull the trigger.

She will immediately go limp in your arms, and you will gently lower her to the floor, sorry that it has come to this. You will take three deep breaths before turning to finish the job.

You will find Joanna at the door of the study.

"I heard a terribly loud noise, dear," she will say. "Did you hear it?"

You will shake your head and swallow hard. You will not be cut out for this, and it will take every ounce of self-control to keep yourself from dropping the gun and running out of the apartment.

"Where's Cindy?"

You will stammer that she went to the restroom, and you came back ahead of her to look at the stamps.

"Are you feeling okay?" Joanna will ask. She will touch your forehead with her cool hand, like your mother used to do when you were a boy. "You seem feverish."

You will swallow again and pull the gun out of your pocket. "I'm sorry, Joanna. Really, I am."

You'll be surprised when she looks away, over your shoulder, and you'll turn your head to see where she's looking.

And that's when you'll see her.

Cindy, like an avenging angel, her white shirt blood-red from the wound in her side, a fireplace poker raised above her head.

"Goodbye, little boy," she will say, as you fall to the intricately woven carpet, and those will be the last words you'll ever hear.

Act V

The 1990s

Assassins

opened on December 18, 1990, at Playwrights Horizons, New York

"Everybody's Got the Right"

"The Ballad of Booth"

"How I Saved Roosevelt"

"The Gun Song"

"The Ballad of Czolgosz"

"Unworthy of Your Love"

"The Ballad of Guiteau"

"Another National Anthem"

"November 22, 1963"

"Something Just Broke"

"Everybody's Got the Right" (reprise)

Music and lyrics by Stephen Sondheim.

Book by John Weidman.

Another National Anthem

by Cheryl L. Davis

He did it. That bacon-egg-and-cheese-on-a-bagel-eating fat man *did* it. Week after week, he buys a bunch of stupid lottery tickets. I tell him he shouldn't waste his money; everyone knows the system is rigged, but he grins like a fool and says, "Hey, you gotta look on the bright side. It never hurts to hope!"

So he "hopes" away twenty or thirty bucks a week—and finally, hope pays off, and he wins!

I betcha he spent more over the years than he won, the stupid bastard. Probably just hit a scratch-off, no big deal. The mainstream media always blow these things out of proportion. Here, lemme see, he won....

Holy shit!

Fifteen. *Million.* Dollars.

Shitshitshitshitshit.

Now the asshole's ruined it for everybody else. Nobody from around here will ever win a giant payoff like that again. You'd think everybody's got the right to win, but "they" won't let it happen. I could buy a ticket every day from here until the world fucking ends, and it'll never happen to me.

It's like that time some jerk got the last ticket into the ballpark for the World Series, so Dad and me had to go home, didn't even get a hot dog, had to watch the game on our crappy TV. Some folks like Dad—like me—it's just never gonna happen for us.

And it's all *his* fault. That fat-ass *mailman*. Winners always win, that's the way the system is rigged. But who knew *he'd* be one of the winners?

* * *

Lynette's slamming the pans again.

"Why *you* didn't buy a ticket, Johnny? It coulda been you! Why didn't you?"

After all the times I told her the system is rigged—

"If it's rigged, how come the mailman won? I saw it on the news!"

As if you can believe what you see on the news. I watched this thing on YouTube, I tell her, breaks it all down for you....

"That mailman, he gonna have a great life now! You'll never see him in this shitty neighborhood again!"

She's right. He must live around here somewhere.

"He say he and his family gonna move to the suburbs. Like we used to talk about."

Sure, yeah, *him* they'll let move to the suburbs. He's a millionaire now. They'd never let someone like me—like us—move to no fancy suburb. Mailboy probably always had an "in," probably knew someone at the lottery who fed him the numbers, that's how he—

"He bought his wife all kinds of stuff while they're looking for their new place. I saw her in the nail salon showing that shit off. Jewelry, red-bottom shoes...she has it all!"

Why does he deserve to win the big prize? He doesn't. Not like I do. I mean, he's a damn *mailman*. That's not work. It's not a *real* job.

"That coulda been you, Johnny. Coulda been *us*."

She says it again and again, like she's singing another national anthem.

So I guess I'll have to fix it.

* * *

"How's it gonna work again?"

Goddamn Leon. Always gotta paint a picture for him, connect the fucking dots. So I do. I tell him and Charlie how we're gonna track the Fat Man, learn his routine. All the way from BEC-on-a-bagel to beddy-bye.

"Why? We gonna hit him on the street?"

We need to know the guy's routine, I explain—*again*—so we know when he's gonna be out of the house. *That's* when we hit him. Hit the house, I mean. The way Lynette's been going on about the stuff his wife is showing off at the nail salon—if he's blowing all that cash on her, he must've bought all kinds of fancy electronic shit for himself. That's the first thing I'd do with that kinda money, go all out on TVs, speakers, gaming equipment. I'd buy out a couple of them stores and set up my own mancave/playroom/wonderland in the basement. And that kinda stuff you can turn over real easy. And don't forget the jewelry. Lynette might like a little shiny something. That'd shut her up. Even a pair of those stupid red-bottom shoes.

So we each take a time slot and watch, figuring out mailboy's routine. He's out of the house at five thirty, on the street all day—but the wife mostly stays home, so daytime's no good. Nights they stay in—and I ask you, what kinda sense does *that* make? With all that green, they just stick around the house? Not me, man. Not with fifteen million bucks in my pocket.

Anyway, that leaves Sunday. They both go to church—where he probably spends the whole service thanking the Lordy for hitting it big and ruining it for the rest of us.

So Sunday it is: we hit the mailtard's house and grab all the expensive shit we can carry.

Only that kinda shit is heavy, and we're betting he's got a lot *of* it. So we're gonna need another pair of hands. Much as I hate it, we'll have to bring Sammy in on the caper.

* * *

Sammy always thinks he's so smart.

"What makes you think the mailman's got anything worth taking?" he says.

So I tell him about the wife and all the bragging at the nail salon.

"Maybe that's all he's *got* is shit for his wife. We're risking a lot for what could be a lot of nothing."

So I tell him I peeked in the bastard's window and saw tons of high-priced shit, just to shut him up. He thinks he's so smart.

"I'll bring my gun," he says.

Hold on, there, cowboy. This is just a quiet little burglary, not a damn shooting gallery.

"If he's got that much stuff, it's gonna take a while to sell. We're gonna have to stash it somewhere and guard it."

That's a bridge for later, I tell him. No guns when we hit the house. I say it again: No. Guns.

He glares, but he knows I'm in charge, so what I say goes.

* * *

I hate Sundays.

"Why you hate Sundays?" Lynette asks. "That don't make sense."

I tell her it's been scientifically proven that Sunday isn't a good day to engage in big things. Here, read this Reddit thread, it lays it out....

"Why you read so much stupid shit about things that don't work or that you can't do? You used to be smarter than that."

She used to listen, to understand. But I guess something in her just broke, somewhere along the line. When I show her I'm a winner, too, she'll pay attention again.

"Where you going, Johnny? Why you up so early, anyway?"

I tell her I'm going to meet some friends. Don't know why she laughs at that. I have friends. And I tell her we're going to the ballgame—that sounds real.

* * *

The mailhole's house is okay. Just. He'll probably buy some stupid McMansion soon. With all his money, after we empty out his house he'll go out and buy new stuff for his castle. When you look at it that way, we're just saving him the moving expenses.

There's Leon, like we agreed. Charlie and Sammy and me climb in the car to nail down our plan.

What's that smell?

"I was running late," Leon says. "I didn't have time for breakfast at home, so I picked something up."

Stupid bastard is eating a BEC. On a roll at least, not a bagel.

"I brought coffee. Regular okay with everybody?"

Who the hell caters a crime?

Leon, that's who.

So is the mailman gone?

"He left right on time for church. All clear!"

All right, then. It's go time.

* * *

"Who the hell are you people?"

Shit. Shitshitshitshitshit. What's mailboy's wife doing here? Sniffling... tissues...is she sick?

"But I saw him leave!" Leon sputters.

Saw *him* leave, but not the wife?

"Like I said, I was running late. I thought she'd already gone."

Leon *thought*? What *with*, the moron? And he was running late, but he stopped for a BEC?

"You watched our house?" yells Fat Man's wife. "You saw my husband leave for church? What are you—are you gonna hurt me?"

Oh, Jesus, now she's crying on top of yelling. And Sammy's reaching into his—oh, no, God, he didn't!

"Shut up," he shouts, "or I'll give you something to cry about!"

"You gonna *shoot* me?"

Didn't I say no guns? What are we, a bunch of assassins?

* * *

At least she's quieter now, with the gag in her mouth. Still crying, though.

"You said you saw tons of expensive shit," says Charlie. "This don't look so expensive to me."

What does it matter *now* what I said, when we got a scared woman tied up in the next room? Which makes this robbery, not burglary, by the way. And with Sammy carrying a piece, we're not just talking armed robbery—we're kidnappers, now.

And worst of all, Sammy's right. There's not much here worth taking.

"So what do we do?" he demands.

We cut out, I tell him. No harm, no foul.

"She saw our faces, Johnny. We can't just leave her here."

He's right again.

Shit.

Shitshitshitshitshit.

* * *

"Who you got there? Why you bring her in our house?"

I can hardly understand what Lynette's saying—her voice always gets squeaky when she's mad.

"Is that—is that Sara Jane?"

I guess, if that's Fat Man's wife's name. Don't look like a Sara Jane to me, but—

"What the *hell* you done, Johnny?"

Goddammit, I hate when her voice gets all squeaky like that.

* * *

"She's your wife," Sammy says, "so she can't testify against you."

Him being all smart again. I don't remind him that my wife can testify against *him*. I mean, he's still got the gun. All he has to do is move his finger,

225

and—

"Kidnappers."

What?

"You said we were kidnappers. So let's *be* kidnappers."

He's just repeating himself now.

"Kidnapping means ransom. So let's get us some millions of dollars in ransom."

Look at Sammy, there, having ideas. I hate that.

We *could* ask for a million or two, I guess, maybe more. The wife isn't bad looking—or at least she wouldn't be, when she's not sick and crying and tied up and in her bathrobe. Fat Man might want her back. We could—we could even ask for the whole fifteen mil. Go for the fucking prize.

We're gonna need a note, I say.

Sammy laughs. "Nobody does notes, these days. We'll call. With an app that changes my voice."

His voice? Whose idea *was* this, anyway?

"*Your* idea was a burglary, and look how *that* turned out."

Fine, like it's *my* fault Leon fucked up.

"Yeah? And who brought Leon in on it?"

Fucking Sammy. Thinks he knows everything. Fine, so he'll make the call. We'll give the mailman a couple of hours to—

"He can't get millions of dollars from an ATM. He'll need time to arrange a wire transfer."

Like Sammy can even *spell* "wire transfer." The check-cashing place is as far as he ever goes. But if he can get us the prize….

So Charlie goes to pick up a burner phone, and Sammy will make the call. And Leon? No one trusts Leon to do any damn thing.

Now all we gotta do is keep the wife on ice. For a week, tops. Just till the ransom is paid.

* * *

"You not gonna keep her here," Lynette squeaks. "Not in *my* house."

226

Fine, rub it in my face her parents left her this house. Luck, that's all that was. It's not my fault mine's bad....

"You gotta take her home, Johnny. When those guys leave, you take Sara Jane back home."

I tell her why I can't, but she's not listening. Do I have to paint her a picture of what'll happen if I keep Sammy from getting his hands on millions of dollars by giving the mailman back his wife for free?

"Sammy, Sammy, Sammy! Who died and made Sammy boss? You got a mind of your own, man. Do the right thing."

The right thing. What the hell *is* that even? I know what it's not: going to jail. Or bleeding out on the floor because I pissed Sammy off.

I finally manage to convince her. At least she's not squeaking anymore. She's not talking to me at all.

* * *

Fat Man's voice is all shaky when Sammy puts him on speaker.

"Let me talk to her, please. Sara Jane? Sara, honey?"

Sammy tells him he's got to pay up first.

"How do I know you haven't killed her already?"

Sammy figured he'd ask that. That's why he took her picture with today's newspaper. He texts it...and mailguy is crying now. Jeez.

"I'll give you anything you want," he whimpers. "Just give me back my wife. *Please.*"

This is going easier than I'da thought. I mean, if someone took Lynette, I'd—I'd—well, I wouldn't cry, I'll tell you that much. If anyone hurt her...I'd kill him, I guess. But I wouldn't fucking *cry.*

* * *

Sara Jane—that's her name, right?—she looks a lot better when Lynette's cleaned her up. And she's not crying and sniffling anymore. She's a little big for Lynette's clothes—but I mean that in a good way. 'Course, I'd never tell Lynette that. I don't want her squeaking at me.

"Can I at least talk to my husband? I won't say anything, I promise. I'm begging you. I just want to know he's okay."

Of course, *he's* okay. He's at home, doing just fine.

"You don't know that. The man can barely take care of himself without me. He's probably forgot to take his medication…please, let me just remind him?"

"Why you don't let her talk to her husband?" says Lynette. "What would it hurt?"

I pull her to the side, remind her about the plan, and everything working out fine so far. For once, *we're* gonna be the winners.

"Oh, I forgot. You can't do nothing unless Sammy says so."

She knows that's not true. I mean, this whole thing was my idea—at least, it started *out* my idea.

"So you can let her call her husband!"

* * *

"Whatcha need the burner for?"

Like it's any of Charlie's business what I need the phone for.

"Did Sammy say it's okay?"

Why does everybody act like Sammy's the one in charge? I am—so I take the phone from Charlie, and that's all there is to it.

I tell Fat Man's wife just to say hi and remind him about his pills, nothing more.

"Of course, of course, whatever you say!"

Lynette hands her the phone, but once she's dialed, I take it back and hold it, so I can hang up if she says anything we don't want.

"Lee? Lee, baby, it's me."

"Sara Jane? Are you okay? Tell me you're okay!"

"I can't talk long, Lee. I just wanted to remind you about your pills."

"My—"

"Hush up and listen, baby. You got to take the pills that are next to my nail polish in the cabinet twice a day—one in the morning, one at night."

"The pills—?"

"The ones next to my nail polish are the twice-a-day ones. The ones on the lower shelf are only once a day. You understand, Lee?"

"The pills next to the nail polish. Right."

"Twice a day, right. I love you, Lee."

"I love you, too, Sara—"

I hang up. No need to listen to their lovey-dovey stuff.

* * *

Sammy rags me about letting Sara Jane call her husband. I tell him just look how calm she is now. It's better not to have a crying woman around the house, let alone a crying woman *and* a squeaking woman. Now all we have to do is wait for the wire transfer.

Our prize. We're finally gonna get the prize.

* * *

You always think they'll come with lights and sirens, the cops. But not these. We didn't even see them until they filled the street, and some asshole was on a bullhorn, calling himself a "negotiator."

"This is because you let her use the goddamn phone," Sammy snarls.

All she did was tell her husband about the pills next to the nail polish.

"Next to the nail polish? What the fuck does *nail polish* have to do with anything?"

It's where his pills were, no big deal.

"No big deal? It gave the cops time to track the location of the burner, you nitwit. And now we got a police negotiator outside the house!"

Sure, like it's all *my* fault. I mean, *he's* King Kidnapper, right? Now how are we supposed to get out of this mess?

"We gotta make a deal," says Sammy with his giant brain. "Trade them a way out for one of the hostages."

One of the—we only have *one* hostage.

"We got the two women. We can give them Lynette."

Give them my *wife*? Put my wife in the hands of some deep-state law-enforcement asshole who'd turn off his bodycam and waterboard her as soon as look at her? Gun or no gun, Sammy, nobody uses my wife as a bargaining chip.

Oh, fuck. Where's all this blood coming from?

* * *

"I love you, Johnny. It's gonna be okay."

Lynette has this big stupid smile on her face. I wanna tell her to shut up: my leg is killing me, and the deep state is gonna take me to some black site somewhere, and I'll never see her again…but she's saying something about me being a hero, beating Sammy up and saving her and Sara Jane from him. I try to correct her, but she's squeezing my hand and motioning her head toward the cop sitting outside my hospital room. She may be squeaky, sometimes, but she's a good woman, and I'm just a knucklehead who's unworthy of her love.

Okay, I guess we'll wait and see how this all plays out.

She tells me Fat Man and Sara Jane moved away already, bought themselves a mansion, and hired a shit-ton of guards.

Moved away *already*? Can't say I blame them, but how long I been out cold?

"Three days, Johnny. Three whole days!"

She squeezes again, and her hand is soft in mine. I forgot how soft her skin is. She always lotions, keeps herself looking good. How could I have forgot about that?

Shit. Shitshitshitshit. I'm still gonna end up in jail.

"You gotta have hope, Johnny. It never hurts to hope."

Great. Now she's talking like the mailman. At least she doesn't—

"You know what? I went by the bodega this morning. I was feeling lucky."

She reaches into her purse and pulls out a scratch-off. A goddamn scratch-off. Doesn't she know the system is rigged? They're never gonna let people like us win.

"The lady who sold me the ticket told me her daughter just made a million dollars off TikTok videos. She's gonna buy them a house and get out of the neighborhood. You see, Johnny? Luck can come to anyone!"

Yeah, sure, right.

My leg hurts like hell, but I force a smile. "All right, Lynette," I say. "Who knows? Maybe you're right. Maybe this time *we'll* get a prize."

Passion

opened May 9, 1994, at the Plymouth Theatre, New York

"Happiness"
"First Letter"
"Second Letter"
"Third Letter"
"Fourth Letter"
"I Read"
"Transition #1"
"Garden Sequence"
"Three Days"
"Transition #2"
"Happiness (Trio, Fifth Letter)"
"Transition #3"
"Three Weeks"
"God, You Are So Beautiful"
"I Wish I Could Forget You"
"Transition #4"
"Soldiers' Gossip #1"
"Flashback"
"Sunrise Letter"
"Is This What You Call Love?"
"Soldiers' Gossip #2"
"Transition #5"

"Transition #6"
"Forty Days"
"Loving You"
"Transition #7"
"Soldiers' Gossip #3"
"Giorgio, I Didn't Tell You in My Letter"
"La Pace Sulla Terra (Peace on Earth)"
"Farewell Letter"
"Just Another Love Story (Happiness/Is This What You Call Love?)"
"No One Has Ever Loved Me"
"Happiness" (reprise)
"The Duel"
"Final Transition"
"Finale (Your Love Will Live in Me)"

Music and lyrics by Stephen Sondheim.
Book by James Lapine.

I Read

by Gabriel Valjan

Suspects don't usually walk into police stations before they're named as suspects, but this one did.

The captain assigned the interview to Detective Bono, who downloaded the file, printed it out, and read what was available on the deceased before proceeding to Observation.

Bono studied the woman through the one-way glass window. "Is that her?" he asked Officer Malo, who manned the camera's controls.

"That's her."

"Why is she here?"

"No idea."

Bono drove past the comment. "She's either guilty of something or innocent."

"It's usually one or the other, Lieutenant."

Bono skimmed the printout's top page. "Or she's mental."

"Where there's no expectations," Malo said, "there are no disappointments."

"What the hell does that mean?"

"Go in and detect."

* * *

Bono entered the room, the folder open to a page. He wished to appear engrossed in the document. That was theater, an act to make the interviewee think the police were unprepared, especially on a case where the deceased had been buried weeks ago. He proceeded *in medias res*, without introducing himself.

"I'm confused as to why you came in, Mrs. Tarchetti."

"It's Miss, Detective. Miss Luisa Tarchetti. I'm here as a preemptive measure. George Bachetti—the deceased—was married."

"And you are not, so you two were having an affair, is that it?"

"Yes. We worked together."

Bono reached for a pen. He clicked it for effect. "Occupation?"

"Ghost singer."

"Pardon me?"

"I fill in for major talent."

That made Bono raise an eyebrow. He took in what was visible of her above the table, the iceberg above the wood. In his experience, most voices never matched their bodies. Bobby Caldwell was whiter than Uncle Ben's rice but sounded darker than Mississippi mud. Luisa was frumpy and frayed as a tired washcloth.

"You were his mistress?"

"Yes," she said. "I have no illusions. I know I'm as homely as Janis Joplin."

"But what a set of pipes on Janis."

She mentioned a song, and he said he had heard it and liked it. He named the singer, but she corrected him and said that *she* had sung it—had been paid well for it, too.

"You ghost-sang it?" he asked.

"Subbing for talent occurs in every industry, Detective, from music to porn to publishing. It's an open secret."

"With your talent, why aren't you a lead act?"

"Because image is what sells. Giorgio knew it."

He flipped the page. "Giorgio? I thought Mr. Bachetti's name was George."

She smiled. "His first name was Giorgio. He said Americans couldn't pronounce Gio, so he went with George. Showbiz is like that: nothing is what it seems."

"I appreciate your candor, but why exactly are you here? There's no active homicide investigation."

"Has the toxicology report come in?"

"You expect us to find something odd?"

"George didn't die the way the media said he did."

Bono searched the folder. "If not a heart attack, then what?"

"Poison."

"Poison?" He tried not to look surprised. "Poisoned by whom?"

"His wife, of course."

Bono leaned forward. "And you think she'll accuse *you* of poisoning him?"

"Yes."

Her monosyllabic answers and demeanor made him think she was experienced, possibly from negotiations with agents or studio execs like George, because she was cool and unflappable. The wrongly accused are passionate about asserting their innocence.

"And there are no other suspects?" he asked. "I mean, he was cheating on his wife, in a competitive industry—and then, of course, there's fraud."

"Fraud?"

"Ghost singing. Tell me about the singer you're ghosting."

"Julie is the sweetest thing, a real gem. She wouldn't hurt a fly."

Bono perused a page. "You said ghost singing is an open secret. What about you and George? Was *that* an open secret? Did his missus know about you two?"

She nodded. "She'll say he threatened to end our affair."

"And did he?"

"No."

He noticed the book next to her. "What are you reading?"

"My favorite novel," she said. "Rousseau's *La Nouvelle Héloïse*. Know it?"

"I can't say that I do. I read people, not books."

"And is that how you solve crimes, Detective?"

"That, and I observe and listen."

"Listen for what?"

"Mistakes. Mistakes are like echoes. I must confess, Miss Tarchetti, I'm confused. The Medical Examiner's report says he died of a heart attack."

"Read deeper, and you'll find there was quinine in his system. Quinine affects the heart."

He consulted the report and found quinine, a medication known for treating malaria. The M.E. noted that George had used it for its off-label treatment of leg cramps, something the FDA frowned upon and had made illegal in the US. George Bachetti apparently traveled a lot, and the report said his London physician had prescribed it.

"I have to ask," Bono said. "Do you have access to quinine?"

"It's more common than you think, Detective. Do you enjoy tonic water?"

"Not my thing."

"Gin and tonic?"

"Please answer the question. Do you have access to quinine or not?"

"Yes. I use it with my bees."

She kept a beehive. Like all converts to a hobby, she rhapsodized on and on about the importance of the insect, how the bee was nature's workaholic. She quoted Einstein's statement that humanity would cease to exist within four years if bees disappeared from the planet. Her honeybees, she said, descended from her penthouse, high above the streets, in search of flowers and gardens.

"You know a lot about bees, Miss Tarchetti."

"I read."

"But you haven't told me about the quinine."

"I use it to train them to avoid certain flowers. Quinine tastes bitter, Detective. I maintain copies of the local flora in a greenhouse on my rooftop and taint the petals with quinine, and the bees learn to avoid those flowers. That's how I control the honey the hive produces."

* * *

Bono called on Donna Bachetti, the dead man's widow, unannounced, because he wanted the element of surprise. He wouldn't allow her the opportunity to mount a scripted defense or have her attorneys present.

Clara, the maid, directed him to the living room.

The apartment was tricked out with all the creature comforts, from a massive flat-screen TV to a palatial deck with a view of the skyline that rivaled LA's. While he waited for Mrs. Bachetti, he admired the bar. The counter's dark polished wood shone under the lights. He leaned over and pulled out the soda gun. He was reading the labels when he heard her voice behind him.

"It looks complicated, but it isn't. Fancy a drink?"

"With twelve buttons, I'd die of thirst before I figured it out."

"Five buttons for carbonated and five for non-carbonated drinks, plus two for still and carbonated water. Electronics and hydraulics make four hundred drinks possible."

He turned the display so she could see it. "And these two below the one for soda?"

She squinted. "T for tonic and Q for quinine. Clara says you're a detective. What can I do for you?"

As he racked the soda gun, her cell chirped. She took the call. It cost him his momentum, but the poor soul on the other end of the call received the full treatment. There was no profanity, but she took the caller to the woodshed and showed him the short stool and the noose made of piano wire. When she terminated the call, she said, "You were saying?"

"T and Q, although I'm mostly interested in quinine."

She seemed nonplussed. "I'm sorry, I don't follow."

"Your husband took quinine."

She shrugged. "No secret there, Detective. George suffered from terrible leg cramps, especially after transatlantic flights. He took pills for them. Anything else?"

"Pills prescribed by his physician in the UK?"

"That's right. Why do you ask?"

"Did he enjoy quinine water, or gin and tonics?"

"He imbibed as much as the next fellow, but he was not a problem drinker. Why?"

"The M.E. indicated no family history of heart disease, yet he died of cardiac arrest."

"It happens, Detective. What's the point of all these questions?"

"For someone who lost her husband two months ago, you don't seem broken up by it."

She met his gaze, eye to eye. "I don't know what you're implying. I loved my husband, Detective, but I didn't kill him. We had our difficulties."

"Financial?"

"No."

"Infidelity?"

"Infidelities."

"Infidelities plural?"

"Yes, plural. What are you suggesting?"

"A motive."

She shook her head and smiled. "I killed my paycheck, is that what you think?"

"Did you?"

"If I wanted to be rid of my husband, I'd've made him walk the gauntlet in divorce court."

"Some women can't afford it," he said, as she stepped behind the bar. He heard ice drop into a glass.

"I'm reaching for the soda gun," she said, "so don't shoot."

He smiled.

"You really need to do your research, Detective. George made good money, but I came by *my* money the old-fashioned way; I inherited it. I own this building and several others."

"The mistresses didn't bother you?"

"You think I stay home and crochet?" She sprayed something into the glass. "Don't worry, it's ginger ale." She pressed another button, and out came something red, which he was certain was grenadine. "I'll admit I never understood why he carried on with that hunchback Luisa. What she lacks in looks, she must make up for in the bedroom." She found a cherry for garnish, dropped it into the drink, and handed him the glass. "Here, it's on the house."

"A Shirley Temple?"

"When you're ready for the adults in the room, I'll make you a real drink." She wrote on a business card. "Call this number. My secretary can provide you with a copy of my daily schedule for the last decade."

"You document everything?"

"Lesson learned after dealing with the IRS and corporate lawyers."

* * *

Julie Hobson entered the room, and he understood without explanation why she was the face of the label's award-winning albums. Technology in the studio could make almost anyone sound ethereal. Fans understood that singers used Auto-Tune to correct pitch, and some lip-synched their songs in live performance.

She introduced herself as Jules and saw his confusion. "My friends call me that," she said.

They sat. He felt old, as in pervert old. She was a midlife crisis personified. Perky for personality and elsewhere, she was like fresh laundry, because you wanted to hug her, feel her warmth, smell her. Petite and charismatic, she commanded a room as if she were the first woman president of the United States. He apologized for being blunt.

"Tell me about your relationship with George Bachetti."

"Strictly professional, one hundred percent."

"Nothing romantic, nothing sexual?"

"Eew, God, no." The words alone would kill a thousand male fantasies. "He was like my grandpa. No offense."

"None taken."

A maid appeared and served non-alcoholic drinks. While he sipped his virgin mimosa, his eyes scanned the walls, hung with awards, gold records, and photos with celebrities. He had to ask her. "How do you live with the F word?"

"You mean fame?"

"No, fraud."

She smiled the smile of a kid with its hand caught in the cookie jar. "You know about Luisa?"

"I know, yes, but the fact that it's accepted doesn't change the reality that ghost singing is fraud."

"Whatever the art form, Detective, there's illusion and there's consent."

"And money," he said.

"And where there's money, miracles happen."

He enjoyed another taste of his drink. "Philosophical, but explain that to me."

She leaned into a cushion. "A bestselling writer hits a dry spell or submits something subpar, and the publisher finds a scribe to fill in the holes. Money. Marketing. Momentum."

She'd gone into the business with her eyes wide open, she told him. She didn't want to have to hawk knickknacks on cable TV when the hot flashes came for her. She had started as a kid doing commercials for toothpaste and then fast food, and now she was a veteran. She had a voice and could dance. She was good, but not *that* good.

As she talked about the lifespan of talented women in the entertainment industries, he thought of his last web search. He'd learned that a typical worker bee lived a month, while—assuming there was no regicide—the hive's queen lived two to three years.

"Image," he said.

"Excuse me?"

"You have it, but Luisa Tarchetti doesn't."

"No, but she has perfect pitch, like Debbie Gibson, which is very rare, and her voice can cover six octaves, like Axl Rose. Unfortunately, she's as ugly as a monkfish."

He thought of the widow and the Shirley Temple. "And George and Luisa had a thing."

"What of it?"

"You knew?"

"Who didn't?"

She explained that she'd been to parties at George's where drugs and drinks flowed. She recalled that George was frisky as an octopus with Luisa. They carried on, and there was no sign of their passion waning.

"And his wife knew?"

"It occurred under her own roof. So long as the bank accounts were fat and the cash registers rang like angels getting their wings, she didn't care. Nothing could ruin her life inside the castle."

"No trouble in paradise, then?"

"None I could tell."

She brought up another party at his place. She'd had too much to drink and staggered into the bedroom to use the en suite bathroom. At George's desk, she found a box stuffed with letters.

She stopped, lost in the chatter in her mind. "Where was I?"

"Letters."

"They were in Luisa's handwriting. Powerful, romantic, heartbreaking stuff, a real whirlwind of emotion. Poetic, too."

"Flowery language?"

"No, not at all. More like a song. The refrain was about a jewel, a priceless gem, but there were two particular lines that haunted me."

"Haunted you how?"

"The two lines were: 'A thousand flights I would captain over oceans and streams/For the wish of every woman to be seen and not in her own dreams.' I've got to tell you, reading that gave me the chills and sobered me up. I felt terrible for her."

"Because she was so in love with him?"

"That, and because I had a conversation with George, a few weeks earlier. He planned to break up with her. I felt awful, reading all that passion and knowing a train wreck was around the corner."

Bono asked one last question. "You keep tonic water?"

"Sorry, I don't. I hate the taste of it."

* * *

Officers brushed past Luisa as Malo read the warrant. He informed her that the police were authorized to search her property for quinine and seize her electronic devices. She was advised to stay where she stood and not interfere with them. Bono was the last to enter the apartment.

"Please hand me your cell phone," he said.

She did. "You won't find anything on it."

"I know. I won't find any calls or texts to George." Seeing officers march by with her computer, he said, "I don't expect to find emails, because you write letters."

A police officer interrupted. "Lieutenant, we're not equipped to search a beehive."

A look of panic on her face. "You can't. Your warrant doesn't extend to bees."

The officer shot her a look. "You got something to hide, lady?"

She dished attitude back. "Those bees are a protected species, and disturbing their hive will raise an alarm. They'll swarm, at best; kill the queen, at worst."

The officer was all testosterone. "I heard smoke calms them. If you interfere, who knows what else will go up in smoke."

Luisa smiled. "Killing those bees would be a felony." She eyed him up and down, which unnerved him. "Go ahead and smoke them. Be sure to keep your uniform on."

This confused him, so he looked to Bono, who answered his unasked question. "Dark clothes make bees aggressive."

Luisa stepped closer to the officer. "An adult male can survive a thousand stings, but some of my bees are Africanized and have evolved to sting like an executioner wasp. The pain is excruciating. One sting, and you'll jump from the deck and consider yourself fortunate if you're dead before you hit the ground."

He sneered, as if he wanted to call her an ugly bitch, but Bono ordered him away.

She faced him. "Why are you doing this to me?"

"You did it to yourself, but I admire your strategy."

"What are you talking about?" she asked.

243

"Thanks to you, I learned a lot about bees, like how you introduce a queen to the hive, for example. Do it all at once, and the workers will kill her. Similarly, if you administer quinine in a massive dose, the recipient gets dizzy, his ears ring, and over time his heart stops. Time is the key, and that's where you were brilliant. Slow and steady doses—the way you introduce a queen to the hive—keep the drug at therapeutic levels."

"Why are you talking about *bees*, for God's sake?" she demanded.

He told her. "The way you introduce a new queen to the hive is to present her inside a cage, accompanied by a piece of sugar candy. By the time her attendants have eaten the candy, they've become acquainted with her, and she can be released into the hive. You did the same thing when you gave George quinine little by little. The difference is that the slow approach has a happy result with bees, but it eventually killed George." He produced a pair of handcuffs.

"What are you doing?"

"I'm going to put you in a cage, Luisa."

"But I *told* you about the quinine. I keep it for my bees. You have no evidence."

He handcuffed her, Mirandized her, and turned her around to face him.

"You wanted me to think his wife killed him, but it was you."

"You're wrong. I *loved* him."

He shook his head. "Maybe at first. But your letter gave you away."

"What letter?"

"The one you wrote about Julie, which he found. Donna showed it to me. I read it."

She went pale.

"The funny thing," Bono went on, "is that he loved you enough to let you go, so you could pursue her—but you didn't give him the chance." He took her arm and steered her to the door. Outside, a patrol car was waiting for them.

"You and Julie would have made a nice couple," he said.

"How did you know I was writing about her?"

He leaned down, whispered into her ear. "You wrote about a priceless gem, a jewel. And her friends call her Jules."

Her eyes went wide, and she put a hand to her mouth.

"I told you," he said, "mistakes are echoes. And I read people."

Act VI

The 2000s and 2020s

Road Show

opened November 18, 2008, at the Newman Theater, New York

"Waste"
"It's In Your Hands Now"
"Gold!"
"Brotherly Love"
"The Game"
"Addison's Trip"
"That Was a Year"
"Isn't He Something!"
"Land Boom!"
"Talent"
"You"
"The Best Thing That Ever Has Happened"
"The Game" (reprise)
"Addison's City"
"Boca Raton"
"Get Out"
"Go"
"Finale"

Music and lyrics by Stephen Sondheim.
Book by John Weidman.

Brotherly Love

by Cheryl A. Head

1933

The seven-story building in east Manhattan was surrounded by taller structures with windows trimmed in Christmas lights. I doubted anyone would notice us on the rooftop at four on a weekday morning. Two men, one in an overcoat cradling another guy wrapped in a quilt, hunched in despair like the lovers in the last act of *Romeo and Juliet*.

Our story was also tragic but not one of romance.

Mama always said I should look after my younger brother. Wilson was the charming rogue, the ne'er do well, the fuckup, but always the apple of her eye. She loved his boldness. His sparkle. His glide. So much so that she'd tricked herself into thinking he was carefree rather than completely lacking in empathy.

* * *

A light snow was falling when I entered a phone booth on Central Park West to call him. I let the phone ring three times. Hung up. Called again and allowed three more rings. That was our signal. Charles, the desk clerk, didn't stir when I entered the small lobby. He'd been the guardian of this building on West 74th since I was a schoolboy and had seemed old even then.

I tiptoed to the elevator and pushed the button for the fourth floor. If anything would wake the neighbors at this hour, it would be the ring of the lift, so I quickly exited, moved to the stairwell, and climbed to the fifth floor. I rapped lightly at the door, and Willy opened right away. He was wearing a T-shirt and shorts, the quilt Mama had sewed for the guest bedroom draped around his shoulders.

"What is it, Addy? What the hell is so important?"

I pushed past him into the narrow hall, my wet overshoes squishing on the marble floor. I switched on the overhead light in the living room and sat on the sofa without removing my coat. Decembers were cold in these old buildings, with their high ceilings and aging wood-framed windows.

"Why'd you do it?" I asked my brother.

Wilson pulled the quilt ends tighter, padded barefoot to a chair across from me, and flopped down. "I don't know what you're talking about." He stifled a yawn and closed his eyes.

"Running that stock scam. Flashing around those certificates like they were worth something."

His eyes fluttered but didn't open. He snuffed another yawn.

"Look at me, Willy. Mama called tonight, crying. She told me all about it."

Our mother was no fragile flower. She'd raised two boys and managed our household without much involvement from her successful CEO husband. I'd witnessed her negotiate a bulk meat sale with a wholesale butcher and stare down the bully in apartment 520 who everyone knew beat his wife. But now, nearly eighty, with chronic gout, Mama lived in a home for the elderly.

Wilson finally peered at me with one eye. "What's the harm? I sold a few dreams to some old people. Most of them haven't had anything to look forward to in years. They all seemed happy when I left."

"Not anymore. The son of one of the residents—a Broadway producer—got wise to your phony goldmine scheme. He's bringing in the police. These are Mama's friends, or used to be, not just marks you con and bounce. Even if you hit the road for a while, Mama can't. She'll get all the blame."

Wilson didn't respond. Still grasping the blanket, he sat up and reached for the bronze cigarette box on the coffee table. His bleary eyes, bare feet, and bunched garb brought back memories of us as kids, when we had a bond linked by blood and true affection. But time had revealed a psychological chasm wider than our two-year age difference.

"Why are you here, Addy? You want me to apologize?"

His legs draped over the chair's armrest, a lock of hair dangling on his forehead, he blew smoke rings. My brother was still boyishly attractive. Charismatic. Family, friends, even some enemies had been caught up in his charm at one time or another. But I was over it. When Mama called last night, she'd already survived a couple of days of confrontation and ostracism. And there was something in her voice I'd never heard before. Shame. It broke my heart and gave me resolve.

"We thought putting the apartment in your name would finally give you some stability."

"We?" Wilson glared. His resentment shimmied across the floor. "You and Mama are always meddling in my affairs, always trying to make me beholden to you. You enjoy it, don't you?" He stubbed his cigarette into the ashtray.

"Where's the money?"

"It's spoken for. I have a line on a real-estate investment."

I looked past Wilson to the dining room's French doors. The six-room apartment was a symbol of upper-middle-class status: Italian marble, lead windows, wood built-ins. The side tables held Tiffany lamps and heavy crystal ashtrays. The mantle displayed framed photos of our American Dream family. When Papa paid off the mortgage, we celebrated with catered lobster and steak, and I had my first taste of champagne. But we also learned that day of Wilson's shellfish allergy, and he had to be rushed to the hospital. That's the way it always was: Mama, Papa, and me taking care of Willy. Those family dynamics, like these rooms, had pretty much remained the same for thirty years.

I circled the living room. Some of the paintings had been removed, their hooks still in the walls. The print Mama adored of some foreign prince, the framed sheet music for "Blue Skies," Papa's favorite song, signed by Irving Berlin himself. They were gone, faded squares marking their outlines. I peered into the dining room. The chandelier was missing, and Mama's sideboard was angled away from the wall.

"Are you selling the furnishings?"

Wilson ignored my question. He pulled the quilt tighter and tucked his feet beneath him. "Don't you have someplace else to be, big brother?" he said. "Like your own home?"

"I mean it, Willy. What's going on? What happened to the paintings? The chandelier?"

"I sold a few things. I was going to tell you later. I have a buyer for the place." He reached for another cigarette. "I'm leaving in a week for Boca Raton."

I slumped onto the couch. Stunned. Staring at the carpet. Mama and Papa had busted their butts to hold onto this place. To keep it in the family. "If you sell the apartment, it'll break Mama's heart. To her, it's part of the family legacy. She was so hopeful."

"Hope is for the little people. It's only what can be counted that counts. Didn't we always say that?"

I shook my head. "*You* always said that."

"Lighten up, Addy. We used to have lots of good times together. I know you're still looking out for me. That's why you came around, isn't it? To warn me about the producer and the police?"

I wanted Wilson to own up to what he'd done and agree to return the money. But he never would. This time, he'd gone too far. He'd disgraced both Mama and the memory of our deceased father. Wilson had wasted his life.

"So, you're going away." I smiled and spread my arms. "Come give your brother a hug."

He hesitated a moment, then rose. I pulled him to me and felt the weight of his head on my shoulder. Just like when we were boys.

I reached for one of the two crystal ashtrays and brought it down hard on Willy's head. His body went limp, but I held him up. I touched the back of his head, and my fingers came away red.

I lifted him over my shoulder and moved to the door. The empty hallway was easy to navigate, and holding onto the railing, I managed the flight-and-a-half of stairs to the roof. Many apartment buildings have an alarm on the roof door, but this one didn't. I shoved it open, and the frigid air slapped my face.

The snow had changed from light to steady. Most of the windows in the surrounding buildings were dark, but a few were still illuminated in the city that never sleeps. I carried Willy to the rear of the building, where the mechanical room faced a brick wall and service alley, and placed him on a grate where warm air escaped the building. I squatted to catch my breath.

As kids, we played on this roof. Shadowboxing like Jack Dempsey defending his heavyweight championship, firing our toy six-guns at imaginary rustlers like Tom Mix, our cowboy hero. As teens, we leaned on this very wall, smoking cigarettes and sipping cognac stolen from Papa's study.

I assessed my coat: wet with blood and melting snow. I'd have to get rid of it, along with the bloody quilt. Bag 'em and stick them in the trash chute, and they'd be burned to ash in the basement incinerator. I also had to make sure there was no blood in the hallway or on the stairs. My fingerprints would be all over the apartment, but that wouldn't be unusual. I'd be sure, though, to wipe my prints from the roof door and railing.

Mama would be inconsolable over Willy's death. I'd tell her he never sounded so down in the dumps. He admitted to the stock fraud and was so ashamed he couldn't live with himself. I'd tell her I went to the apartment to take care of him.

My last problem was how to get out of the building unnoticed. The daily newspapers were delivered to the lobby at four-forty-five, and Charles would sort them and deliver them to the apartments. If I was lucky, I could slip out the service door while he was on his rounds.

My watch read four twenty-two. I had to act now, before the early risers began to stir. I lifted my brother and cradled him in my arms. He felt heavier than before.

When he spoke, my legs buckled, and we collapsed in a heap.

"What—what did you say?" I asked, staring into his blinking eyes. His eyelashes and hair were coated with snow.

"Thanks for looking out for me, Addy," he whispered, then raised a hand to touch his face. "My head hurts. Oh, Jesus, why is it so cold?"

He instinctively gathered the quilt around him. I yanked it away and propped him up. "Come on. Lean on me."

I drag-walked him to the three-foot roof wall, squatted to secure his legs in my arms, and lifted him to the ledge. He resisted my efforts but was too groggy to fight.

"What kind of game is this, Addy?" he asked.

"No game, brother. Not this time," I replied and shoved him over the edge.

* * *

I wiped the floor, doorknobs, and railings with water and soap, then threw the blood-soaked coat and quilt and the wet rags down the trash chute. I took the stairs to the lobby. I was lucky: Charles wasn't at the desk. I didn't look back as I exited the service entrance.

Traffic was light, and it was still snowing when I detoured into the park. Ten minutes later, I stopped at home to feed the cat. Then, for the second time in three hours, I walked to Willy's apartment.

Charles sat at the front desk. It was just after six, and I acted out a pantomime of concern for my brother. Strangely, I felt absolutely no remorse about what I'd done.

I called the police from Willy's apartment to report him missing, and when a couple of patrolmen arrived, they searched the apartment and the stairwell. One of them suggested they might look on the roof, and twenty minutes later, they returned with the news that Willy had been found in the alley. He'd apparently jumped from the rear of the building. Charles had identified him. I declined the cop's invitation to look at the body.

By eight thirty, the police were everywhere. The apartment door was open, and neighbors gathered in the hall for a peek at the goings on. I was tired and sat on the couch with my head in my hands. One of the cops had made a pot of coffee and offered me a cup. "No, thanks," I said.

An increase in activity at the door made me look up. An NYPD detective had arrived, and he was in conversation with Charles and one of the patrolmen. I caught him staring at me from the front door. A few minutes later, he came over and flipped open a notebook.

"Mr. Mizner, I'm Detective Hollis," he said, sitting where Willy had been a few hours ago. He looked at the side table, then placed his hat there. I was glad I'd remembered to take the ashtray with me. Hollis wasn't much older than me. Taller, thinner, maybe mid-thirties. His hat and overcoat were of good quality, and he wore crepe-soled brogues, the policeman's friend.

"Nice apartment," he said, looking around.

"It's been in our family thirty-five years," I said.

"You don't live here?"

"No. But I'm not far away—on 66th, just off the park. This is—was—my brother's place."

The detective jotted in his notebook. "Our officer found your brother in the alley just after seven. It appeared he'd fallen from the roof an hour or two before. Oddly, no one saw or heard anything." The detective paused to look at me. I returned the stare. "When it's snowing like this, the city can be very quiet. Snow muffles the chaos."

Papa had introduced us to many patrolmen over the years—New York's finest, he called them. Most were working-class guys who started on foot patrol and retired still walking a beat. This guy was different. He dressed well and talked like he read poetry instead of police reports.

"I have to tell my mother what's happened," I said. "She shouldn't hear about this on the radio or from one of the neighbors."

"I understand she's at Chapins, in Queens. The old folks' home."

"A residence for elderly women," I corrected him.

The detective read my tone. "I see. Well, I need you to stick around. I have questions for you."

"I told the two officers everything I know. I don't have anything to add."

"There are always things witnesses remember later."

He noticed me flinch at the word "witnesses."

"We're interviewing the neighbors on this floor," Hollis continued. "And we've spoken with the desk clerk. He says he's known you and your brother since you were boys."

I nodded. I had to play it cool with this policeman. Willy and I had known men like him. Willy called them "misses," as in "hit or miss." You'd hit on the guys you could con, but some men couldn't be flattered, tempted, or strung along. They were the misses, and Hollis was one of them. But I had no choice.

"Charles has become a bit of a busybody in his old age."

Hollis studied me, then stood. "You can call your mother. Or I can send a patrol car to her, uh, residence, and one of our officers can speak with her. But like I said, I need you here."

I glared at him.

He conferred with someone from the medical examiner's office while I phoned Mama. When I heard her voice, mine choked. When I got out the story I wanted her to believe, she screamed. And when the phone suddenly disconnected, I crumpled to the floor. It was a few minutes before I regained my composure. When I did, Detective Hollis was staring.

"I still need to ask some questions," he said, gazing down at me. "Let's talk in your brother's room."

He headed for the middle bedroom. I pulled myself up and followed, found him standing at Willy's dresser, holding a framed photograph of the two of us when we were thirteen and eleven. "The Mizner brothers. The golden boy Wilson, and the level-headed Addison." His voice held a bit of derision. "A few of the neighbors said you were inseparable as boys. The janitor says he had to shoo you off the roof all the time."

"So?"

"So, is it true you and your brother haven't been so cozy since your mother moved out?"

"We haven't seen each other very much, the last couple of years."

"But you came over this morning because he called you and sounded suicidal?"

"I never said that. He called, upset, but I didn't think he'd kill himself. I'd never heard him sound so depressed, though, so I offered to come over."

"How long did it take for you to arrive?"

"Maybe a half hour. I got dressed and walked over."

"From 66th Street?"

"That's right."

"Did your brother say why he felt depressed?"

I sat on the bed, staring at the floor and forming my lie. I didn't want Hollis to know about the stock scam at Mom's residence. But maybe he already knew. "He'd had a business deal go bad." A lie built on an element of truth is always more effective.

"That's happened quite a bit, I understand." Now Hollis was sorting through the clothes hangers. "Lots of bad luck, I hear."

"He's had a few enterprises go south."

"Enterprises? I've heard they were more like shady deals."

"That's why he was feeling so down. He'd seen the error of his ways."

"Mr. Mizner, I received some news before I got here this morning. Your brother was assaulted before he fell to his death. Bashed on the head with a blunt object. So we're dealing with a homicide, not a suicide."

I felt blood rush to my face. *Damn. I thought sure the impact of a seven-story fall would cover up the head wound.*

Hollis watched my surprised reaction for a few seconds, then continued his perusal of the contents of Wilson's closet. Suddenly, he spun to face me. "Mizner, where's your overcoat?"

"My overcoat?"

"Yes. You didn't walk out in the snow without a coat, did you?"

"Uh, no. I guess it's in the hallway. There's a hat stand—"

"Let's go take a look," Hollis said, heading out the door.

"Here it is." I removed a worsted wool coat from the rack and handed it to the detective. "See, it's still a bit wet."

"Charles says this is Wilson's coat. He says your mother gave each of you boys an overcoat three Christmases ago. Yours was black, and your brother's was dark blue. He thought it was odd when he saw you wearing this blue one this morning."

"Well, Charles is wrong. He's a desk clerk, and not privy to everything that goes on in our family."

"Then where's Wilson's overcoat? It's not in the closet."

I shifted from one foot to the other and looked toward the front door. Two uniformed officers stood guard, their thumbs tucked in their belts. They eyed me like they already knew I was guilty.

"Why don't you sit down, Mr. Mizner," Hollis ordered.

I took the couch again, and Hollis returned to the armchair.

"Did you know your brother had purchased train tickets to Boca Raton? He was leaving next week."

"No," I lied. "I didn't know."

"Did you know he was selling the apartment?"

"Who told you that? Oh, let me guess: the desk clerk."

"Charles says Wilson has had a half-dozen potential buyers in and out of here over the last month."

I held the detective's eyes as they slowly shifted from me to his notebook. He was calculating my responses, sizing me up. He wouldn't say another word until I did.

"Look, I don't know where Willy's coat is. Maybe someone stole it. With strangers coming in and out of the apartment, who knows what's missing? Several valuable paintings that were in this room are gone." I gestured toward the discolored walls. "Along with other things."

"Like the match to this?" He raised the second crystal ashtray from the side table.

I'm positive he saw me swallow before I answered. "I don't recall that it was part of a pair."

Hollis again paused the interrogation. He scribbled in his notebook, then laid it aside and stared at me. I felt sweat gather at the nape of my neck. The detective thought he was smart, but so was I. He had no evidence I'd killed Wilson. He couldn't place me in the apartment when Wilson died, and he didn't have a motive. I was agitated but still in control. I never raised my voice, never let my gaze waver. I'd successfully negotiated scores of business deals, and this guy wasn't so different from others I'd convinced to buy my story.

"Here's what I think, Detective. My brother was feeling despondent. Maybe he was low on cash, regretting having to sell the apartment. Ashamed, even. He couldn't sleep, and he was overwhelmed with fear that he was a failure. He went up to the roof, and in a rash moment, he jumped."

"What about the head wound?"

"Maybe he lost his footing on the roof and bumped his head. It was snowing. And the other officer said he was barefooted. Now, if you don't have any other questions for me, I need to go see my mother. She isn't strong anymore, and this could kill her. Wilson was—"

"Her favorite?"

I stood. "I'm leaving, Detective Hollis, unless you plan to arrest me. May I have my overcoat?"

Hollis signaled one of the officers, who handed over the blue coat. The two policemen at the door reluctantly parted to let me by.

* * *

Charles registered surprise when he saw me come out of the elevator and avoided my eyes as I passed by the front desk.

"Good day, Mr. Mizner," he said, as I opened the front door.

"You talk too much, Charles," I replied.

I wished I'd worn gloves as I turned up the collar on Wilson's coat and headed south. When I got home, I'd shave and change clothes, then hail a taxi for the ride to Queens. But first, a quick errand.

The city always did a wonderful job of decorating for the holidays. In the daytime, the Christmas trees were unremarkable, but at night, with the colored lights sparkling and snow falling, they were magical.

I stepped into Central Park, where several inches of pristine snow covered the grass. A woman walked her dog on the slushy path, and a few people hurried along on their way to wherever. Nobody seemed interested when I paused at the first decorated tree. I crouched in front of a display of metal cubes painted to look like festive gifts and reached behind the pink box, groping until my fingers found the ashtray. I shoved it into the same pocket it had rested in a few hours earlier. I'd get rid of it for good near Mama's place.

I returned to the path and hurried to my apartment. Before I turned the key in the lock, I heard Cleveland's meow. I stepped inside—and stopped. Hollis and the two cops who had guarded Willy's apartment stood in my vestibule. I shoved both hands into my pockets.

"Found your coat," Hollis said. "In the basement of your brother's building." He signaled one of the officers, who held up two paper bags. Paper bags that ought to have been ashes by now. "Lucky for us, the maintenance man was running late for work this morning. He hadn't had time to fire up the incinerator."

The detective gave me a cocky smile. "What's that in your pocket, Mr. Mizner?"

Here We Are

opened October 22, 2023, at the Shed's Griffin Theatre, New York

ACT I

"Here We Are (Overture)"

"Who's Hungry? (The Road 1, Part 1)"

"Are We Not Blessed? (The Road 1, Part 2)"

"Only Just the End of the World (The Road 1, Part 3)"

"Café Everything (Toast 1)"

"Waiter's Song"

"If It Isn't the Food (The Road 2)"

"Bistro à La Mode (Toast 2)"

"It Is What It Is"

"Such an Afternoon (The Road 3)"

"Osteria Zeno (Toast 3)"

"The Soldier's Dream"

"Did You Leave a Tip? (The Road 4, Part 1)"

"Marianne (The Road 4, Part 2)"

"Oh, Look, Here's the Embassy!"

"Bishop's Song"

"End of Act One"

ACT II

"Entr'acte"

"Digestion"

"Shine"

"Hesitation"

"Double Duet"

"Marianne and the Bear (Interlude 1)"

"Wandering (Interlude 2)"

"Snow (Interlude 3)"

"Hesitation (reprise)"

"Exit Music"

Music and lyrics by Stephen Sondheim.
Book by David Ives.

Only Just the End of the World

by Alison Louise Hubbard

"I believe my husband is trying to kill me," Marianne whispered through the confessional's mesh screen.

There was a long pause before the priest said, "Have you gone to the police, my child?"

"I can't. It's impossible." Her face burned. The priest would know who she was. Recently arrived from Dublin, he had become a pet of the glitterati in their East Hampton community. Elegant in his black silk robe, with a twinkling sense of humor and bright blue eyes, he seemed to be a fixture at every party. Marianne's friend Claudia called him "The Sexiest Priest Alive."

"Impossible?" he said. "And why is that?"

"He's friends with the cops! My sister adores him, my parents depend on him. I'm the only one who suspects him. I think I'm losing my mind, Father. I'm completely alone."

"You are not alone," the priest said.

He slid an appointment card under the window. On it was written: *Private Session @ Café Buñuel. Eight o'clock tomorrow evening.* It was signed *Rev. Fr. Dean Jones.*

* * *

The next day, Marianne met Claudia at Bistro à la Mode, where they went every Monday. They called themselves the "ladies who brunch." Marianne was nervous and distraught; Leo had prowled around downstairs for most of the night, talking on the phone with someone, and their French bulldog Frederika had a urinary tract infection and needed a walk at four in the morning. But missing lunch with Claudia would definitely arouse suspicion. Besides, Marianne was hungry.

She wore Prada, and Claudia wore Ferragamo. The blood-red soles of their Christian Louboutin spike heels complemented their Chanel lipstick and nail polish.

The service at Bistro à la Mode was dismal as usual, although they were the only ones in the restaurant. Marianne's stomach growled as she watched the waiter, Raffael, fold and refold napkins into swans. Claudia blathered on about her children's camps and the prizes they had won in the water balloon toss and sack race. Marianne chimed in about her daughter Janey building huts in Port-au-Prince. Knowing Claudia had a mouth like a megaphone, Marianne kept her secrets about Leo and the priest to herself. Her biggest regret was that she couldn't ask Claudia what she should wear to meet the priest.

Claudia leaned over the table. "So, Marianne, I want the truth. Does this make me look fat?"

Marianne eyed Claudia's outfit, an oversized one-piece jumpsuit dotted with colored circles.

What she wanted to say was, *Send in the clowns.*

What she *said* was, "Not at all. Not really."

Claudia opened her eyes so wide her false eyelashes nearly touched her eyebrows. "What does 'really' mean?" She stuck out her Botoxed lower lip. "Go ahead, Marianne, tell the truth. I can take it."

"Claudia, your outfit has a discreet charm," she began, but just then, Raffael, who had a faux-French accent and a talent for interrupting a conversation at the worst possible moment, appeared at their table.

"The usual vodkatinis, ladies?" he said.

"That sounds good," Marianne said. "We'll start with the Manna from Heaven salad and the sourdough bread with the salted, flagellated butter.

And some of the Petite Marmite. Oh, and two decaf latte mochaccinos with soy milk. Anything else, Claude?"

Claudia was crossing her arms to hide the pouffy front of her jumpsuit. "Water," she said. "That's all, just plain water. For two."

The waiter stepped back, affronted.

"Water? I am so sorry, madame, but we have run out of that."

Claudia stood up. "Well. Some service. I'm leaving."

She stormed out of the restaurant. Marianne followed as fast as her spike heels could carry her, but Claudia was already rounding the corner, jumpsuit flapping in the breeze. As Marianne made her way to her bright yellow Lamborghini, she was intercepted by her sister Fritzy, decked out in a camouflage shirt, matching shorts, and combat boots. With her pink cheeks, blond braids, and beret, she looked like a cross between Heidi and Che Guevara.

"Any plans today, Fritzy? Starting another revolution?" Marianne said.

"Starting one? I've been fighting one my entire life, thanks to my family," Fritzy said.

"What have we done now?" Marianne said.

"You're all petit bourgeois capitalists, that's what! You wear designer clothes, drive super-expensive sportscars, spend days at the spa, travel first class to Paris, buy thousand-dollar-an-ounce perfume, eat out six times a week, own French bulldogs—"

"Leave Frederika out of it," Marianne said. "The rest of it is only just stuff."

Fritzy's eyes flashed. "It's only just the end of the *world*, that's all!"

"What do you want from me, Fritzy?" Marianne tapped a Louboutin on the pavement.

"Twenty-five dollars," Fritzy said.

"You're kidding, right?"

"It's not for me," Fritzy said. "It's for the starving polar bears. But I'm sure *you* wouldn't understand what it's like to be hungry."

Marianne's stomach growled again as she wrote a check and handed it over. In her check register she scribbled, *Marianne and the Bear*. Yes, Fritzy was a bear. A *cross* to bear. No matter how much Marianne had tried to train her sister up to be a fashionista or introduce her to eligible bachelor traders and surgeons, Fritzy insisted on being a terrorist. She was twenty-two but looked seventeen and had never had a manicure or facial in her life.

Marianne was in college when her mother discovered she was pregnant with Fritzy. Mama had been forty-four, Marianne's age now. Even as a toddler, Fritzy had preferred machine guns to dolls. And now, with Mama gone and Papa in his dotage, Fritzy had become Marianne's *bear*.

* * *

She sat at the wheel of her Lamborghini for a long time, afraid to turn the key in the ignition, thinking of *The Godfather*. But Leo wouldn't kill her that way, she decided. He cared too much about the car. No, he would use poison, or pills, or a tiny stiletto bikini cut that would barely leave a wound.

"*La petite mort*," her elderly professor had said in her French philosophy class at Vassar, "refers to the female orgasm. An ephemeral moment of complete ecstasy. But it also refers to a state of mind: free of desire, joy, or pain. *La petite mort est liberation totale.*"

How long had it been since Marianne had experienced that sense of freedom?

* * *

That night, she walked up and down the aisles of her closet, choosing an outfit to wear to her assignation with Father Jones. She settled on a bright-red silk Prada dress and matching satin Chanel ballet flats with rosebud appliqués. The priest was a man of God, but he was also a man.

Leo was in the great room, watching a ballgame, highball in hand. Perfect. She put on her black Burberry raincoat and lace veil, hoping to slip out, but he came up silently behind her.

"Where are you going?" he demanded.

She jumped. From the great room, she heard an excited announcer and a cheering crowd.

"To church," she said.

"Marianne." His eyes bored into her. "Are you meeting someone? Tell me the truth."

She looked down. "Of course not."

He pulled her chin up and looked into her eyes. "I hope it's not your crazy sister."

"I told you, Leo." She stepped back. "I'm going to church."

* * *

Gripping the wheel, backing out of the driveway, she was terrified Leo would follow her; he had done it before. She was relieved to see only blackness in the rear-view mirror.

The priest would help, she was sure of it. It was important to appear mature, not paranoid. She took her travel vial of Shumukh perfume from her purse and applied a dab to her wrist.

The scent of the perfume brought her back to a long-ago liaison with Leo. She: a waitress in a restaurant in Turtle Bay Gardens, a girl from a working-class Italian family on scholarship at Vassar, supporting herself with summer jobs. He: older, married, employed at his father's firm, wearing a tailored gray suit, hair sleeked down with Brilliantine, offering her a gift in a black leather tufted box.

"Open it," he'd said.

The box opened sideways to reveal a tiny gilt bottle made to resemble a carousel, with miniature horses and a bird on top.

"I can't accept this," she'd said, but he was already breaking the seal, offering it to her on the palm of his large hand.

"Put it on. It's magical. One drop will take you to paradise."

She'd obeyed, and Leo buried his face in her neck, breathing deeply, then moving his mouth to kiss her.

So it began.

* * *

268

The sign for the Café Buñuel was hidden by trees, and she nearly missed it. Looking over her shoulder, she passed through the wrought-iron gates and climbed the winding steps up and up, drawn by the ragged sound of a saxophone. Couples passed by, laughing, arm in arm, making her feel lonelier than ever. Here she was, a forty-four-year-old woman, sneaking out to meet a priest because there was no one else in the world she could trust.

When they feel agitated, some women have a little valium—or a little wine, she thought. *But me, I have a little priest!*

But Father Jones was not so little. In fact, beneath his black silk robe, he had looked quite ripped.

When she got to the stairs leading to the café, she heard quick footsteps. A figure stepped out of the shadows.

"Well," he said. "Here we are."

"Father," she said, amazed. "Aren't we going to the café?" She pointed upstairs.

"No, no. That would be too dangerous—you know how people talk around here. Come into my cathedral, my dear."

She followed him to an abandoned terrace, shoes crunching on broken glass, passing broken concrete, avoiding the spikes of discarded umbrellas. His firm hand came up on her shoulder to steer her.

He motioned toward an old wrought-iron garden table, where a bottle of wine and two glasses had been set out for them. "Sit," he told her. "The chairs are rusty, but the view is spectacular, don't you think?"

They looked out over the Long Island Sound at twinkling lights and sailboats far below. Hunger gnawed at her as the smell of cooking wafted down from the café, something savory and familiar that reminded her of London. Meat pies? Shepherd's pie? But then another scent—the putrid day-old remains of last night's food, discarded all together now in a dumpster far below—reminded her of where she was.

Something jangled. Her heart beat like a drum, distant at first, then so loud she feared he would hear it. They were completely alone here. From the Café Buñuel a floor above, the saxophone seemed to sound a warning note.

Couples were standing near the window, arms entwined, oblivious. In a haze of hysteria, she imagined she was in a surreal world, a character in a play. No, a musical! And the people in the café were characters in musicals, too. She imagined music, downbeats, melodies, characters dancing in formation across a stage, and thought about the killers in the musicals she knew— Sweeney Todd, John Hinckley, Chino—and imagined them watching her through the window, preparing not to destroy her but to protect her from her husband.

If only, if only!

But when she looked up, she saw only the bourgeois *nouveau riche* of East Hampton, dressed in silks and satins, decorated with glittery earrings and tennis bracelets, lost in their own world of plenitude. What had possessed her to come to this place alone, with this stranger? She held her raincoat tightly closed, not wanting him to see her dress.

He poured wine into the glasses and handed one to her. He held up his glass, and she did the same.

"To," she said weakly, but had no idea how to continue the toast.

"To being alive," he said. His blue eyes, which looked gentle, lamb-like during mass, were shrewd. She noticed his white collar was shredded at the edges.

"Where did you go to seminary, Father? What town in Ireland?"

Those eyes pierced her. "God, but you're naïve," he said in a Brooklyn accent.

She stood up, but he yanked her down. "Sit, Marianne. We're going to see this through."

He reached across the table and tugged open her raincoat to reveal her red dress. "Don't tell me you came here to talk about your husband."

"But I did! I did!"

"In those shoes? What are they, Manolo Blahniks?"

"Chanel," she said softly.

"Give 'em here, lady," he said.

Numbly, she bent, removed her flats, and handed them to him.

"Very nice," he said, stroking the silk. With a sudden motion, he tossed

270

them over the railing into the water. "Oops," he said.

She jumped to her feet.

"You're not going anywhere without your shoes," he said. "There's broken glass all over the ground."

Tears fell down her cheeks. The band started an agitated Carmen Miranda-style samba, and she saw flitting shapes moving in the window above like panicked citizens fleeing some apocalypse. He grabbed her wrists so tightly she cried out.

"Shut up," he ordered. "Now, what did you come here to tell me? You think your husband is trying to kill you?"

"No, I—I didn't mean it. I must have imagined it—"

"You little fool!" He laughed and bent her wrist so she thought it would break.

"You're a devil!" she cried hoarsely.

"No, no, my dear. Think of me as an angel—an exterminating angel, putting shallow, self-centered women like you out their misery."

"Let me go!" she cried, twisting free of his grasp, sprinting across the broken glass.

She fell, sobbing as shards of glass cut her hands and knees. Someone reached under her armpits and lifted her up.

"Leo!"

"Yes, me," her husband grinned. "I could divorce you, Marianne, but I've gone through one divorce already, and I have no intention of going back to that particular square one. Much easier to make a clean break this time."

She looked from Leo to the priest and knew they were a couple.

"We are planning to go away together," the priest said, confirming her unspoken thought.

"And you, my dear, will not get a penny from me," Leo said.

"But what about Janey?" Marianne said.

"Oh, she'll be taken care of. You're the one who's expendable." He turned to the priest. "Go ahead, Henrick."

"Me?" the priest said. "She's *your* wife! I thought you were going to do it."

"We'll do it together," Leo said.

271

They surrounded her, moving in. Henrik reached up to put his hands around her throat.

A gunshot whizzed over their heads.

"What the—?" Leo said.

Fritzy emerged from the shadows, holding a pistol. "Get away from my sister!" she shouted.

"Put the gun down, Fritzy," Leo said in a patronizing tone. "You're too old to play with toys."

Fritzy pulled a grenade from her belt. "I'm going to pull this pin and blow the two of you to bits, if you don't unhand my sister."

"Don't worry," Leo said. "She doesn't have the guts. She's a wuss. A poseur."

Henrik looked doubtful. "You sure?"

Fritzy raised the grenade, pulled the pin, and tossed it.

The two men ducked, and the grenade hissed and spun through the railing, exploding when it hit the water far below.

"Let's get out of here, Leo," Henrik said.

"Go! I don't care! Just leave me alone!" Marianne said. "I don't want anything from you!"

"Oh, no, my darling. Not a chance. I've learned not to leave loose ends behind. And you, my dear, are a loose end."

Marianne froze as her husband came forward and clamped his hands around her throat. Helpless, she felt herself slip away into a dream.

It is what it is, she thought.

From a distant part of her consciousness, she heard a gunshot. Leo's hands dropped, and he fell to the ground. Dazed, Marianne looked up to see Fritzy pitch her gun over the rail.

Heads peered out of the upstairs window, and a policeman emerged from the darkness and knelt to feel Leo's pulse. Standing slowly, he shook his head and looked back and forth between Fritzy, Henrick, and Marianne. "Which one of you shot this man?"

Henrik pointed to Fritzy, and Fritzy pointed to Henrick.

"The priest did it," Marianne said. "He shot my husband and threw the gun into the water."

There was shocked whispering from above, and a woman's voice called, "That beautiful priest?"

"Those people know me," Henrick said in a thick Irish brogue. "I'm part of this wonderful community." He smiled. "You're a Catholic, aren't you, officer? Irish? Italian? Perhaps you, too, have taken communion from—"

"My name's Krupke, Officer Krupke." The cop folded his arms. "I'm Jewish."

"Well, anyway, this young woman is unstable," Henrick said. "One look at her tells you that. She did it, as God is my witness. I tried to bring her to the Lord, but she was a hopeless transgressor. And now she has killed her sister's husband in cold blood!"

"Don't listen to him," Marianne said. "He's an imposter."

"Remove your robe, sir," the cop said.

"What? Why?"

When Henrick hesitated, Krupke pulled Henrik's robe up to reveal six knives and seven guns strapped to his waist and legs.

"All right, sir, I'll ask you to come with me," the cop said.

"I didn't do it! It was the girl!" Henrick whined, as he was led away.

"Let's get out of here," Marianne said to her sister. "I don't know about you, but I'm starving. How does dinner at the Osteria Zeno sound? It's French deconstructivist cuisine."

"I *am* hungry," Fritzy admitted.

They descended the stairs and got into Marianne's Lamborghini.

"I thought you were mad at me," Marianne said. "My lifestyle, my materialism, my capitalism."

"What difference does all that make?" Fritzy said. "You're my sister, and nothing's gonna harm you. Not while I'm around."

Who's Who in the Cast

FLEUR BRADLEY is the author of dozens of short mysteries which have appeared in publications including *Thrilling Detective* and *Dark Yonder* and have been reprinted in *The Best Mystery Stories of the Year*. She also writes mysteries for kids, including the Anthony- and Agatha-nominated *Daybreak on Raven Island* and *Midnight at the Barclay Hotel* and the Double Vision trilogy. Originally from The Netherlands, she now lives in a small cottage in the foothills of the Colorado Rockies. *www.ftbradley.com*

JOHN COPENHAVER is the author of *Dodging and Burning*, a historical crime novel that won the Macavity Award for Best First Mystery in 2019, and *The Savage Kind*, which won the Lambda Literary Award for Best LGBTQ Mystery in 2021. He is a founding member of Queer Crime Writers, an at-large board member of Mystery Writers of America, and a cohost of the *House of Mystery* radio show. He's also a faculty mentor in the University of Nebraska's Low-Residency MFA program and teaches creative writing and literature at Virginia Commonwealth University in Richmond (VA), where he lives with his husband, artist Jeffery Paul Herrity. His new novel, *Hall of Mirrors*, is a sequel to *The Savage Kind*. *www.johncopenhaver.com*

BRIAN COX is a fiction writer, newspaper editor, playwright, *New York Times* crossword constructor, and founder of Pencilpoint Theatreworks in Ypsilanti, Michigan. His story "The Surrogate Initiative" was included in *The Best American Mystery Stories 2020*. His play *Clutter* won the Wilde Award for Best New Script, and his children's plays *Stone Dragon Stew* and *Welcome to Candy Kingdom* have been produced in the US and internationally. In the late 1980s, he served for several years as the managing editor of *Alfred*

Hitchcock's Mystery Magazine. He and his wife Dana have two children, Elijah and Annie.

CHERYL L. DAVIS has received WGA Awards for her soap writing, the Kleban Award for her work as a musical theater librettist (for her musical *Barnstormer,* about Bessie Coleman, the first Black woman flyer), and seven Audelco Awards for her play *Maid's Door,* which was presented at two National Black Theatre Festivals and is included in *Holy Ground: The National Black Theatre Festival Anthology.* She received her AB from Princeton, her J.D. from Columbia, and her M.S.J. from the Columbia School of Journalism. She is the general counsel of the Authors Guild and, in her copious free time, worships Stephen Sondheim. *www.cldplay.com*

JOHN M. FLOYD is the author of more than a thousand short stories in publications including AHMM, *Ellery Queen's Mystery Magazine, The Strand, The Saturday Evening Post, Best American Mystery Stories,* and *Best Mystery Stories of the Year.* A former Air Force captain and IBM systems engineer, John is also an Edgar nominee, a Shamus winner, a six-time Derringer winner, and a recipient of the Short Mystery Fiction Society's Golden Derringer for Lifetime Achievement. *www.johnmfloyd.com*

JOSEPH GOODRICH is an Edgar-winning dramatist whose plays have been produced around the world. His work has appeared in *American Theatre,* EQMM, AHMM, *Mystery Scene,* and *Crimespree.* He's the author of the novel *The Paris Manuscript,* the nonfiction book *Unusual Suspects: Selected Non-Fiction,* and the editor of *Blood Relations: The Selected Letters of Ellery Queen, 1947-1950* and *People in a Magazine: The Selected Letters of S. N. Behrman and His Editors at the New Yorker.* An alumnus of New Dramatists and a former Calderwood Fellow at McDowell, he lives in New York City. *www.snapbrimfedora.com*

CHERYL A. HEAD is a former television producer and broadcast executive. She is the author of the award-winning Charlie Mack Motown mysteries, whose female protagonist is a Black, queer private investigator. *Time's Undoing*, her 2023 stand-alone novel, was shortlisted for the Los Angeles Times Book Prize and the Agatha, Lefty, Nero, Macavity, and Strand Critics awards, and nominated for the Best Hardcover Novel Anthony. She is the chair of the national Bouchercon board and lives in Washington (DC) with her partner and rescue pooch.

J.A. HENNRIKUS is the author of ten novels in three series and several short stories. A theater fan whose talents lie offstage, she has had a long career in performing-arts administration. Musical theater feeds her soul, and she has seen many, many Sondheim shows over the years. She still teaches arts administration to theater students, and she serves as the executive director of Sisters in Crime. *www.jhauthors.com*

ALISON LOUISE HUBBARD turned to crime fiction after a successful career as a musical theater lyricist, with many productions, publications, and national tours of her shows, for which she has received the prestigious Kleban award and two Richard Rodgers awards. Her short crime story "Belladonna" won the Slippery Elm Literary Journal Prize for Prose in 2021, "Wildflowers" appeared in *The Saturday Evening* Post in 2022, and her historical novel *The Kelsey Outrage: The Crime of the Century* was published in 2024. *www.alisonlouisehubbard.com*

REBECCA K. JONES is a criminal appeals attorney in Phoenix (AZ) by day and a crime writer by night. Her Mackenzie Wilson novels—Goldie finalist *Steadying the Ark, Stemming the Tide,* and *Staying the Course*—are published by Bella Books, and her short stories and translations have appeared in EQMM and other places. *www.rebeccakjoneswrites.com*

JEFFREY MARKS has contributed numerous profiles of mystery authors to *The Armchair Detective, Mystery Scene,* and other publications, and is the author of *Who Was That Lady?* (a biography of Craig Rice), *Anthony Boucher: A Biobibliography,* and *Atomic Renaissance: Women Mystery Writers of the*

1940s/1950s. He is the editor of five anthologies and is currently working on a biography of Erle Stanley Gardner and running Crippen & Landru Publishers. He lives in Cincinnati (OH) with his husband and three dogs.

LISA NANNI-MESSEGEE is a playwright and screenwriter who writes both solo and with her husband Todd Messegee. She writes large-cast historical dramas, twenty-five of which have been produced across the country by high schools, community theaters, and colleges. She's scripted five movies, notably *Holiday for Heroes* and *Christmas Homecoming* for Hallmark Movies and Mysteries. Her first sf/adventure novel, *The Triumvirate*, will be released in 2025.

JOSH PACHTER was the 2020 recipient of the SMFS's Golden Derringer for Lifetime Achievement. His stories appear in EQMM, AHMM, *Black Cat Mystery Magazine, Mystery Magazine, Mystery Tribune*, and elsewhere. He edits anthologies (including Anthony finalists inspired by the songs of Joni Mitchell, Paul Simon, and the Beatles) and translates fiction and nonfiction from multiple languages—mainly Dutch—into English. *www.joshpachter.com*

MICHAEL PORTANTIERE is a theater journalist, author, and photographer. One of three panelists for the podcast "This Week on Broadway," he has previously worked as a writer and editor for such publications as *InTheater* magazine, *Playbill, Backstage*, and *TheaterMania*. His theatrical photos have appeared in the *New York Times* and other publications, and he is the creator of *CastAlbumReviews.com*, a website featuring thousands of reviews of hundreds of recordings, written by a large stable of contributors.

DAVID SPENCER is an award-winning musical dramatist, author, critic and teacher. His principal theater credits include two musicals as lyricist-librettist with composer Alan Menken (*The Apprenticeship of Duddy Kravitz* and *Weird Romance*), two as composer-lyricist for Theatreworks/USA with librettist-director Rob Barron (*Phantom of the Opera* and *Les Misérables*), and the Public Theatre's *La Bohème* (English adaptation). His published books include *The Musical Theatre Writer's Survival Guide* and *The Novelizers: An Affectionate History of Media Adaptations and Originals, Their Astonishing Authors—and the Art of the Craft*. Teaser, Pran, and Gadge were co-created with Jerry James. *www.davidspencerworks.com*

JEFFREY SWEET divides his time between writing *for* the theater and writing *about* it. His best-known plays are *The Value of Names, Flyovers, Kunstler, Porch, The Action Against Sol Schumann* and *American Enterprise*, plus *I Sent a Letter to My Love*, a musical he wrote with Melissa Manchester. His books include *Something Wonderful Right Away* (about Second City), *The O'Neill, The Dramatist's Toolkit*, and *What Playwrights Talk About When They Talk About Writing. www.jeffreysweet.blog*

MARCIA TALLEY is the Agatha- and Anthony-winning author of twenty novels featuring Maryland sleuth Hannah Ives and the editor/author of two collaborative serial novels, *Naked Came the Phoenix* and *I'd Kill for That*. Her short stories appear in more than a dozen collections and have been reprinted in many year's-best anthologies. A longtime Sondheim fangirl, she set her novel *This Enemy Town* around an amateur-theater production of *Sweeney Todd. www.marciatalley.com*

GABRIEL VALJAN is the author of the Company Files and the Shane Cleary mystery series. A nominee for the Agatha, Anthony, Derringer, and Silver Falchion awards, he won the Macavity for Best Short Story in 2021 and the Shamus for Best Original PI Paperback for *Liar's Dice* in 2024. A member of the Historical Novel Society, International Thriller Writers, MWA, and Sisters in Crime, he lives in Boston and answers to a tuxedo cat named Munchkin. *www.gabrielvaljan.com*

JOSEPH S. WALKER is the president of the Short Mystery Fiction Society. His fiction has appeared in EQMM, AHMM, *The Saturday Evening Post, Mystery Tribune,* and other magazines and anthologies, has been nominated for the Edgar, Derringer, and Shamus awards, has won the Al Blanchard award twice, and has been reprinted in *The Best American Mystery and Suspense* and *The Mysterious Bookshop Presents the Best Mystery Stories of the Year*. *www.jswalkerauthor.com*

KRISTOPHER ZGORSKI is the founder and sole reviewer at the crime fiction book blog BOLO Books and contributes a column on digital crime-fiction resources to *EQMM*. In 2018, he was awarded the MWA Raven Award for "outstanding achievement in the mystery field outside the realm of creative writing" and was nominated for an Anthony. "Ticket to Ride," his first published short story (written collaboratively with Dru Ann Love), won the Agatha, Anthony, and Macavity awards for Best Short Story of 2023. *www.bolobooks.com*

Acknowledgments

My thanks to the authors who enthusiastically contributed stories, to Shawn Reilly Simmons and Verena Rose at Level Best Books for greenlighting my eighth "inspired by" anthology, to my wife Laurie Pachter and daughter Rebecca Jones as always and for always…and, most of all, to the late, great Stephen Sondheim, for writing the songs that inspired the stories contained in this book.

About the Editor

Josh Pachter is the author of more than 130 short stories. In 2023, his first novel—*Dutch Threat*—was a finalist for the Agatha, Macavity, and Lefty awards; in 2024, his first book for younger readers—*First Week Free at the Roomy Toilet*—was an Agatha finalist. Three of the seven previous volumes in his "inspired by" series were Anthony finalists. He was the 2020 recipient of the Short Mystery Fiction Society's Golden Derringer for Lifetime Achievement.

AUTHOR WEBSITE:

  www.joshpachter.com

SOCIAL MEDIA HANDLES:

  www.facebook.com/josh.pachter/

bsky.app/profile/joshpachter.bsky.social

Also by Josh Pachter

EDITED BY JOSH PACHTER

- *Friend of the Devil: Crime Fiction Inspired by the Songs of the Grateful Dead*
- *Happiness Is a Warm Gun: Crime Fiction Inspired by the Songs of the Beatles*
- *Paranoia Blues: Crime Fiction Inspired by the Songs of Paul Simon*
- *The Man Who Solved Mysteries: More Short Fiction by William Brittain*
- *Monkey Business: Crime Fiction Inspired by the Films of the Marx Brothers*
- *Only the Good Die Young: Crime Fiction Inspired by the Songs of Billy Joel*
- *The Great Filling Station Holdup: Crime Fiction Inspired by the Songs of Jimmy Buffett*
- *The Further Misadventures of Ellery Queen* (with Dale C. Andrews)
- *The Misadventures of Nero Wolfe*
- *The Beat of Black Wings: Crime Fiction Inspired by the Songs of Joni Mitchell*
- *Amsterdam Noir* (with René Appel)
- *The Man Who Read Mysteries: The Short Fiction of William Brittain*
- *The Misadventures of Ellery Queen* (with Dale C. Andrews)
- *Top Fantasy: The Authors' Choice*
- *Top Science Fiction: The Authors' Choice*
- *Top Crime: The Authors' Choice*

WRITTEN BY JOSH PACHTER

- *First Week Free at the Roomy Toilet*
- *Dutch Threat*
- *The Adventures of the Puzzle Club and Other Stories* (with Ellery Queen)
- *The Tree of Life*

.

www.ingramcontent.com/pod-product-compliance
Ingram Content Group UK Ltd.
Pitfield, Milton Keynes, MK11 3LW, UK
UKHW040634240325
5122UKWH00033B/293